Books by Lynn Florkiewicz
in the Linford Mystery Library:

LORD JAMES HARRINGTON
AND THE SPRING MYSTERY
LORD JAMES HARRINGTON
AND THE SUMMER MYSTERY

LORD JAMES HARRINGTON AND THE CORNISH MYSTERY

While on holiday with his wife Beth in Cornwall, James learns that a local fisherman vanished during the recent opening procession of the Cornish Legends Festival. When more men disappear in broad daylight, he can't help but put his sleuthing hat on. If they were kidnapped, why is there no ransom demand? What are the flashing lights off the coastline? Who is the eccentric woman on the moors? Have the Cornish Legends really come to life? As James delves into the mystery, he realizes his questions come at a price . . .

LYNN FLORKIEWICZ

LORD JAMES HARRINGTON AND THE CORNISH MYSTERY

Complete and Unabridged

LINFORD
Leicester

First published in Great Britain

First Linford Edition
published 2018

A catalogue record for this book is available
from the British Library.

ISBN 978–1–4448–3826–8

Published by
F. A. Thorpe (Publishing)
Anstey, Leicestershire

Set by Words & Graphics Ltd.
Anstey, Leicestershire
Printed and bound in Great Britain by
T. J. International Ltd., Padstow, Cornwall

This book is printed on acid-free paper

1

With no light, there was nothing. It was dark: unbroken dark, unnerving, disorienting.

It was ideal.

Far enough away; close enough to watch.

The plan would work well here. The details were finalised. It was foolproof.

It was nearly time.

2

'It's no use,' James said, leaning on one of the kitchen counters leafing through a Hygena brochure. 'We'll have to move out. We can't stay here; it'll look like a building site.'

Beth groaned, admitting he was right.

'It should only take a week at the most. We're going to have to make a decision. We can't stay at Harrington's — it's full.'

Harrington's, the country house that had been in James' family for centuries, was now a thriving hotel catering to the rich and famous, its success based on excellent service, quality, and above all, recommendation — this was now *the* place to stay in Sussex. James and Beth ran the business and lived just up the road in a smaller yet roomy red-brick house on the outskirts of the pretty village of Cavendish.

Their discussion about moving out had gone on for most of the morning.

They'd decided to strip the entire kitchen out and install a new, fresh, modern design. Beth insisted she wanted something in keeping with the times; featuring bubble-gum colours that lightened the feel of a room. Beth had reminded James it was 1959 and the existing cupboards belonged in a museum. They'd chosen Formica worktops, fitted cupboards, a washer/drier and room for what the Americans called a breakfast bar. A New World cooker stood in its box ready to be installed.

With Harrington's full, they had two choices. Live among the rubble and dine out or book a holiday and trust the builders to get on with it. It didn't take them long to decide. A holiday it was and discussions were now in place about where to go.

3

Colm Fiske screwed his face up hoping it would loosen the gag and dislodge the blindfold. He'd stopped fighting the rope: its strands had rubbed into his wrists, leaving them raw and angry.

Kicking his feet did nothing to loosen the bindings around his ankles. His heart banged in his chest. Resting his head back against cold, jagged rock, he took a deep breath. It was cool; a dry air but he could smell the ocean. He jerked forward and roared through the gag knowing, deep down, that no one would answer. Whoever had brought him here had gone.

Or were they watching? A silent observer lurking in the shadows?

He drew his knees up and shivered.

He could stand a gale force storm in the Atlantic, heaving the nets in and risking life and limb to earn a wage; but being kept in a dark hole, more silent than a grave, forced every muscle to tense.

4

Cavendish basked in sunshine as June blazed in and pushed the spring showers into history. The blossoming trees and summer buds had burst into life and Ernest Appleton, the Harringtons' gardener, was working his magic on the landscape. Those tiny seeds he'd propagated in the winter months had been folded into the soil and were now shouting a big hello to the world.

If it weren't for the builders' imminent arrival, James would have happily remained exactly where he was. The English garden was in full bloom and Appleton had planted a wonderful selection of delphiniums, foxgloves, geraniums and roses. Their scents mixed with the smell of freshly mown grass. The borders had flowered into a riot of colour and, although the brochure showing their holiday destination was inviting, at this precise moment he could have easily stayed exactly where he was.

He and Beth were on the terrace that ran the length of their house. Bees hovered above lavender that grew along the wall. Goldfinches, blackbirds and blue tits flittered close by, wary of any sudden movement. The gentle birdsong floated on the breeze. On the wrought iron table in front of them was a jug of Pimms with a combination of fresh summer fruits, lemon slices and sprigs of mint floating on the surface of the liquid.

James rolled his sleeves up, placed a straw hat on his head and studied the map of South West England. 'Cornwall is certainly one of the most scenic counties in England,' he said as he sipped his drink. The ice cubes clinked on the side of his glass. He picked out a sodden strawberry and popped it in his mouth.

Beth dragged her chair closer to examine the area. 'Whereabouts is Polpennarth?'

He leant in; his index finger traced the southern coastline of West Cornwall and finally came to a halt. 'Here.'

'Goodness, that's about as far west as you can go.'

'Yes, it's pretty near Land's End. Full of quaint little coves and inlets and this, according to the brochure, is one of the best. It has a harbour, a pub, a couple of restaurants, a fish market and a few shops. There's quite a vibrant community; it's a typical Cornish retreat. You can probably walk around it in an hour; but says there are some lovely rambles along the cliff-tops. There's also a festival on while we're there.'

'Oh, that'll be perfect. I do hope Stephen and Anne will be happy with our news.'

The Reverend Stephen Merryweather and his wife, Anne, had moved to Cavendish just a couple of years previously and the four of them had hit it off straight away, forging a friendship they knew would last forever. The doorbell chimed. Beth sprang up.

'That'll be them.'

Five minutes later, the young couple had joined them on the terrace where

Anne was quick to compliment Beth on her outfit.

Beth smoothed down her floral sleeveless frock. 'Thank you. You know I made it years ago but it's one of those dresses I simply can't throw out.'

'And why should you?' said Anne, feeling the fabric, 'The cotton is crisp and it's so summery, perfect for this weather.'

Stephen, also sporting a straw hat, peered at the map. 'You're th–thinking of Cornwall too?'

James gave the Merryweathers a knowing look and winked at Beth.

Anne narrowed her eyes. 'What are you planning?'

'Well, old thing, we rather hoped you wouldn't mind if we joined you in Cornwall. I know it's your anniversary and all but — '

'Oh James, how wonderful,' said Anne. She turned to Stephen. 'Isn't that wonderful?'

'That i–is marvellous news but what about Harrington's? This is y–your busy time, isn't it?'

James topped their glasses up and

explained that their twins, Harry and Oliver, who were on their summer break from Oxford, would be taking the reins.

'They're staying here to make sure the builders behave. Harry did a pretty good job of being Lord of the Manor over Christmas and I believe it's time for him to fly solo. Paul and the regulars are there so they can put them right if they slip up. And we're only away for a week.'

James had called a staff meeting at Harrington's to tell them of their plans to take a holiday. Paul, their experienced and professional *maître d'hôtel*, assured him that he and his staff would oversee things, along with Harry and Oliver.

'W–well, Harry certainly sh–showed his worth when you were sorting out that awful business with Olivia Dupree and the Major.'

James groaned. It had been just before Christmas that the famous singer, Olivia Dupree, was poisoned at Harrington's, leading to an interesting yet disturbing mystery to solve. He smiled to himself. Harry had been quick to insist he didn't want anything to do with detective work but then had actually found himself enjoying it. James sent a silent prayer up to ask that nothing untoward should happen in their absence. Anne broke his thoughts.

'Are you actually going to stay in Polpennarth?'

Beth took up the conversation. 'Yes. When you said you were going there for your anniversary, we thought we'd try and get accommodation nearby and take you out to dinner to celebrate.'

'Oh, what a perfect time we're going to have! And it's so kind of you to remember us.'

'A–are you not stopping at the same caravan site as us?' Stephen's eyes twinkled as he held his hands up. 'I–I'm sorry James. I w–would like to see you living in a caravan.'

James allowed Stephen his witticism. 'I'll have you know that I spent quite a bit of time in my youth, camping, but I make no bones about it, my preference is for something a little more luxurious. I will visit your caravan and I'm sure I'll find it quite acceptable but I know I'd rather be in a hotel.'

Beth confirmed that they'd booked bed and breakfast accommodation at The Polpennarth Hotel on the quayside. 'We're fortunate they had a cancellation. It only has six rooms and overlooks the harbour and the beach. And you know there's a festival on at the moment.'

'No, we didn't,' said Anne. 'What is it?'

James lifted the map and retrieved a small brochure. 'The Cornish Legends festival. They hold it every year and it celebrates all the local folklore down there: giants, pixies, mermaids, pirates, smugglers. If it's related to Cornwall, it's likely to be celebrated.' He flicked through the pages. 'Some of these characters are really quite dark.'

He went on to describe mermaids that lure swimmers into the ocean, murderous smugglers, hobgoblins that lurk in the shadows of fishermen's cottages and mischievous fairies who prance about playing tricks.

'Ooh,' said Anne, 'it sounds spooky, doesn't it?'

'It does rather and they're all part of a number of parades that go on throughout the week. And there's a fairground too.'

'Th–that sounds pretty jolly, doesn't it? We must spend p–plenty of time together.'

James wagged a finger at him. 'No no no; this is your wedding anniversary and we'll meet up when you feel you want to. You booked this some time ago and I'm sure you've made plans of your own. We felt a little cheeky barging in on your celebrations but — .'

'Nonsense,' said Anne. 'It'll be wonderful to meet up and explore together.'

'And are the children coming?' said Beth, adding her concern over whether they would all squeeze into a caravan, especially with two boys aged nine and eleven.

'Oh, yes. The dog too. We've hired one of the larger caravans so there's plenty of room. It's got two single beds for the boys, one double and a kitchen.'

During the next hour, the four of them pored over the map and the various brochures Beth had sent for. They exchanged the addresses and telephone numbers of where they were staying and arranged a meeting point for the first evening: they settled on a pub called The Pilchard Inn. The leaflet depicted an ancient pub that looked out to sea, with the harbour wall to one side and the beach the other. A swing and slide occupied a tiny garden for the children to play on. With arrangements in place, they said goodbye to the Merryweathers.

Beth tidied the glasses away and James stepped into the lounge and switched the radiogram on. It was an old relic and although they'd purchased a more modern transistor for the kitchen, James had a soft spot for it because it had belonged to his parents. Although it took some minutes to spring to life he couldn't imagine parting with it. He hoped that when they decided to decorate this room, there'd be a place for it. He turned a dial to tune it in clearly. The news had already begun.

'Boat-builder, Christopher Cockerell, will be testing a revolutionary new form of transport in the Solent, Hampshire.

Described as a cross between a boat and land vehicle, the hovercraft is propelled on a cushion of air created by its own fan power.'

James felt his pockets and brought out his cigarettes. 'Good Lord,' he muttered as he listened to the rest of the story. Beth joined him, wiping her hands on a towel. 'I say, Beth, there's a chap here who's developed a boat that hovers across the sea.' They continued listening.

'Following the launch of this particular prototype, there are now plans to build a 40-ton vehicle capable of crossing the English Channel.'

They gave each other an astonished look. He lit his cigarette as the next news item came on.

'And finally, police in Polpennarth are perplexed over the disappearance of a man who mysteriously vanished on Monday.' James turned the volume up. 'The man, a resident of the village in West Cornwall, went missing whilst taking part in a busy festival parade.'

Beth's jaw dropped. 'I don't believe it. James, you must have a sign on your head that advertises for mysteries.' She shook her head, folded the towel and gave him a look worthy of a headmistress. 'Don't you dare get involved in any shenanigans down there.' She returned to the kitchen.

James picked up the *Daily Express* and examined each page until he came to a small heading: *Polpennarth Man Missing — Are Pixies to Blame?* He folded the newspaper into a more manageable size and read it.

'Mr Colm Fiske, 30, went missing in the small fishing village of Polpennarth on Monday. Mr Fiske, born in the village, was taking part in the opening of the Cornish Legends festival when he vanished. Although the main street was busy, no witnesses have come forward. Mr Fiske is a fisherman and knows the area and tides well; but searches to date have proved unsuccessful. Locals insist that Cornish Pixies are to blame. The police have dismissed these rumours and continue to search the area.'

James let the paper fall onto the table. He stood at the window and watched Appleton tend to the rose bushes. 'How can a man simply vanish off the face of the earth in a busy village? How can no one have seen that?'

Beth announced she was taking some books back to the library. 'I'll call in to Graham's and get a couple of pork chops for tonight.'

James went through to the study where he scanned the shelves for books on folklore and traditional customs. He tapped the spine of one that caught his eye, slipped it out and sat at his desk.

''ere he is,' said Bert, peering around the door.

Surprised to see his old friend, James said, 'I thought you were at the races?'

'Derby day was yesterday, Jimmy boy.'

'Of course it was.' He couldn't imagine Bert being anywhere else that week. His Cockney friend was a frequent visitor to horse-racing meetings and the Epsom Derby was one of the premier events on the calendar. Though Bert was a gambler and a wheeler-dealer, he and James had formed an unlikely friendship since childhood. James had no idea where he actually lived or what he did.

The wily character always seemed to steer clear of the subject or give an ambiguous answer. He certainly didn't hold down a regular job. If James needed to contact Bert Briggs, he had three telephone numbers: the bookmaker's, a pub in Brighton and a man who ran a stall at Petticoat Lane market in London's East End.

Judging by the items Bert sold, James had come to the conclusion quite early on in their relationship that his friend 'procured' stock from somewhere other than legal sources. Personally, he turned a blind eye, preferring the phrase 'ignorance is bliss', especially as his other good friend, George Lane, happened to be a Detective Chief Inspector.

'Whatcha doin'?'

'Trying to find out about pixies.'

Bert let out an infectious and suggestive chuckle and the many lines on his face creased like the contours on a map. James couldn't help but giggle along with him.

'Blimey, you gone soft or somethin'? What d'you wanna know about pixies for?'

James mentioned the festival in Polpennarth and Bert was not slow to mention the missing local, Colm Fiske. James knew he must have looked astonished. 'How on earth did you know about that?'

'Same as you — I listen to the news. And I know it's intrigued you 'cos you're staying there in a few days. You're nosing about aren't you?'

'We're celebrating the Merryweathers' — '

'Don't give me that, d'you think I'm stupid? Bloody pixies. You don't believe any of that codswallop, do you?'

'Of course not. I'm interested to know why the locals do though. Myths and legends occasionally have their roots in something factual.'

Bert sat down next to him. His sleeves were rolled up and he smelt of Golden Virginia. He pulled the open book toward him. 'I though' pixies were s'posed to be the ghosts of small babies. What's that gotta do with this bloke going AWOL?'

James held a finger up to suggest that he had discovered more. He pointed at the text. 'That's only part of the story.

According to this, the pixies in the south-west also have a different connotation. They cause people to lose their way, even if they're familiar with the area. Now this Colm Fiske chap is apparently a local, a fisherman and resident who knows the place like the back of his hand.'

'Load o' cobblers. If it is a pixie, it's someone dressed up as one. The papers haven't got any news this week, they're grasping at whatever they can find. They turned up something yesterday about some woman who reckons she's a reincarnation of Queen Victoria. What time you leaving?'

'We're making an early morning start on Saturday — probably around four o'clock. We'll need to stop off a few times to let the car cool down.'

'And did you book this to chase the mystery or were you definitely going?'

James raised an eyebrow and reminded Bert that their kitchen was being fitted while they were away. 'This is a holiday. Nothing more, nothing less.'

His old friend grinned and James conceded that Bert knew him too well.

He and Beth were excited about their holiday, of course they were. They hadn't been away for some time. But he couldn't hide his desire to know more about the missing fisherman. The fact that the man had disappeared in a busy high street, and in the middle of an opening parade, intrigued him.

5

They received the warmest of welcomes from proprietors Vivian and Desmond Simms as they entered Reception with their suitcases. It was a rectangular area with a tiny front desk ahead of them. To one side stood a rack containing pamphlets and maps and, on the wall, posters advertising local events.

Desmond dashed forward to help. 'Lord Harrington, Lady Harrington, welcome to The Polpennarth Hotel; only hotel in the cove and in the best position too.' He introduced his wife, Vivian.

James put the couple at around their mid-fifties and he warmed to them straight away. Some people seemed to have that ability — an unseen aura that enveloped you and made you part of their family. Vivian reminded him a little of her namesake, Vivian Vance, who played Ethel in the popular American TV comedy *I Love Lucy*. She had a similar build and looks to match; and her husband he couldn't help but liken to Spencer Tracy.

Desmond clasped his hands together. 'Now, how about a nice pot of tea.'

Beth let out a delighted sigh. 'Oh Mr Simms, that would be lovely. It's a long journey but now we've seen the view, well worth it.'

'If you're comfortable with it, we'd much prefer you to call us Desmond and Vivian.'

James took his sunglasses off and confirmed that they were more than comfortable with it and that, likewise, they needn't bother with the formalities of Lord and Lady.

Vivian stepped back with a startled look. 'Are you sure? I don't want to upset you by being too informal.'

He assured her that the rules about dealing with the gentry that had existed before the war had long gone; he was keen to embrace a more informal approach. 'Not everyone is comfortable with it but we're more than happy with first names. Need to move with the times and all that. Do we need to sign in?'

Desmond hovered and Vivian rolled her eyes at him and told him to ask. He swallowed hard. 'I've a book out back about rally driving and you're in it. I wondered if you'd sign it.'

James couldn't hide his surprise. 'Good lord.'

Desmond didn't wait to be asked. He dashed to the room at the back of reception and came out triumphantly holding up a large hardback book. 'It's all about the big rallies to Monte Carlo. When I heard you were coming I thought I recognised the name and there you were. You're mentioned a couple of times and there's a photo of you.' He'd already marked the page and held the book open. 'There, look.'

James studied the grainy black and white photograph showing him as a young man holding a trophy aloft.

Beth squeezed his arm. 'You're a celebrity.'

'I've told everyone here that I've not only got a Lord staying here but that he's a famous rally driver too.'

James played down his status, insisting

that he'd only come second in that race. 'I didn't fare so well in the others. It was a long time ago.'

'But you haven't lost your passion. You wouldn't be driving that lovely Austin if you weren't bothered.'

Beth agreed. 'It's his pride and joy and I'm sure he'd race again if the chance came up.'

Vivian chivvied Desmond to prepare the tea. He excused himself as Vivian motioned for them to sit down. To the side of the glass front doors there was a round table with two comfy chairs and an outlook toward the ocean. Two cushions occupied the low, wide window sill. They made themselves comfortable as she brought over the visitors' book.

'We've put you in the double room just above. You've a nice view out to the bay and a small bathroom. Probably not what you're used to — '

'I'm sure it'll be perfect,' said Beth with a reassuring smile.

'You run your own hotel, don't you?'

James went through a brief family history about moving into a smaller property and converting the old family home into Harrington's. 'We've been open for some time now and gaining a reputation — an excellent one, thank heavens. And how long have you been here?'

'Just on five years. We moved from Torquay in Devon — had a hotel there but it was a twenty-room monstrosity that needed constant care and attention. You may as well have dug a hole and thrown money in it. We wanted something smaller and cosier.'

Desmond returned with a tray and placed it on the table between them. 'Tea and some of Viv's Dundee cake.'

Vivian handed them the visitors' book, then perched on the windowsill and prepared the tea. 'I hope you don't think I'm being cheeky but would you mind signing as Lord and Lady Harrington? It'll do our business good to have someone of your stature here.'

'Vivian!' Desmond baulked.

James held a hand up as he brought out his fountain pen. 'We're happy to, Vivian. We do the same when we have someone with some clout staying with us.'

Desmond gawped. 'Really?'

'Really.' James went on to explain that regardless of which end of the business one was in, be it a bed and breakfast or the Savoy, recommendation was always the best form of business. Before he put his pen away, he signed Desmond's book and a rush of pride flashed through him. How lovely to be remembered and in such an out of the way place too. Extraordinary.

Beth went on to offer some tips for encouraging custom and then told them of their latest venture, painting courses. 'We're always on the lookout for new things. It keeps business coming in.'

Over the next ten minutes, the four of them chatted like old friends and James learned that the couple were originally from London and had moved to Torquay to take over the twenty-room monstrosity. Desmond had been a messenger for the merchant banks in the City of London. Vivian had remained as a housewife, bringing up their only son who was now, himself, working in London. Beth explained their reason for visiting Polpen-narth and Desmond began suggesting places to visit.

'The Pilchard Inn is about a five minute walk from here; they do nice pasties in there. The landlord's name is Bidevin and his mum makes them fresh every day. If your friends need any groceries, then Gretchen runs the store by the harbour. The best fish and chip shop is run by Vic and Flora and you mentioned about your friend's anniversary. Well, there's a nice restaurant called The Sardine a bit further along, run by Jonah Quinn.'

'It sounds as if you have everything covered,' James said as he handed the visitors' book back to Vivian.

'And you know we have the Cornish Legends festival on for another week.'

'Yes, we saw the bunting and flags zig-zagging across the road as we came in.'

'And that's already started, hasn't it?' asked Beth.

Desmond reached across to the rack that held a number of leaflets about the area. He picked one up and gave it to Beth. 'Started on Monday with a huge parade. From tomorrow, we celebrate one specific legend every few days and there's either a parade or some sort of gathering to mark that particular character. Your friends' children will love it.'

James thanked him and saw his opening. 'And Polpennarth was in the news recently. Have they found that chap that went missing?'

Vivian's reaction confirmed that she loved to gossip. She immediately sat forward with some animation to go through what happened. 'One minute he's walking along the high street, next minute, he'd vanished — just like that — not a word to anyone. It wasn't in the middle of the night, neither. Broad daylight it was.'

'And no one saw anything?'

'Not a thing.'

Desmond added that it had been crowded. 'It was the day of the opening parade and he just disappeared. And no one's seen hide nor hair of him since.'

'Dear, dear!' said Beth. 'Is he married?

His wife must be worried sick.'

'Oh yes, married he is to a lovely girl. Quiet little thing she is — not from round here.'

'And Fiske, he's local?' asked James.

'Born and bred,' said Desmond, who went on to explain that he'd been a fisherman, man and boy. 'Generations of fishermen in his family — knows the area, knows the tides and the currents. That's what makes this so strange.'

'The *Daily Express* mentioned that the locals felt this was the work of pixies.'

Desmond roared with laughter. 'Some of the older residents believe in all this nonsense. I mean, this festival is great for a bit of fun but some of 'em take it all too seriously. There's a few of them put in a petition to ban it a couple of years ago — said it'd cause trouble and that the goblins would come out. Hah! I ask you — talk about living in the Dark Ages.'

Vivian agreed and checked her watch. 'Now, you've had a long drive, so I expect you'd like to get to your room and freshen up.'

Two minutes later, James and Beth

30

closed the door on their hosts and took in their surroundings for the next week. They were in a large room with a high ceiling and a double bed with an eiderdown embroidered with country flowers on a rose trellis. There were two wardrobes and chest of drawers, together with a cabinet on either side of the bed. In front of the huge bay window were two arm chairs and a pair of binoculars on the windowsill. James wandered across and picked them up.

'I say, this is rather good isn't it? We should do this. We have some stunning views from some of our rooms. If we want to relax we can just sit here and watch the world go by.' He scanned the horizon. 'Water's like a millpond and there are plenty of children building sandcastles on the beach.'

Beth joined him. 'A beautiful beach too. It's a natural cove, isn't it?'

Boulders and rocks lay at each end of the cove. He could make out small children with fishing nets and tin buckets poking around in the puddles, collecting crabs and small fish; something he'd done himself at that age. A couple of men were standing further up on the rocks sea-fishing and a number of families were enjoying picnics on the beach and playing games.

It was close to four o'clock and he suggested to Beth they take a stroll down to the harbour to get their bearings.

★ ★ ★

They began at the harbour wall, just along from the hotel and estimated it would take about an hour to walk around the village. With the sun shining down from the clearest of blue skies, they began to explore. They meandered in and out of small shops selling anything from shells and colourful tin spades to fishermen's smocks and fishing tackle. Tourists stood pondering which souvenirs and postcards to send home.

The freshness of the sea air was invigorating and every few yards the smell of fish, chips and pasties wafted past. A seafood vendor selling cockles, mussels and winkles looked up from behind his stall and waved hello. The long drive down was soon forgotten.

Bunting criss-crossed the road all the way up the hill where, a signpost pointed towards the fairground. Billboards were posted outside several shops, advertising the festival and inviting people to buy a programme for more detailed information.

'I'll get one of those, Beth. It'll be good to read up on all of these characters and know exactly when and where things are happening. Shall I get one for the Merryweathers too?'

'I think so. There'll be some activities for Luke and Mark, I'm sure.'

He looked up at the shop sign. Gretchen's, the shop was called. As they entered, the bell above the door jingled.

It was a shop that couldn't really decide what it was meant to be. There were newspapers, magazines and sweets, small toys, buckets and spades, rubber rings and hundreds of ornaments of all shapes and sizes depicting the Cornish legends. At the far end were shelves of groceries, cereals, tinned produce and bottles of fizzy drinks.

Beth picked up a large plastic mermaid and pulled a face. 'I thought about getting a present for Stephen and Anne.'

James grinned, took the figurine from her and placed it back on the shelf. 'I rather think they wouldn't thank you for that.'

He heard some movement behind the counter. He turned to see a lady who he presumed was Gretchen. She was a lady in her sixties, less than five feet tall, with the most mischievous expression he'd ever seen. If anyone could pass for a naughty pixie, it would be her. Her eyes twinkled and her summer dress was easily three sizes too big for her. He wondered if she'd do better buying children's clothes.

'Ooh,' she chuckled, 'strangers in town.' She chuckled again. 'Have to warn the Sheriff.' Another chuckle. 'Tch, too many Westerns on the television. I do love a Western, don't you?'

James and Beth confessed they did like to catch the new serial, *Wagon Train*.

'One of my ancestors was a cowboy for a short while,' said James.

Gretchen put her hands to her mouth. 'How exciting.'

Beth swung round. 'Are you leading us on?'

He assured her he wasn't. 'He was my grandfather's cousin I think, or great grandfather's cousin; something like that. Yes, he was a banker in Chicago, I believe, but headed west. I should find out more about him.'

Gretchen gently clapped and James couldn't help but smile. The woman's childlike wonder was refreshing.

'I take it you're Gretchen?'

She stole a quick peek over her shoulder. 'Last time I looked. Gretchen Kettel.' She chuckled as she sang a few bars of *Polly Put the Kettle On*. 'You're visiting are you?'

Beth went through their reasons for travelling as James purchased two festival programmes. After a few minutes they bade Gretchen goodbye with an assurance they would be sure to see her over the next few days. Out on the pavement,

James wrapped an arm around Beth and laughed.

'What an extraordinary woman. She reminds me of a little sparrow flitting about, always twitching, never still.'

'She's adorable and I want her living in Cavendish.'

They wandered further along the high street. Flags and balloons hung from every available space and colourful cardboard effigies of mermaids, pixies and other Cornish legends were placed at various intervals along the pavement. Small alleyways and cobbled streets threaded off the main road where residents displayed hanging baskets cascading with summer blooms. Two local policemen were sealing off the end of the road.

Beth nudged him. 'There's The Sardine. That's the place Desmond and Vivian recommended for dinner.'

'And there's The Pilchard Inn where we're meeting the Merryweathers later,' said James. 'That's where the landlord's mother makes the pasties. We'll have to try those. Can't come to Cornwall and not have a pasty.'

The pasty was unique to Cornwall and was a staple food for miners during the previous century. Filled with chunks of beef, potato, onion and swede, the pastry band was thick so that miners could hold them easily. A traditional home-made pasty could not be beaten and James had already made a mental note to have at least one while they were there.

Beth checked her watch and suggested they get back to change and freshen up. 'I'd also like to get a cardigan if nothing else. I would imagine the sea breeze brings a chill in during the evening.'

As they turned, they bumped into one of the policemen. He was a young, fresh-faced man who apologised and introduced himself.

'PC Cardew Innes,' he said in a mild Cornish burr.

James shook hands with him. 'James and Beth Harrington.'

'Welcome to Polpennarth. You're not just Mr and Mrs Harrington though, are you? Not according to the Simms. Sorry but word spread the minute you made a booking. I don't think we've ever had a Lord and Lady here before.'

Beth assured him they were no different to anyone else but Innes stood straight and frowned.

'Oh no, your Ladyship. That won't do. You are Lord and Lady Harrington and that's how I'll address you.'

James bit back a grin and indicated the activity. 'You're closing the road off?'

Innes explained that the first of the character parades would start the next day. 'We had the opening parade which is just a general march up the street and then we celebrate each of the Cornish legends. Tomorrow is Old Bogey.'

'Goodness,' said Beth, 'who's Old Bogey?'

The young man gave a description of a solitary individual who came out at night; was horribly evil and loved to interfere with people. 'They're dark, have menacing red eyes and give off a nasty smell.'

Beth grimaced. 'Sounds horrid.'

'Oh, it's just a bit of fun. Some of the locals will dress up as Old Bogey. They use black greasepaint, wear tall top hats and run around trying to scare people. You should come.'

'We will,' said James. He then asked about the missing Colm Fiske. 'Have you found him yet?'

'Not a dicky-bird. It's like someone's whisked him off the face of the earth.' He leaned in. 'Some of the old ones are saying that the piskies have had him.' He straightened up and cleared his throat. 'Not that I believe in any of that.'

Beth queried his use of the word 'piskie'. 'Don't you mean pixie?'

'Cornish term for 'em is piskie.'

'I say, do you have an Inspector investigating?' said James.

'Oh yes. He's come up from Penzance. Inspector Jarvis Wormstone. Used to work at Scotland Yard in London so he knows his stuff.'

'And how's his investigation coming along?'

'Not a sausage. No one saw anything. No one heard anything.'

'But it was a busy day?'

'Very busy; first day of the festival. It

was mid morning so it was all in full swing; plenty of people about.' He checked the road and spotted a blind gentleman with a white stick trying to cross it. 'I'd best get over and give Mr Atherton a hand.'

'Will you keep me posted on the investigation? Sleuthing's a bit of a hobby for me and this is intriguing. You know where we're staying.'

'I can only let you know what's out there for the public to know.' He moved on.

Beth linked an arm through his. 'You really are the limit, James. We're on holiday, not delving into a mystery. I'm sure this Jarvis Wormstone won't thank you for poking your nose in.'

'He doesn't need to know, does he? It's odd don't you think? A man going missing in the middle of a busy street, and with the parade going on as well.' He felt Beth tug him back.

'Who on earth is that?'

He followed her gaze. His eyes settled on a strange figure prancing along the road in a long green cloak and a fur

balaclava. She wore several bead neck-
laces and a pair of ram's horns fastened
to her head with string.

She came to a halt, stared at PC Innes
and stabbed a bony finger at him. 'I curse
you!' She cried, then turned on her heels
and ran up a side street.

'Good lord!' Said James.

'Maybe she's part of the festival.'

'Mmm, do you think? She doesn't
appear to have a good impression of the
local constabulary.' They made their way
back to the hotel. 'Perhaps we'll discover
her identity in the pub tonight.'

6

They found a vacant wooden picnic table on the small rocky outcrop to one side of The Pilchard Inn. There were six benches in all and most were taken by holiday-makers. Wherever people sat, there was an uninterrupted view of the beach.

Mark and Luke, dressed in blue shorts and Aertex shirts, tugged Stephen's arm.

'Dad, can we go play on the beach please?' said Mark.

'And can we take Radley, too?' added his brother eagerly.

Radley, as if understanding everything that had been said, gazed up to Stephen in anticipation.

Stephen handed the lead over. 'Stay within sight and no g–going in the water.'

They cheered and raced down the sandy wooden stairs to the side of the pub.

James and Stephen made for the bar.

'We've been transported to a p–pirate ship.'

They each gave a slow shake of the head. The bar was heaving and they jostled among not only customers but all things seafaring. An abundance of ornaments and relics from old ships and fishing boats decorated every spare inch of space, from floor to ceiling. Fishing nets with weathered buoys and plastic fish hung from the rafters. Attached to the walls were ships' figureheads and maritime artefacts rescued from wrecks. Giant cannons with chipped cannonballs stood guard by the door and a ship's wheel was fastened to the front of the bar. To the side of them was a life-size pirate with a moth-eaten parrot secured to his shoulder.

It was warm and the smell of beer, hops and pasties was an enticing one. The ancient oak bar was around six feet long with very little space behind for staff. Two young women were busy serving customers when a tall bear of a man with dark hair and a bushy beard came up from the cellar stairs and placed his hands on the bar. James put him at about thirty although he found that beards always put years on a man. Often, when they shaved them off, they looked much younger. The barman scrutinised him. He had to shout to be heard above the chatter and spoke with a strong Cornish brogue.

'All right? Just arrived?'

'Yes, this afternoon. We're here for the festival and to celebrate our friend's wedding anniversary.'

The man held a hand out. 'Bidevin. Bidevin Tallack.'

'Ah, you're the landlord. I say, is that a Cornish name?'

'It is. Bidevin is the Cornish word for hawk. You wanting a drink?'

James put an order in for two gin and tonics and he and Stephen opted for local ale. 'Can you suggest one?'

'We've our own little brewery just outside of the village. Polpennarth ale. Want to try it?'

'A–absolutely,' said Stephen.

James enquired after the pasties.

'All gone today. Mam bakes 'em fresh every morning. Come mid-morning tomorrow and they'll be a new batch out.' He placed the drinks on the bar and reached under the counter for a tray. 'You're Lord Harrington?'

James did a double-take. 'How on earth did you know that?'

Bidevin raised an eyebrow. 'Locals chat. Desmond was raving about you being a racing driver and I was having a natter with Cardew Innes earlier. He was quite taken to be introduced to you. A real Lord, he said.'

James rolled his eyes. 'I'm happy not to stand out from the crowd. By the way, this is Stephen Merryweather. He's our vicar back home and one half of the celebrating couple.'

'Welcome and happy anniversary. You've come at a good time.'

'Y–yes, the festival looks very entertaining. O–our children will love it.'

James leant on the bar. 'Shame that you've had some bad news with that chap going missing.'

Bidevin shrugged as he accepted payment. 'I'm not crying over him. He had the hump with me the previous night 'coz I chucked him out. Have to do that sometimes with Colm; he don't know

45

when to stop.' He leaned over the bar and brushed the hair from his forehead. 'See that? Colm did that. Tried to punch me but lost his balance. He's a big bloke, Colm, but not as big as me. Mind, he's a good fisherman, Polpennarth man. Strange one though, him going missing. He'll pitch up. Prob'ly sleeping it off in a ditch somewhere.' He gave James his change and moved to the next customer.

Back at their bench, Stephen asked whether James was going to investigate Colm Fiske.

Anne looked on in anticipation. 'Oh, do say you are. We could do it between us. And we have a dog. It'll be like Enid Blyton's Famous Five.'

Stephen groaned. Beth gave James a knowing look. 'It's no use you saying you're not going to. You've already started asking questions.'

'A–and there are some odd c–characters floating about. Have you seen that woman in the cloak?'

James sat up with a start. 'Yes, did you?'

Anne explained that she'd shown up at

the caravan site. 'The owner told her to sling her hook. That's the expression he used.'

'B–but not before she shouted that Colm Fiske had it coming to him.'

'How extraordinary.' He told Beth and Anne about Colm being thrown out of the pub. 'The young Fiske doesn't appear to have endeared himself to people, does he?'

Beth reminded him that this was a small community. 'I'm sure if you fall out with someone here, it would be awkward. Everyone knows everyone else.'

Anne agreed. 'People are prone to take sides in such a remote village.'

'The owner of the site said he didn't know C–Colm well but he seemed a n–nice man.'

James supped his ale and watched Luke and Mark on the beach. The children were deep in thought about where to put the next turret on the sand-castle. Radley barked furiously, demanding a stick or ball to be thrown. Two other children stood nearby and Mark was quick to invite them to help.

He scanned the surrounding tables. Their neighbours were clearly tourists. The residents all had healthy, rugged complexions; unlike the visitors who had arrived with city paleness about them or who'd caught too much sun on their first day — their faces red and sore. A few people would be dabbing calamine lotion on that night.

'I wonder where he lives?'

Beth caught her breath. 'You're not going round there are you?'

'Absolutely not, no; but I did think we could accidentally bump into his wife and offer some empathy and support.' He looked at Stephen. 'You didn't bring your dog collar, did you?'

Stephen raised an eyebrow. 'I did not. I would introduce myself to the v–vicar here and glean some information but he's on holiday himself.'

Anne fanned herself with a beer mat. 'Beth, there's a Women's Institute here, do you think we should spend an evening with them — there's bound to be some gossip there.'

James couldn't help but laugh. 'Will

48

you listen to yourselves? You sound like the Snoop Sisters.'

The remark caused some amusement. Rose and Lilac Crumb, two elderly spinsters back in Cavendish were renowned for their nosiness and for making two and two come to seven. James had nicknamed them the Snoop Sisters a few years ago and was careful about the conversations he had if they were in earshot. If they couldn't hear what you were saying, they'd simply make assumptions and spread the rumours regardless.

Anne finished her drink. 'Four people are better than one. We've always been on the periphery of your investigations and we're in a lovely position to pry. No one knows us here — we're just curious tourists.'

'Well, I've heard it all now. You all admonish me for meddling and here you all are setting up a plan of action.' He noticed Beth frown. 'Darling, you have reservations?'

'We're behaving as if this were a game,' she answered. 'It's not. The things you've been involved with have been dangerous. People have been killed and we've been put in perilous situations. We don't know the villagers. We'd have to speak with everybody to even get close to what is happening here. How can we possibly investigate this? Remember, this is supposed to be a holiday.'

He rested his elbows on the bench. 'Beth's right. We're here to celebrate your anniversary. We can't go around meddling in people's lives. And we already have conflicting information about Colm. Bidevin is not his biggest fan and your man at the caravan site appears to like him.'

Anne's shoulders dropped. 'You're right.' After a few seconds she sat upright and suggested that it wouldn't hurt to simply listen or ask some innocent questions. 'We may discover something and we could simply pass it on to that Inspector man.'

Stephen sighed. 'No, I–I agree with Beth but I've a feeling you're not g–going to let it go, are you? Your interest is already piqued.'

James suppressed a grin. 'We could do as Anne said. Ask a few questions; simply tourists on holiday interested in the local mystery.' He sought Beth's approval. 'Are you happy with that? You have to admit, it is compelling. How can a fit young man, who knows the area, simply disappear into thin air?'

Beth heaved a sigh and met everyone's gaze. 'If I see anyone doing anything more than that, I will put a stop to the whole thing. No one does anything silly.' She singled out James. 'Or wanders off without a word to anyone.'

'Understood.'

Stephen finished his beer. 'A–another round. I thought the l–landlord might know who that odd-looking woman was.'

James swigged the last of his ale. 'Yes, come on, that'll kick start our observations. Ladies, the same again?'

Anne added an order for lemonade for the boys.

With instructions in hand, the men returned to the bar where Bidevin took their order. 'So, you'll be watching out for Old Bogey tomorrow?'

51

'Ah, yes, we're looking forward to it. I've a feeling we're going to see some odd sights over the next few days.'

'Not wrong there.'

'I–I saw an odd sight earlier.'

Bidevin set one pint on the bar and began pulling the next. 'Oh yeah, and what was that?'

'An e–elderly lady with horns on her h–head.'

'Ah, you've bumped into old Nibbin.'

James exchanged a startled look with Stephen. 'Nibbin?'

'That's right. Lives up on the moors. Comes down now and again for provisions. Don't like anyone or anything; keeps herself to herself and you don't want to be crossing her.'

'Is she a Cornish lady?'

'Polpennarth born and bred. Her uncle was the same, running about on the moors with a colander on his head spouting on about nature and Mother Earth.' He placed the second pint on the bar and prepared the remaining drinks. 'She's harmless. Likes to scare people but she has a bit of fun with it to be honest.

Likes Mam's pasties.'

He took payment and moved on to the next customer. James and Stephen threaded their way through the crowds to join Beth and Anne.

'Well,' said James. 'We've found out a little more about our cloaked lady.' He went on to outline their discussion with Bidevin and the eccentricities of Nibbin. 'I can't imagine why she'd want to kidnap Colm Fiske.'

'I can't imagine she'd be able to,' said Anne. 'It sounds as if that fisherman is a big man — she didn't look strong enough to tackle someone like that.'

'Perhaps,' said Beth, 'she put him into some sort of mesmeric trance and seduced him into going with her.'

'Or she's doing something to him to satisfy a pagan worship thing.'

James rolled his eyes and reminded Anne that her imagination was, perhaps, a little too active. 'She has her opinion on Colm though, judging by that comment you heard at the caravan site.' A shadow crossed over them and he looked behind to see Desmond Simms. 'Ah, Desmond, do you want to join us?' He introduced the Merryweathers. 'We were just discussing your little mystery down here with the missing fisherman.'

Desmond perched on the end of the bench next to James. 'Yes, odd isn't it? Still no word and Evelyn's worried sick.'

'Evelyn?'

'His wife.' He picked out a young, dark haired lady chatting near the roadside. 'That's her there.' He got up. 'Nice to see you all. Me and Viv are taking a hilltop walk. See you in the morning if not before.'

James studied Evelyn Fiske. She stood with a buxom blonde lady who he could imagine wouldn't pull any punches. Evelyn looked as if she was in her late twenties. She had long chestnut brown hair and her shoulders sagged. There was an ingrained weariness about her, as if she'd had worries for some time. When she looked toward them, he found himself being surprised. There was fear in her eyes. He'd expected concern and worry. Was this the reaction of a wife missing her husband? He threw the question out.

'I'm sure I would look harried if you were to go missing,' said Beth.

'I–I see what you m–mean though. She looks old, as if she's had an awfully h–hard life.'

'Perhaps she has,' said Anne. 'I can't imagine being a fisherman's wife is a bed of roses.'

Evelyn and her companion walked toward them and sat at the vacant table alongside. The buxom lady slapped the bench with her hand.

'What you need is a stiff brandy, that'll sort you out. At least you can do a few things now. No scurrying around like a church mouse.'

Evelyn shrank. 'Hilda, I don't think I'll have a brandy — perhaps a small bitter shandy.'

'Nonsense, brandy'll put some life into you. And coming to the festival tomorrow will put a glow in your cheeks. You're not to sit moping around, Evelyn Fiske; you're not to feel sorry for yourself, things are looking up for you.'

Hilda marched into the pub, leaving Evelyn to fiddle nervously with the clasp of her handbag. James caught her eye and raised his glass.

'Cheers. Are you local?'

The young woman's eyes darted here and there as if the devil himself were going to leap out. 'Yes, yes I am.'

'We're down for the festival. I suppose you go every year or even take part.'

'Oh no, no, Colm — ' she twisted her ring. 'I do some cakes for the WI stall.'

'We do the same for ours, back home,' said Anne. 'Does your WI let other members in for the evening? Me and Beth are keen to pop into your meeting if that's all right.'

Evelyn fiddled with her hair. 'Well . . . I suppose it's all right. You'd have to ask Hilda, the lady I'm with. Oh I don't know! She may say no.'

James held his hands up in apology. The conversation had appeared to increase her anxiety. 'It's absolutely fine if it's a no-go. The girls will just have to miss out for a week.' He watched her fasten and unfasten the top button of her cardigan and asked her if she was well.

'Quite well, thank you.'

He noticed a quiet exhalation of relief as Hilda approached and thrust a drink in her hand. 'Get that down you, it'll warm the cockles of your heart.' She plonked herself down next to her and Evelyn repeated Anne's request about attending the WI. Hilda swung round. 'Glorious. Always happy to meet members from further afield. We're preparing for some festivities later in the month. City people are you?'

Beth explained who they were, where they were from and why they were visiting. Hilda asked direct questions that required little in the way of detail. Where was Cavendish, how many residents, how long had the WI been there; she had the grace to look astounded when Beth advised her it had been one of the first to be formed.

Hilda swigged her pint of ale down in twenty seconds. 'We started in '47. Thirty members and counting. Meet once a week.' She slapped the table with the palm of her hand and brought Evelyn out of her daydream. 'Come along Evelyn, we can't sit here all night. I've to deliver sandwiches to Tris and you can't mope about on your own.' She helped the young woman to her feet and asked them if they were attending the festival the next day.

They confirmed they would be.

'Jolly good. See you there. You won't recognise me, I'll be in character. Come along Evelyn.'

Once she was out of earshot, Stephen puffed out his cheeks. 'G–goodness, she's a whirlwind, isn't she?'

James agreed. 'A more assertive version of our Dorothy Forbes, don't you think?'

Dorothy, the self-appointed director of the Cavendish players, was positively gentle compared to Hilda. Beth put in that Hilda reminded her of James' sister, Fiona. 'She has that loud, extrovert personality.'

Anne remarked that she felt Fiona would be more tactful with someone whose husband was missing. 'Hilda seemed incredibly unsympathetic, didn't you think?'

The general opinion was that it was odd for Evelyn to be drinking in a pub a couple of days after her husband had disappeared. Ladies rarely drank in pubs alone although James felt Hilda would dismiss the notion and insist she had as much right to do so as anyone else.

He pondered. It wasn't Evelyn drinking that bothered him so much; more her demeanour and body language. That young lady was fearful, not worried or upset. And Hilda's comments seemed untimely, bearing in mind the circumstances. What was it she'd said: '*Things are looking up for you; you can't sit around moping.*' What an odd thing to say to a lady whose husband had just disappeared.

Beth brought him out of his musings. 'I'm surprised Evelyn's attending the festival. I wouldn't have thought she'd be in the mood for such gaiety.'

'Most peculiar. I think we need to keep our eyes peeled and our ears pinned back tomorrow. There's something troubling Evelyn. Whether it's her husband I don't know but that woman has the worries of the world on her shoulders.'

Stephen checked his watch and called

for Luke and Mark to come up from the beach.

Mark shouted back. 'Look at our sandcastle.'

Luke added, 'And we've made a moat for the water.'

Radley barked and wagged his tail.

Anne waved them up while telling them how lovely their structure was.

'W–we must be getting along. The parade starts at midday tomorrow. We'll look out for you in the high street.'

With arrangements in place, James and Beth wandered hand in hand along the promenade toward their hotel. Above them, a string of coloured lights fixed to lampposts lit their way. James looked along the coastline and saw a flashing light. 'Did you see that?'

Beth looked across. 'What?'

'It's gone now. Looked like a light flashing out at sea. It may have been on the cliff top; hard to say.' He squeezed Beth's hand. 'I wonder what the festival will be like.'

'We'll soon find out. Hopefully no one will vanish in front of our eyes.'

7

The participants of the Old Bogey parade gathered just along from the hotel. There must have been around a hundred villagers who had made a supreme effort and dressed up for the occasion. They jostled for space on the road. The remaining villagers and several hundred tourists and visitors lined the pavements and promenade from the hotel to the far end of the high street.

Old Bogey's costume consisted of a tall top hat, tails, a loose white shirt, trousers that were a little too short and hobnail boots. Last minute preparations saw people helping one another out by smearing black greasepaint over their faces. Some carried dolls that, in their day, had probably been the pride and joy of girls in the village but were now hideously deformed by their new owners with missing eyes and squashed faces.

The crowds clapped to a constant rhythm of a drum and Morris men in white hats with flowers pinned on played accordions and fiddles. It reminded James a little of the tune played at their own scarecrow festival; a mesmeric melody that played around and around without pause. It was uplifting and James couldn't help but feel inspired by the laughter and enthusiasm the whole ceremony communicated.

The balmy breeze carried with it the smell of the sea and the occasional aroma of fish and chips. Three or four men lined the route, selling hot dogs from stands, alongside the more traditional ice-cream carts. Children waved the black and white Cornish flag in one hand and kept a firm hold on their ice lollies in the other. Most men had Box or Ilford cameras hanging around their necks, ready to capture the moment. A Master of Ceremonies arrived with a long wooden staff. He pounded the tarmac and roared out his request for silence. The crowd hushed. The musicians softened the melody, the drummer muted the drum.

'Old Bogey be out tonight. Whether
the moon be dull or bright,
It makes no difference to the Bogeyman:
He's coming for you if he possibly
can.
He's hiding in cupboards all dark and
dusty.
Will he get you or will he get me?
Old Bogey's out tonight; Old Bogey's
out tonight.'

The volume of the music increased; the
man held the staff high and yelled, 'OLD
BOGEY BE OUT TONIGHT!'

The parade began and a stream of Old
Bogey characters shuffled behind the
Master of Ceremonies. James and Beth
marvelled at the spectacle. Everyone
taking part reverted to character, especially those who had adopted a creeping
gait. Bidevin was easy to spot with his
huge frame, bushy beard and exaggerated
swagger. He growled at the children who
sheltered between their parents' legs. On
seeing James and Beth, he stood upright
and broke into a wide smile.

'All right?'

James and Beth grinned back as he reverted to character. Just behind him was a lady who yelled a loud 'Hello!' At first James wondered who on earth it was and then remembered the voice behind the greasepaint. It was Hilda, her blonde hair tucked up inside the tall hat.

Beth squeezed his arm. 'The Bogey man is quite gruesome looking, isn't it? What does Old Bogey represent?'

He reminded Beth that this was one of the most famous of the legends and one that reached most cultures. 'I believe most parents at some time will threaten their children with the Bogey man if they don't do as they're told.'

The musicians followed the characters accompanied by the pounding of a huge bass drum. The man beating the rhythm was a tall, wiry man who didn't seem big enough to carry such a thing. James wondered if he'd make it to the fairground. An open top lorry, made to look like a prison, passed by with a few residents behind its bars shouting for help. The crowd fell in and tagged behind the parade.

They advanced slowly and were showered with vibrant flowers, ribbons and coloured confetti. James and Beth shuffled along with the masses and sang along with a *la-la* to the tune as it continued its repetitive melody. Toward the middle of the high street, James spotted Stephen's straw hat. Fortunately, he was a tall man and easy to spot. He grabbed Beth's hand and guided her through the crowd and onto the pavement.

Luke and Mark jumped up and down tugging at them. 'Did you see the Bogey man? Did you see how many there were? Did you see the big drum?'

James and Beth answered every question patiently and suggested they rejoin the throng.

Anne steered the two boys ahead of them and ordered them to stay in sight. She shouted to make herself heard. 'Where does the parade finish?'

'According to this,' James waved his programme in the air, 'just over the brow of the hill. There's a large green there with a fairground.'

'Will there be dodgems?' asked Mark.

'And swings?' Luke added.

'Will there be see-saw?'

Stephen placed a hand on each of their shoulders and assured them they wouldn't miss out. 'W–we have a week here, s–so you have plenty of t–time for rides.'

The boys skipped in time with the music. James looked around. 'Where's Radley?'

Anne explained that Radley had made friends with two Border collies and a lady who owned them was going on a long walk. 'She offered to take Radley and we agreed. We thought it would be better than the poor thing being trampled on.'

They fell back a little to make themselves heard.

'The l–lady with the dogs is a writer. Her name's Kerry Sheppard.'

James asked what sort of books she wrote.

'Non-fiction,' replied Stephen, who went on to detail that she was down for the festival as she was writing a book about folklore and customs.

Beth suggested they invite her to Cavendish. 'I'm sure she'd have plenty of material with the amount of things we celebrate. Is she with family?'

Anne replied that she'd travelled alone. 'She doesn't believe in women being home-makers. She doesn't believe in men being the breadwinners and thinks that women have every right to be independent. I can't imagine her with a family although she is very attractive and quite feminine.'

'Well, I guess that's similar to Elsie.' Elsie ran the local café between the villages of Cavendish and Charnley. She'd remained single and adored running her own business. 'I say it shows some guts to branch out like that, don't you James?'

'Yes, I do. I would imagine that writing is a rather lonely job if you're having to travel all the time. It'd be interesting to meet her though and find out what she's researched; especially if she's been travelling the length of Britain.'

Stephen suggested they come up to the

caravan site one evening. 'We could have a chat with her, perhaps arrange something for early evening. L–leave it with me.'

'Oh look,' said Beth, 'there's that Nibbin woman.'

They'd reached the green and although the music continued, the expansive area had allowed everyone to spread out. People dispersed to stalls selling burgers and many hopped on the fairground rides. Nibbin scurried here and there chattering to herself and calling out odd phrases that made no sense. The ram horns had been replaced by some old rope netting and tied to this was a plastic lobster. James suppressed a grin and turned to Beth who had diverted her attention elsewhere. Her focus was Evelyn Fiske who still had an air of fear about her. Hilda and a few other women surrounded her and seemed intent on encouraging her to enjoy herself.

Stephen stood alongside him. 'I–I find that a little odd, don't you?'

James concurred. 'I'm all for empathy and support but those women appear to be oblivious to Evelyn's situation.'

'A–and Evelyn still looks more fearful than worried.'

Luke dragged his parents over to the merry-go-round, insisting they all choose a horse. Mark, who had already clambered on one, called over. 'Come on Uncle James.'

'Come on Uncle James,' Luke repeated his elder brother's request. 'Auntie Beth, you can sit next to me.'

Their friendship with the Merryweathers had been cemented quickly and the boys had taken to calling James and Beth Uncle and Aunt. James nudged Beth onto the merry-go-round and they chose painted ponies alongside Luke. The automated organ launched into *I Do Like to be Beside the Seaside* and the horses began to rise and fall. Mark and Luke shouted excitedly. 'We're winning, we're winning!'

James gazed across the green as his horse gently galloped round. The Old Bogey characters had lost their scariness as most were digging into candy floss and Cornish pasties. Bidevin was wiping greasepaint off his face. He spotted them and waved. James and Beth waved back as the horses began to slow down.

Luke pointed. 'Can we go on the swing chairs?'

Stephen raised his eyebrows. 'Sh–shall we meet you later?' he said to the James. 'I can't believe y–you're going to want to go on rides all afternoon.'

They agreed to meet at five o'clock by the entrance to the park. James and Beth wandered around the green. There were stalls selling sandwiches, pies and drinks. Alongside these were craft and art displays created by local people. The WI had a large marquee tent at the end. Beth nudged him.

'Come on, that's where the gossip will be.'

Inside, the WI had set up a small café where James ordered tea and home-made cherry scones. They found a spare table and sat down. As they cut into their scones Hilda dragged a chair over and joined them. She still had her costume and make-up on but the black had become streaked from the heat.

'Phew. Outfit's far too heavy for this weather. Roll on tomorrow, that's what I say.'

'Oh,' said James, 'what's tomorrow?'

'The Fairy family. Not so much to wear and no greasepaint involved. How are you enjoying it?'

Beth said they were enjoying it very much and commented on how nice it was to meet some of the locals, including Hilda.

'We're a welcoming bunch.' She swung round, scanned the area and startled James when she bellowed. 'Tristram.'

A man of around thirty looked up and acknowledged her. He picked up a fruit juice and wandered over. He was fit and trim with a crop of almost white hair that stuck up at the front, making him look boyish and charming. Judging by his weathered complexion, James surmised that he spent a lot of time outdoors.

'Tris, this is Lord and Lady Harrington.'

Tristram reached over and shook hands with them both. 'Tristram Roscarrock.'

'My husband,' Hilda stated.

'I heard we had a Lord and Lady in the village.'

James complimented him on his outfit. He carried a pair of old boots and the obligatory tall top hat was under his arm. He'd washed the greasepaint from his face although traces remained by his ears. Tristram looked down at his feet. 'I had to take these off, they're not conducive to walking far. Belonged to my grand-dad and he had smaller feet than me.' He looked at Hilda. 'I'll probably head back to the sanctuary in a while.'

'Sanctuary?' James said.

Tristram explained that he helped run a sanctuary for animals and birds. 'We get all sorts come in from the sea, seals and birds; also get animals hit by cars, that sort of thing. At the moment, we've a few seals washed up due to the storms last week. They need a little love and attention.'

Beth put a hand to her chest and let out a sigh. 'Oh the poor things — is that all voluntary?'

'Some of it. There's half a dozen of us work full time. I work alongside Hans. We tend to do most of the rescues. He's on his own at the moment — gone off to the headland to free some birds. We're pretty busy but I didn't want to miss the parade.'

'This sanctuary, how do you fund it?'

'Donations mainly. We're a registered charity and a lot of the Cornish people do fund raising for us. We tend to get quite a bit when the newspapers show a baby seal washed up. They are incredibly cute.'

'Tris can't bear to see animals abused,' said Hilda. 'The man can't even kill a fly — he has to let it go.'

Tristram blushed. 'I'm a grown man so I s'pose it sounds a bit silly.'

James assured him it sounded nothing of the sort. 'It's people like you that keep the rest of us focussed on what's right. I don't particularly like cruelty to animals but I don't do anything about it — you do.'

'You hunt foxes?'

'Tristram!' Hilda said with a fierce glare.

Her husband shrugged and James held his hands up. 'Personally no but most villages have hunts and Cavendish is one of them. The farmers appreciate that it keeps the fox population down.'

'They could do it another way, Lord Harrington.'

'I agree,' said Beth, 'but it's a double-edged sword, isn't it? The foxes need to be kept under control and it's difficult to find them without the dogs sniffing them out.'

James suggested they postpone this discussion for another time. 'It's a lovely day and I'd hate to argue with you over something that I'm not actually involved in. Perhaps we could visit the sanctuary one day. Is it open?'

Tristram beamed at the opportunity to promote the place. 'It's open every day between ten and four.' He felt in his jacket pocket and brought out a leaflet. 'Always have some of these to hand. Here. Why don't you pop over?'

They bade him goodbye with a promise that they would call in.

'I say, Hilda, has he always worked there?'

'Yes, man and boy. I don't know what

he'd do if he didn't have that. He'd be hopeless in an office; he gets seasick so couldn't be a fisherman if his life depended on it. He's an outdoors man. That sanctuary is right up his street. If that closed down I think he'd become a shepherd or something.'

Beth asked if she knew Nibbin, whereupon Hilda let out a whoop of laughter. 'Everyone knows Nibbin. I take it you've seen her.'

'Is that her real name?'

'No idea. Always known as Nibbin. There was another one, a father or uncle, but he died.' She laughed again. 'She doesn't harm anyone but she's not all there as far as I'm concerned.' She clapped her hands together. 'Now, I must get on. These cakes won't judge themselves. No doubt I'll be seeing you later or at the fairy parade tomorrow. Enjoy your afternoon.' She marched off.

Beth turned to him. 'Hilda and her husband are very different, don't you think?'

James agreed. 'He's a very gentle, considerate individual and she is loud and assertive but they seem to rub along well together. They say opposites attract.' He put his scone down with a comment that they were not as nice as Grandma Harrington's recipe. 'Come on, let's go and enjoy what's on offer.'

They spent the next couple of hours studying art displays, discussing the skills of the local craftsmen and joining in with the fairground activities. James won a coconut and Beth bagged a goldfish in a jam jar. After hanging onto them for several minutes, they decided to hand them to the nearest child, who was over the moon with her gifts and went racing off to show her parents.

James checked his watch. 'We've half an hour before we meet the Merryweathers. Shall we sit over there and have a cold drink? I'm getting a little foot weary.'

They made themselves comfortable in a makeshift café where they had an excellent view of the green and, to their right, the coastline. The sun glinted off a turquoise sea and small waves splashed onto the beach. They could see the distinctive roof of The Pilchard Inn;

distinctive as it had a life-size model of a small fishing boat bolted to the chimney with a model of a fisherman on board, looking through a telescope.

Beth touched his arm and pointed. He shifted in his seat and watched a young woman in her early twenties. She meandered aimlessly, her eyes flicking about.

He sat up. She wore the same fearful look as Evelyn Fiske and she wrung her hands mindlessly.

Beth put her glass down. 'Do you think she's all right? She looks terribly frightened.'

The woman came closer to them, all the while scanning the crowds and checking her watch. She stopped a passer-by who checked his own watch for her and moved on. The merry-go-round played a cheery tune and children raced among the crowds giggling and playing tag. Tourists and villagers ambled by, wrapped up in the festival, checking their programmes to ensure they missed nothing, oblivious to the woman looking so lost. As she neared them, James was about to get up to help when Hilda strode up to her.

'Debra, whatever's the matter? You look as if you've lost a pound and found a penny.'

'I can't find Bevis. He told me to meet him here at four thirty and he's not here; he'll go spare if he thinks I'm late.'

'Whatever for? You're here aren't you? I'll give him a piece of my mind if he blames you for being late.'

Debra grasped Hilda's hand. 'You mustn't do that. Oh no, you mustn't do that. Promise you won't.'

James exchanged a concerned look with Beth. The two women were just yards from him. He got up and enquired after the young lady. 'You seem a little preoccupied. Why don't you join us? You can wait for your friend here.'

Debra caught her breath. 'He's not a friend, Bevis is my husband.'

James steered her toward the empty chair at their table. 'Well, we're seated on the perimeter here so we can look out for him.' While Beth settled her down, he turned to Hilda. 'What does this Bevis look like?'

Under her breath, Hilda described him as a fool. Then she pulled her shoulders back and reverted to the booming voice he'd become used to. 'Mid-twenties, black hair slicked back and thinks he's Elvis Presley. Tch, I ask you, these youngsters need their heads bashing together. He's average height, a little overweight and needs to be here for his wife. He thinks he knows everything and it'll be Debra's fault if he pitches up late, you can be sure of that.'

'But why?' Beth put in. 'She's been here for a good five minutes. We saw her walking toward us.'

Debra wrung her hands on her skirt. 'Don't fret about me, please. I'll be fine. Don't go blaming Bevis, he don't like it.'

James suggested he and Beth sit with Debra. 'I know you have a lot on, Hilda. We'll defuse the situation if one arises.'

Hilda jutted her chin at Debra. 'She's like a mouse cornered by a cat. She can never do right according to Bevis. Surly individual he is. Never used to be. She's better off without him.' She thanked them for sitting with her, turned on her heels and strode toward the WI tent.

Beth sought another glass and poured some lemonade. Debra's eyes darted about the green as if she dreaded seeing her killer bearing down on her. James pushed the glass toward her. 'When did you last see Bevis?'

'Breakfast time. I'd cooked him a bacon sandwich at five o'clock.'

'Five o'clock!' said Beth. 'That's early.'

'The fishermen come into harbour around then. I wrap the sandwich in paper and he takes it with him with a flask of tea. Five o'clock sharp he likes it and he's out the door at five past.'

James felt in his pocket for his cigarettes. 'I take it he's something to do with the fishing industry?'

Debra confirmed that he was and that he worked closely with the people from Billingsgate market in London, where supplies from all fishing communities made their way to then to be sold on to restaurants and stores. James sat back as Beth coaxed more information from her. Debra, it transpired, was from the small town of Okehampton in Devon, the next county along, and met Bevis when she was on holiday in Polpennarth. She smiled ruefully and suggested that things were much better then.

'Oh dear,' said Beth, 'you're too young to be having problems, surely.'

'Sometimes people marry too quick, don't they? Oh we get along fine, but it's a hard life. Not much wages come in for a fish trader. We struggle quite a bit. Can't remember the last time we had a proper joint of meat for dinner. Always fish 'cos Bevis gets it cheap.'

James tried to summon up the image of life down here. On a bright summer's day, it was an idyllic setting with the waves lapping at the shoreline, Punch and Judy on the beach and drinks at the pub while watching the sun set over the ocean.

But things must be difficult in the winter when the sea whipped up in frenzy; fishermen lost their nets and sometimes their lives as they battled with the elements. He could imagine the gales slamming against the cottages as if God himself was telling them to leave this place. Unless you owned a thriving business, daily life must be incredibly challenging. He put his head back and blew out tobacco smoke.

'Was Bevis part of the festival today?'

'He drove the flat-back lorry with the jail on the back.'

'Old Bogey's lair?'

'That's it.'

Beth recalled seeing it and picked the lorry out in the car park. 'He's obviously here. Perhaps he's got caught up with friends.'

Debra clenched her handbag. 'Not Bevis, no. If he says meet at four thirty, he means it.' She checked her watch and grew pale. 'I hope I didn't misunderstand him. He said the café next door to the hoopla stall. There's not another one.'

Beth exchanged a concerned look with James who suggested to Debra that she relax and enjoy her drink.

The young woman's eyes met his and her haunted look sent a shiver through him. 'He's friends with Colm Fiske. P'haps Old Bogey's taken him. He's locked 'em both away somewhere.'

James struggled to comprehend such an outrageous claim and suggested that there was probably a more logical explanation than an old folk tale.

She leapt up and almost spat her words out. 'Don't mock it. Old Bogey's not funny, Bevis says so, says he'll come and get me if I don't do things and now Bevis is missing. He's done bad things too, you know, I'm not the only one.'

The outburst attracted attention. A bald, middle-aged man, who looked like a city banker in his dark suit, shirt and tie, stepped in. 'What's the problem here, miss?'

'My husband's missing. Old Bogey's got him. He took Colm and now he's taken Bevis.'

PC Innes pushed his way through the small crowd. He patted Debra's hand. 'I'm sure he's fine, Debra. You know Bevis; he's prob'ly had a few drinks and lost track of time.'

'No! You all keep saying that but he wouldn't — not if he's meeting me.' She poked the man in the suit. 'You're the

83

copper, you should be out looking for him.'

James realised who this gentleman must be. 'Inspector Wormstone?'

The Inspector scrutinised him with a frown. James held a hand out and introduced himself and Beth and how they had heard his name. 'We've been sitting with Debra.' He went on to confirm that they'd thought the same as PC Innes.

Beth referred them to the parked lorry and said that Bevis must be in the crowd somewhere.

A heavy set older man in his sixties with grey hair, piercing blue eyes and mahogany skin strolled over. 'What's all this,' he growled. He turned to Debra and spoke in a gravelly voice. 'You all right?'

Debra went through it all again. James discreetly rolled his eyes at Beth who gave a light nod back. He was beginning to wonder if this young woman simply wanted some attention. Wormstone broke up the conversation to ask who the older man was.

'Enoch Pengilly. Fisherman. You spoke

to us fishermen two days ago when Colm went missing. Debra's right. If Bevis said he'd meet her here at a certain time, he'd be here. He's not here so he's missing.'

'But his lorry is there,' said Beth with an incredulous look. 'He's only twenty minutes late.'

'Don't mean nothing. It's not his lorry; he was just asked to drive it. I ain't seen him.' He called across to a crowd of men who, judging by their complexions and clothing, James guessed were fellow fishermen. Had any of them seen Bevis? No, was the resounding answer.

Wormstone turned to PC Innes. 'You know what he looks like?'

'Yes sir, we went to school together.'

'Well don't just stand there, go and look for him.'

Innes jumped to it and ran toward the biggest crowd on the green. Wormstone opened his notebook and took down Debra's contact details. 'We can't do much at the moment because he's not really missing yet.'

Enoch swore under his breath. ''Course he's missing. He ain't here is he? You won't find him here.'

'And how can you be so sure, Mr Pengilly? He may have been taken poorly or have been waylaid.'

The old fisherman pursed his lips. 'If he was poorly, my men over there would know and Bevis don't get waylaid when he's meeting his missus.'

'Be that as it may, I can't put him down as a missing person when he's only been missing for half an hour.'

'W–what's going on?' Stephen said to James, who was pleased to see a familiar face. He steered the Merryweathers and Beth back to their table and went through what had happened.

Anne couldn't hide her astonishment and James gave a curt nod. 'You're thinking the same as us. A lot of fuss over not a great deal. The man could be wandering about here and lost track of time.'

'Why is she so adamant he's gone?'

'A–and isn't a little odd for someone that age to b–believe in Old Bogey?'

Beth agreed that she felt the same and gave her own opinion of Bevis. 'She seems to take everything he says as gospel. He says he's going to be here at a certain time, he'll be here. She won't listen to common sense. It seems a little over-zealous.'

Anne commented that Bevis sounded the same as some of the youngsters at the summer festival the previous year. James groaned. He remembered them all too well, with their leather jackets and quiffed hair, strutting about with undesirable attitudes. Perhaps Bevis was going through a similar phase, although he thought it unusual for a married man with responsibilities to behave in that way. He caught the eye of a passing waitress and requested lemonade for the Merryweathers.

Hilda reappeared and approached Jarvis Wormstone. 'Inspector, the man is obviously missing. Do your job and find him. If he's with Colm you'll get the pair of them. A feather in your cap.'

'Mrs Roscarrock, we have this in hand. Unless you have some information about the whereabouts of Colm and Bevis, I don't need you here.'

'I haven't any information, Inspector, but these two ladies are part of our community and part of my WI. We're their support. Always have been. I won't interfere with your investigations but I need to be here for my friends.'

James watched as PC Innes returned with a forlorn shake of the head. Hilda snaked a protective arm around Debra and led her away telling the Inspector that he knew where to find them.

Inspector Wormstone instructed Innes to file a report. 'You never know,' he said, 'it may be connected to Colm Fiske.'

The crowd dispersed. Hilda had led Debra toward the WI tent where half a dozen ladies dashed to her aid. James chewed his lip. A hand waving in his face brought him out of his day-dream. He focussed and saw Beth, Stephen and Anne looking at him.

'Sweetie, you look as if your brain is working overtime,' his wife said

James turned and pulled his chair in. 'This is all very odd.'

Anne's eyes sparkled. 'Have you stumbled on something?'

'Not stumbled upon, no. It's just an observation. Colm Fiske, resident, went missing mid-morning in the middle of the opening day of the festival. No one saw him disappear. No one has any information. Now, this Bevis chap is presumed missing. The place is heaving with people and no one saw him go. These men, strong young men, have disappeared with no witnesses whatsoever.'

'T–taken in plain s–sight, James.'

'Mm?'

'If the p–place is heaving, people often don't see things. Unless you were a–actually examining a s–situation, you wouldn't see someone disappear.'

James lightly tapped the table. 'The only way you'll see something untoward is if it *appears* untoward. That means one thing.'

Anne tilted her head, inviting the answer.

'If these men haven't simply wandered off, it means they've been kidnapped. And if they disappeared without a struggle, it means that Colm and Bevis knew their kidnapper.'

There was a collective sharp intake of breath.

'How else can they disappear in a crowd of people? If they were kidnapped by a stranger, they'd put up a fight — yet no one reported a struggle.'

Beth, Stephen and Anne slowly nodded in agreement. James held a finger up. 'You know what else is puzzling me? Evelyn Fiske and that Debra woman. Neither of them strikes me as a carefree, happy woman. They have a haunted look about them.'

James sat back and returned his attention to the WI tent. The way those women flocked to Debra was unnatural. Yes, of course, they would want to comfort a woman whose husband was missing but he'd been gone less than half an hour. They're consoling her as if he were dead. He glanced across to Enoch Pengilly and the fishermen. They huddled shoulder to shoulder chatting and smoking; a fraternity that stuck together. What secrets did they have? He felt sure that if there were any, they would remain confined to the group.

He swung round. 'Something odd is going on here. People know more than they're telling. Stephen, Anne, what are your plans tonight?'

Stephen explained that they had to get back to the caravan site because Luke and Mark were spending the evening with the family next door. 'I have to go and rescue them in a while. They're over there trying to win a huge bag of Spangles.'

Anne whispered. 'But, we could book a table at The Sardine or go for fish and chips at that little chippy in the harbour.'

James instinctively leaned forward' Why?'

'Because we overheard that Inspector earlier telling someone he was dining at The Sardine tonight. And that young policeman said he was having fish and chips after a pint. It might be a — '

'Splendid,' James interrupted with a broad smile. He pecked Beth on the cheek. 'Wormstone's from Scotland Yard. I may telephone George to see if he knew him and if he's likely to be approachable. My guess is that he's not.' He turned to the Merryweathers. 'Shall we meet you at the harbour wall and decide where to pounce?'

Anne scrunched her shoulders up. 'How exciting.'

8

Colm gulped the water down. 'Who are you? Why're you doing this?'

The blindfold tightened. He received no reply. His captor checked the bindings around his ankles.

'You'll be sorry. Once I find you out, you'll be sorry.'

A hand squeezed his neck. His bravado quickly vanished. 'Please, please, I'll do what you say. Tell me what you want.' The gag returned, tight and uncomfortable. He put his head back. The footsteps retreated and faded away.

How long had he been here? The blackness stripped time away. Was it night or day? His appetite had gone but without knowing when the next meal would come, he'd eaten the scraps of pasty fed to him.

What was the point of this?

What had he done?

Would he ever be found?

His stomach lurched. What if he died here?

9

At the hotel, James asked Vivian if he could use their telephone. 'I'll pop some money on the side.'

Vivian was more than happy and showed him into their living quarters. 'Phone's just there. I'll be on reception if you need me. We've got a couple of guests arriving anytime now.'

He closed the door and lifted the receiver. After what seemed an eternity, he was put through to his old friend Detective Chief Inspector George Lane, who couldn't hide his surprise at hearing from him.

'Is everything all right?'

'Everything is fine, George. The weather is glorious, the festival is a good deal of fun, the hospitality is beyond expectations and it's wonderful to have a break from the routine. Do you know if Harry and Oli are coping at Harrington's?'

George assured him they were. 'I popped in on the way home yesterday and everything seems to be running well. But you've only been away one full day, James. What's going on?'

James silently cursed George's intuition and then gave him a brief outline of what had been happening in Polpennarth. George knew of the case, but only from what he'd read in the newspaper columns.

'You say another man's gone missing?'

Further clarification of the afternoon's events followed and before too long, his friend was up to date with everything.

'Did you ever work with this Wormstone chap? Do you think he'd mind me poking my nose in?'

George indicated that he thought he'd mind very much. 'No policeman wants an amateur sticking their oar in and Wormstone won't be any different.'

'The constable seems happy to share information.'

'Well, he would do, wouldn't he? He's probably bowled over by your charm and status. Get further up the ranks and you won't get that sort of worship, James. You know that from your dealings with my Inspector.'

James afforded himself a wry smile, remembering only too well that he received short shrift from Inspector Collins on the two occasions he'd crossed paths with him. 'Well, enough of that. As I've got you on the telephone, do you know Wormstone? What's he like?'

There was a brief silence and James visualised George at his desk, surrounded with buff folders, pondering the question.

'I've never actually worked with him but he had a reputation.'

'Good or bad?'

'Oh good, very good. He was entrusted with complex cases and solved all of them; except one.'

James dragged a dining room chair over and sat down. 'And?'

'Sent him over the edge. It was a particularly brutal case — a child went missing and Jarvis Wormstone found the body.'

'Oh good Lord. Did they find the killer?'

'No. And that's what got him. He told me that he wouldn't have minded any other criminal he'd convicted walking but he couldn't bear the thought of a child killer being free.'

'So are you saying that he left and joined the force down here?'

'I know he went off sick. Off for months he was. One of his closer colleagues went round to him one day and apparently he broke down. Just sat and cried. Must have caught him at his lowest. Anyway, a few months later, he gets back to work but wants somewhere quieter where the most he'd have to deal with would be theft or the odd punch-up. The job in Penzance was ideal for him so he moved down there.'

'He seemed a bit of a pompous oaf when I met him. I feel a little sorry for him now.'

'Oh, he can be a pompous oaf, if he wants to be. If he's back to his normal self, he probably is but I think that incident took something away that he'll never get back.'

James thanked George for this insight

and reminded himself that it was wrong to make a judgement on first impressions. George asked what he was going to do. James winced. On reflection, he didn't know what to do. This was supposed to be a holiday; a break with Beth to get away from things. The Merryweathers were here to celebrate, not to get involved in any unpleasantness. George asked if he were still there.

'Sorry, yes, just thinking. Well, we're having dinner with Stephen and Anne tonight and we understand that this Inspector Wormstone is dining at the same place. We thought we might ingratiate ourselves with him.'

'Ingratiate away but tread carefully, James. Don't go in all guns blazing. If you do that, he'll shut up shop and tell you to back off. If I were you, I'd just get on and enjoy your holiday. Oh by the way, what's your telephone number there?'

James peered at the centre of the dial and read out the number.

'Bert was asking where you were. He and Gladys are coming down to some race meeting in Devon. They said they might take a trip and meet up with you.'

James saw his delight reflected in the mirror on the wall. Bert had rediscovered an old friendship with a lady called Gladys during the past year and they were to be seen together more often these days. 'How splendid. Tell him we look forward to seeing them.'

After finishing the call, he placed half a crown by the telephone and made his way upstairs where he went through the entire conversation with Beth. She poured two glasses of sherry and put them on the table by the bay window.

James stared at the refreshments. 'Where'd you get the sherry?'

'I put it in the luggage with two glasses.' She gave him a mischievous smile. 'Anne said she does this when they go away.'

'She's a sly one, that Anne, isn't she? Likes us to believe she's the typical vicar's wife and all the time, she's chomping at the bit trying to get involved in mysteries and sneaking sherry into her luggage.' He took a sip. 'Jolly good idea though. George said we should tread carefully with Wormstone and that we should just enjoy our holiday.'

'Perhaps he's right but we may as well get tonight organised.' She went on to say that she and Anne had taken a detour via The Sardine before parting. 'We discovered that Jarvis Wormstone is dining at seven and the constable normally pops into the fish and chip shop around nine after he's had a pint. So, we can nab Wormstone straightaway and pass by the fish shop on the way home.'

James knew he must have looked bemused. 'You two are delightfully devious.' He held his glass up. 'Here's to an enlightening evening of talking crime.'

10

The Sardine was a converted terraced house with six tables of four in what would have been the living room. One table was occupied by an elderly couple; other than that they had the choice of where to sit. The proprietor waved hello. He was in his fifties with a crew cut and goatee beard. He wore black trousers, a Breton shirt and a black beret. James would have described him as Bohemian, more at home enjoying a cigar in a smoky jazz club in London than running a business in Cornwall.

The restaurant itself was plain, with wooden tables and chairs, white curtains and napkins to match. It had a homely, cosy feel to it and the owner had created the atmosphere of a gathering place for friends. He signalled that they should take the table by the window looking onto the promenade. The menu cards were already on the table. The owner came across and introduced himself as Jonah Quinn and asked for their drinks order. To James' surprise, he spoke with a plummy accent. Jonah confirmed he'd moved from Kensington, in London, eight years previously.

'Kensington,' said Beth. 'That's a big adjustment, moving from the metropolis to such a small village.'

'I was a banker in the city and hated every minute of it. I tried city life but it wasn't for me. I wanted to get as far away from London as I possibly could. That meant either Scotland or Cornwall. Cornwall's climate is better and I had more chance of making a living here than in the remote glens of the highlands, so here I am.'

'D–did you burn your suits?'

Jonah laughed. 'Not literally, no. I gave them all to a charity shop and turned into a beatnik. Not my expression but that's what some of the locals here describe me as.'

'So you opened a restaurant?' said James. 'That's a completely different path to take. Had you done this sort of thing before?'

'Never, but I didn't do anything when I first arrived. I became a beachcomber for a while. I had plenty of savings and spent the first two years being something I'd always wanted to be. Didn't have to answer to anyone or anything. No wife, no children; just me and a sense of freedom.'

Beth smiled. 'You sound as if this was a much needed break from things.'

Jonah explained that life in the city was stressful for him and his manager was unforgiving of any mistakes. 'Not that I made many but it made for an unpleasant working situation. Most of my colleagues were married and had responsibilities so they simply had to put up with it. I wasn't so tied down.' He brought out a notepad and pencil. 'Now, what do you want to drink? We're fully licensed but limited with stock. That means I don't do fancy cocktails, only the popular ones.'

A quick discussion resulted in an order for two whisky and sodas and two gin and tonics. James studied the menu. Most of the Polpennarth cafés and restaurants served fried fish or pasties and he was

104

pleased to see more variety here. Anne and Beth requested the same dish more or less straight away.

'Moules marinières.' They chorused.

'I'll feel as if I'm on the French Riviera,' said Anne. 'I've only had the dish once and that was on a day trip to the Kent coast.'

James and Beth were fortunate as they'd visited the French Riviera numerous times so mussels in garlic and white wine were not such a rarity for them.

He and Stephen took their time, aware they were stalling for the arrival of Wormstone. James finally decided on Dover sole with a lemon sauce and fresh garden peas; Stephen requested an explanation of prawn provençale.

'My speciality,' said Jonah as he poured the drinks. 'It's a Mediterranean dish; prawns, tomatoes, parsley and basil with a splash of white wine. Very tasty.'

'I–I'll have that.'

James held his hand up. 'I rather think I may change my order to the same. It sounds wonderful.'

As Jonah jotted the order down, Jarvis

Wormstone entered the restaurant and stood for a short while, deliberating about which table to occupy. He met James' gaze with a silent greeting. James did the same and allowed the Inspector to make his choice and sit for a couple of minutes. When he was satisfied the man was dining alone, he winked at Beth and pushed his chair back.

'I say, Inspector, if you're dining alone, you're welcome to join us.' He was fully prepared to be disappointed, believing the Inspector to be distant and wanting to be alone with his thoughts. To his surprise, Wormstone accepted the invitation. He collected his jacket from the back of his chair, loosened his tie and moved across. Jonah pulled another table over to give them plenty of room.

'It's kind of you to ask,' said Wormstone, his bald head tanned from being in the sun all day. 'Not many people invite a police inspector to dine with 'em, especially when he's poking his nose into things.'

Beth assured him that as they were tourists, they were not too worried about what he might be doing here.

Anne sympathised with the fact that he had to investigate alone. 'Do you not have a team of people?'

The Inspector wagged a finger. 'Not down here, no. I have PC Cardew Innes, local lad who's a bit wet behind the ears. Still, he'll do. I've got rooms in a bed and breakfast up the hill.' He placed his order with Jonah and settled back in his chair. 'So, you're all on holiday?'

James was keen to probe but knew that doing so would cause the Inspector to put the barriers up. As they sipped their drinks and made their way through dinner, the conversation was light-hearted and inquisitive: where were they from; what did they do; was this their first trip to Cornwall? In exchange, Wormstone explained that he was from Cambridgeshire and had joined Scotland Yard twenty years previously. He didn't go into detail about why he'd left but he did confess that he preferred the way of life in Penzance where he was now based. He waved his knife in the air.

'The most we get in Cornwall is a

skirmish outside a pub and the odd robbery. Quite busy during the tourist season with things going missing or the odd couple not paying their bill but that's about it.'

A kick in the shins from Beth confirmed to James that this was his opening. He reached across for his glass. 'I expect this little mystery you have here is something you can get your teeth into, isn't it?'

Having drunk three glasses of wine, Jarvis Wormstone was flushed and relaxed. James surmised he'd no reason to question their interest; the last hour had been spent putting him at his ease. Wormstone's eyes widened.

'I must admit, it's been good to use the old brain cells. Quite a conundrum too, I can tell you.'

'Oh? Why's that?'

'You've not been following it?'

Stephen put in that they knew only what they'd read in the papers. 'I–I wasn't sure what to m–make of it as they said the men disappeared in broad d–daylight. I said to Anne this was probably some sort of mistake. You know how the press are.'

'No mistake. Two men missing. Both vanished in a tiny village in the middle of the day with crowds of people milling about.' He shook his head. 'No one's seen anything. One minute they're there and the next,' he clicked his fingers, 'they've gone. I don't mind admitting that I'm stumped.'

'Perhaps they're doing it as a practical joke or something,' suggested Anne. 'You know what young men can be like.'

'Oh I know only too well, Mrs Merryweather. If I was in London, I'd agree. But the men down here are hard-working. These men that have disappeared are married, so a day's work lost is a day's pay lost. From what I've heard, they're men's men and don't suffer fools gladly. They're not weak either. There's nothing to suggest they've left home. You don't wander off without spare clothes and some money. It's sounding more like an abduction. If they've been kidnapped, then it must be a big fella that's got 'em, that's all I can say.'

'Does that mean you've had a ransom

demand? Isn't that what's supposed to happen in a kidnapping?' asked James.

Beth teased him for reading too many Paul Temple books. The Inspector confirmed that James was right. 'Normally always a ransom demand but these men have got nothing. They're in the fishing trade — there's no money in that. They live day to day depending on the catch. If the weather's bad and they can't get out in the boats, that's it, they don't get paid.'

'That's an awfully hard existence,' said Beth.

James agreed and looked at Wormstone with some confusion. 'So what do you think has happened?'

He shrugged. 'I've no idea. We've searched the village, been up on the cliff-tops, looked along the beaches. Nothing.'

'No marital problems?'

'Not that I can establish. You were with that Debra woman this afternoon. Personally I thought she was jumping the gun. Her husband had simply not turned up on time. Now, of course, it looks like she was right 'cos he hasn't come home.'

'What did you make of her, Inspector? I found her a little odd. Didn't you, Beth?'

Beth confirmed that she did. She leant on the table and met the Inspector's gaze. 'She seemed incredibly timid, almost frightened of her own shadow.'

'Yes, yes, she did,' Wormstone said and was of the opinion that a handful of the women he'd spoken to were like that. 'That Colm Fiske's wife is similar. They're not all like that of course. Have you met that Hilda woman who heads up the WI? Fearsome creature.' He shuddered at the thought.

It was pretty clear that Inspector Jarvis Wormstone couldn't, or wouldn't, provide anything more. The wives of these victims had no indication of their husbands' whereabouts. The fishermen were equally perplexed and the community, as a whole, was baffled. James checked his watch. It was nearly eight thirty and he was keen to catch PC Innes. As the young man was from Polpennarth, he believed he could shed some light on the personalities involved. He gestured to

Jonah for the bill and insisted that he pay for the Inspector who stumbled over his sincere thanks.

'Think nothing of it. Can't have a hard-working policeman eating alone and paying for the privilege. Perhaps we can do it again in a few days' time, give you a break from the routine.'

They said goodbye to the Inspector and James held the door open for everyone to leave. Jonah came across and thanked him for his custom. As James turned to leave, the owner tugged his sleeve. 'I reckon that writer's got something to do with those kidnappings.'

James indicated to Beth that he'd catch up with them. He turned to Jonah. 'The writer?'

'Kerry Sheppard, her name is. She was in here last night. She had quite an altercation with Fiske on her first day here.'

'Really?'

Jonah went on to explain that Miss Sheppard was researching folk-lore and was mocking Fiske for believing in fairy stories. 'Sounds like she's interested in the customs of England but doesn't necessarily believe in them.'

James suggested that many researchers would be the same. 'She may have been commissioned to write the book.'

'Perhaps. But she's condescending of men in general. And she apparently laughed at Bevis in his leather jacket. Laughed to his face. I mean, Bevis isn't Elvis but there's nothing wrong in copying your hero, is there?'

James agreed that there wasn't and was reminded of the many times Beth had copied the style and fashion of Audrey Hepburn; chic and elegant, yet homely and welcoming. He suggested Jonah relay those thoughts to the Inspector but the man dismissed the idea.

'You're pals with him. I don't speak to the police.'

He closed the door on James who stood for a couple of seconds thinking about Jonah's parting statement. *I don't speak to the police.* What possible reason did he have for steering clear of them? Did Jonah have a past?

He caught up with Beth and the

Merryweathers and imparted Jonah's allegation. Stephen and Anne couldn't help but laugh.

'Y–you haven't met Kerry yet. W–we must introduce you.'

Beth took that comment to mean she was the most unlikely suspect.

'She's a fiery, independent young woman who knows what she wants,' said Anne.

'She is also incredibly s–slight of frame. I c–can't see her manhandling stocky young f–fishermen about.'

'Unless,' said Anne with a mischievous glint in her eye, 'she's discovered a way of overpowering them. Her hatred of men could be such that she's stockpiling them away somewhere.'

'Anne!'

They continued joking all the way to the fish shop. The smell of fried cod and chips greeted them ahead of their arrival and although they'd eaten a wonderful meal at The Sardine, James couldn't help but crave a portion. He pushed the thought to the back of his mind and suggested they round the evening off with a cup of tea. The fish and chip shop was solely take-away but the owners did put out a couple of plastic tables and chairs on the pavement.

'I say, Beth, why don't you and Anne grab one of those tables. Stephen and I will order the teas.'

He and Stephen joined the queue at the counter. It was a typical fish and chip shop with coastal themed tiles on the surrounding walls, a plastic ornament of a fisherman in oilskins and huge jars of pickled eggs and onions on display. He heard the bubbling fat and the hissing sound of fresh potatoes being poured into the fryer. To the side of him was a glass heated cabinet where several portions of golden battered cod rested. Further along were deep-fried sausages and four enormous Pilchard Inn pasties. He salivated and commented to Stephen that although full he would love to tear off a piece of cod and try it. Stephen suggested they must have a portion at some point during the holiday.

'Luke and Mark love f–fish and chips.'

James patted his stomach. 'I think we'll

need to go for a long walk to get rid of this excess food. Perhaps we could stroll up to your caravan site tomorrow and meet Kerry Sheppard.'

'It's h–hardly a stroll. Uphill all the way but, it'll c–certainly build up an appetite.'

They ordered four teas and introduced themselves. The man behind the counter, wearing a blue and white apron, brought out a basket of chips from the deep fat fryer and gave them a shake. He introduced himself as Vic Chenery. He was a thin, wiry man with a chiselled face and short, black hair. He called out to the room at the back.

'More cod please.'

A woman appeared with a tray of fresh fish.

'This is my wife, Flora.'

Flora, shorter than her husband and twice the width, put the tray down and nodded at the fryer. 'Those chips'll be overdone if you cook 'em much more.' She said a quick hello to them. 'I won't shake hands 'cos I stink of fish. You're stopping with Viv and Des, aren't you? A Lord and Lady I heard.'

She told them to go and sit outside. 'Vic'll bring the tea out. Vic, get those chips out or we'll have to throw 'em away.'

As they turned, a young man grinned at them. 'Hello.'

At first, James wondered who it was and then expressed his surprise. 'PC Innes?'

Cardew Innes was dressed in jeans and a checked shirt. He looked like a teenager without his police uniform and helmet. His hair was smoothed back with Brylcreem.

'I say, I didn't recognise you at first. You're obviously not on duty.'

'No, no, finished two hours ago. I've just had a couple of pints at The Pilchard and come in for some chips.'

Behind them, Flora admonished her husband again. 'You've not put enough batter on, put 'em through again. Honestly, do I have to do everything around here?'

Innes pulled a face at James who suppressed a grin and invited the young man to sit with them.

They gathered around a small table where Innes sprinkled vinegar on his chips along with a generous helping of salt. He used a wooden fork to prod a solitary chip and held it up in triumph.

'Can't beat fresh cooked chips.' He pushed the bag to the centre of the table. 'Help yourself if you want one.'

It was clear to James that everyone was keen to dig in but too polite to do so after they'd had such a delicious meal. He stirred his tea. 'So how's the investigation going, Cardew? Do you have an idea of who did it and where those men are?'

Cardew swallowed his food. 'Not officially no but the locals have all had their say.'

James raised an eyebrow and invited the young man to elaborate. Fortunately, he was more than happy to do so.

'Well, the mad Nibbin is a suspect in just about every crime around here, whether it's kidnapping or someone's bottle of sauce gone missing. Most of the older people, Polpennarth folk, say it's Old Bogey or the Knockers or Spriggans.'

James exchanged bewildered looks with

everyone and Cardew smiled in apology.

'Spriggans and Knockers are two of the Cornish legends for the festival. We've had Old Bogey today. He lives in the shadows and comes out at night to scare you witless — I think everyone has the Bogeyman whatever country you're in. But the Spriggans and Knockers are Cornish and a little more sinister.'

'In what way?' asked Beth.

'Spriggan is a name given to a family of fairies. They're supposed to be related to Piskies but they're more menacing. Piskies are mischievous but fun, they play practical jokes on you but not with any bad intentions. But Spriggans, well they're darker. Dangerous. They hang out in ruins and on windswept crags and live among the standing stones.' He munched a couple more chips and continued. 'Their most common trait is to lead people into swamps or toward crumbling cliff-tops and watch them fall or struggle till they die.'

'Good lord,' James exclaimed.

Stephen scratched his forehead. 'P–people really believe all of this?'

'Oh yes. Well I suppose these myths and legends have to start from some basis of fact, don't you think?'

Anne commented on the Merry Maidens and Stephen stared at her. 'W–what are the Merry M–maidens when they're at home?'

'I read about them in a leaflet. They're a collection of standing stones in Cornwall that are thousands of years old. Apparently, they're the remains of young women who danced on the Sabbath and, because of that, they were turned to stone.'

'That's right,' said Cardew, 'there's also some more stones a little further away who were the pipers. There's quite a few of those sort of stories connected to standing stones.' He sat forward. 'And some people have received electric shocks from those stones.' He gave them a 'what do you think about that?' look.

James sipped his tea and asked Cardew about the other group of legends, the Knockers. The young man sprinkled more salt on his chips.

'Ah, yes, the Knockers. Some folk say

that Knockers and Spriggans are the same thing but Knockers confine themselves mainly to the tin mines. The miners would hear knocking when they worked down the mine and that signalled where they should be digging.'

'S–so the Knockers were an underground f–fairy godmother.'

'I suppose they were but you have to treat them with respect. If any miner offended a Knocker, they'd be led down dangerous places and be lost in the mine forever.'

Anne shivered. 'That sounds horrible. What sort of things did the miners have to avoid?'

'Whistling, spying, making a sign of the cross; all that sort of thing'd annoy them. To be on the safe side, a lot of miners would leave some of their lunch where they'd heard knocking to apologise for anything they might have done.'

'And what do these Knockers look like?' asked James. 'Same sort of get up as the Spriggans?'

Cardew described a sinister character, dark and menacing and explained that the

Knockers had their own parade in a few days. 'The Spriggans are similar in mentality to the Piskie and they're all part of the Fairy family. It's the turn of the Fairies tomorrow. Should be a good turn out and good fun too as it's more geared up for the children.'

'Do *you* believe that fairies are responsible for these kidnappings?'

The young man answered with a wry smile. 'No, your Lordship, I don't. But there's plenty here that do and you'd best not mock 'em. They won't appreciate it.'

'Who in particular?'

'Like I say, most of the old ones, mainly Polpennarth born. Most of 'em won't admit it to strangers. Gretchen Kettel down in the little gift shop. Bidevin and his ma. Old mad Nibbin who lives on the moor and those two that went missing. Their families are from Polpennarth so they grew up believing in that stuff. All the historic families here believe.'

Anne reminded him that he also grew up in the village.

'Ah but my family come from Essex. Moved down here with Dad's job. He drives the lorries round the farms, picking up the milk churns. Maybe there is something to it. After all, no one's seen 'em since.' He looked up with surprise. 'Speak of the devil.' He called out to Gretchen who scurried across; her over-size dress billowed in the breeze.

She chuckled. 'Tch, where would Cardew be without his chips?' Her sparkling eyes darted from one person to another with a quick hello to each of them.

'I've just been telling our visitors about the Knockers and Spriggans and how the village think they're responsible for those missing men.'

'Oh yes. Yes. No doubt about it. And there'll be more, yes, yes.'

James asked her why she would think such a thing.

'Once they start, they don't stop. Mischievous buggers. Doesn't do to bring them to life every year. They do it in plain sight you know and no one sees them. Too fast.' She checked her watch. 'Time for my hot chocolate. Cheerio.'

She scurried off as quickly as she came.

'I say, Cardew, do you know Colm and Bevis? What sort of men are they?'

'Rough around the edges. Colm is a big man, proud and stands no nonsense. He finds the fishing hard, as do a lot of 'em. He's seen friends die out there in the ocean. It's made him a hard man and he takes it out on others sometimes, fighting and scrapping. Bidevin's thrown him out of his pub so many times, I've lost count. Last time he said it would be his last; that he wouldn't set foot in The Pilchard again. No love lost there, especially after Colm insulted Bid's mum. No one insults her and gets away with it.'

'What w–was that about?'

'He reckoned the pasty recipe was in the Fiske family before the Tallacks got hold of it. They do a roaring trade in pasties and it's a much easier life cooking pasties than battling the elements to catch cod.'

James and Beth met each other's gaze. That was surely a motive. He asked Cardew about Bevis.

'Easily led and mainly by Colm. He's latched onto Fiske for some reason so tends to support his battles.'

'Has he been banned from the pub too?'

'Bevis? No, only Colm. He overstepped the mark.' He pushed himself up from the table. 'Right, I'd best be on my way. Nice to chat. Enjoy the festival tomorrow.'

They said goodbye to Cardew with the promise they were likely to see him at the Fairy parade. James felt an excitement swirl in his stomach. Bidevin has motive and Bevis considered the fisherman a role model; he might have been sucked into something unpleasant.

And all this business about the Cornish Legends being responsible — surely these legends didn't exist. This must be someone taking advantage of the folklore.

Back in their room, James slipped his dressing gown on and poured a nightcap for them both. Beth perched on a stool at the dressing table brushing her hair. He looked out of the bay window and a light out to sea caught his eye. Reaching for the binoculars, he scanned the ocean and settled on an area not far off the coastline. He zoomed in further but couldn't make out any boats or ships. It flashed intermittently then stopped. It was eleven o'clock, the same time as on the previous evening. He turned to Beth.

'Most odd.'

'What's that, darling?'

'Well, last night I saw some lights out at sea, flashing as if they were sending a message to shore. Blow me if it's not there again and at exactly the same time. I can't see a boat out there though.'

Beth wrapped her gown around her and joined him. She studied the horizon. 'I don't see anything.'

'It was definitely there.'

'Was it like a signal or something?'

'I don't know. It was intermittent so I suppose it could be.'

He held Beth's hand as they gazed across the harbour and out into the darkness. It was late evening; who would be signalling to shore at that time of night? Was this connected to the missing men? And did Knockers and Old Bogey exist? He admonished himself for even thinking such a thing. The person, or persons, behind this were brazen and happy to abduct people in broad daylight. He'd have to keep his eyes peeled the next day. If these men were going missing during the parades, why shouldn't others? Gretchen Kettel seemed certain that more would disappear. He wondered if Wormstone would bring in some extra police to keep watch.

11

James patted his stomach and complimented Vivian on her cooking. He and Beth had enjoyed a sumptuous cooked breakfast with crispy bacon, poached egg, mushrooms, fried bread and a sausage. 'I believe our chef at Harrington's would be impressed with this and that's a difficult feat.'

Vivian noticed the brochure by his arm. 'You thinking of going up to the Sanctuary?'

'I don't think Beth would permit me to leave Polpennarth until she's seen some seals.'

Beth dabbed her lips with her napkin. 'They look adorable. The weather's holding today so we thought we'd pop in for an hour.'

'They'll be glad to see you, I'm sure. Are you going to the parade? It's the fairies today.'

James confirmed that they'd spend an

hour watching but was mindful that there were other things to do and see. 'My wife and Anne are going to visit the WI and we've some walks we want to go on as well.'

Desmond strolled in with a plate of breakfast for a fellow guest. Having overheard the last piece of the conversation he suggested they schedule their outdoor activities that day. 'There's rain coming in later. Fortunately, there's a day off from the parades tomorrow so it won't spoil anything too much. Have you got a wet weather plan?'

James hadn't really thought about it although he and Beth didn't mind getting drenched providing they were dressed for it. 'My father used to say there was no such thing as bad weather, just poor clothing.'

'And,' added Beth, 'having somewhere warm to come back to.'

Vivian and Desmond assured them that the heating went on during wet days to take the chill out of the air and that the immersion would be on for a hot bath. Another couple entered the dining room and there was a quick hello between guests. The Simms went to attend to them.

'I say, Beth, we could always take the Merryweathers up on their offer to meet Kerry Sheppard. After hearing what Jonah Quinn said last night, I'd be interested to meet her.'

Beth picked up the leaflet for the Sanctuary. 'How about we watch the beginning of the parade with the Merry-weathers, then drive up to the Sanctuary and have a walk across the cliff-tops? The rain's due early evening so we could visit Stephen and Anne for supper.'

'Good idea.'

⋆   ⋆   ⋆

The fairy parade took place on the beach. It was a smaller affair to the Old Bogey celebrations of the previous day and geared toward the youngsters. Most of the people taking part were children and James guessed that few men were keen to dress up as pixies and fairy kings and queens. He imagined that the numbers would swell again once the darker characters reappeared later in the week.

In the short time they'd been here, James had already come to recognise a few of the locals.

* * *

Nibbin, for once, seemed to fit in with the whole concept of fairies and wore a hat that appeared to be made of leaves. Flora Chenery from the fish and chip shop stood in a group of a dozen women including Hilda, Evelyn and Debra. No doubt, poor Vic was back at the shop preparing fillets of fish for the lunchtime trade. James had the feeling that Vic did as he was told in that marriage. Thank goodness Beth didn't nag like that.

Wormstone and PC Innes stood on the promenade surveying the scene.

The giant Bidevin and an accordion player led the procession and the landlord had somehow managed to maintain his masculinity even though he wore a ridiculous outfit. He moved gingerly in long brown shoes that curled up at the toes, brown tights, a knee-length green and red stripy jumper and on his head a knitted green and red striped pointed hat. He skipped ahead of the children with a knobbly wooden staff in his hand. Excited youngsters followed his every move, copying his dancing in time with the melody.

Mark dragged his brother along. 'Come on.'

Luke ran alongside him with Radley and they followed for a few minutes until Radley decided chasing balls was much more fun.

The tide was out, leaving a huge stretch of golden sand where the organisers were inviting people to enter a competition. Stephen waved the boys back and read a piece of paper handed to him by a local.

'Children and a–adults are invited to construct a s–sandcastle that fairies live in.'

Luke jumped up and down. 'Let's make a castle.'

Mark studied the beach. 'Shall we make it here, Mum?'

Anne spread her hands wide. 'Why not?

We're out of the way of the parade and the tide will take a while to reach this far.'

Without a moment's hesitation, the boys picked up their spades and started digging. They instructed each other on who was to do what: dig trenches, build a moat; construct corners and different-sized turrets; there must be a drawbridge and they needed water to help mould the turrets. They raced toward the shoreline with their buckets.

James shook his head. 'They really are a blast of energy, aren't they?'

The beach was transformed into a hive of activity as plans and discussions took place over what a fairy sandcastle would look like. Dads hammered in windbreakers and Mums prepared their family areas for the next few hours, laying out tartan blankets and picnic essentials of flasks and sandwiches.

Stephen opened up a couple of deckchairs. 'A–are you joining us or have you plans?'

Beth outlined their day and invited them to join them at the Sanctuary and for a walk later. James put forward the suggestion of supper with Kerry. Anne explained that the boys had been invited to the Sanctuary by their neighbours up at the caravan site.

'We thought we might have a rest this afternoon but we'll try and invite Kerry to supper and we can pick her brains. Shall we see you at the site around six? Oh, and we'll keep an eye on things here.' She positioned her deckchair to face the crowds.

'Operation 'Spot the Kidnapper'. Mum's the word.'

James exchanged a bemused look with Stephen. He and Beth made their way up the steps to the promenade and greeted Wormstone and Innes.

'Any news on your missing men?'

Innes shook his head.

Wormstone loosened his collar. 'Not a sausage. I don't get it, I really don't. Those men knew one another, of course, but that's about it. They didn't belong to any clubs or attend any functions at the same time. They've no criminal record, just the odd skirmish outside the pub. They didn't have any hobbies. I'm baffled.' The Inspector scrutinised him. 'You're quite interested in this, aren't you? Innes here was telling me you were asking questions. Can I ask why?'

'You can indeed, Inspector, and it's simply that I'm interested. I like puzzles and I am extremely puzzled by what has gone on here. I can assure you that I am not involved but if we stumble over any gossip we think you may need to hear, we'll let you know.'

Wormstone gave a curt nod and, as they walked on, they heard the Inspector telling Innes to check them out.

★　★　★

In ten minutes, James had folded the roof down on the Austin Healey and they were making their way up a winding hill away from Polpennarth. He could see stretches of road ahead and went up and down the gears, relishing a proper drive. His short spell as a rally driver was one he would never forget and he felt the blood pumping as he put the Austin through her paces.

Beth held on to her straw hat and pushed her sunglasses up the bridge of her nose. 'You're reliving your Monte Carlo rally, aren't you?'

Although she sounded stern, they grinned at each other. James couldn't help it. A nifty sports car with the roof down, sunshine, the perfect rally road with bends and crests. The only difference between this road and the one in Monte Carlo was that this one led to a seal sanctuary. He had a sudden longing for the sophistication and casinos of the French Riviera. In the distance, a tractor trundled toward them. He went down through the gears and pulled into a small lay-by. Once it had passed, he pulled away.

'I say, Beth, do you fancy going to Monte Carlo or Nice again? We haven't been for quite some time.'

'Oh darling, I'd love to. In fact, there are a few places I'd like to revisit. That little hotel in Naples, skiing in Switzerland. We've gotten out of the habit, haven't we?'

James agreed. Running Harrington's

was marvellous and he couldn't believe how successful it had become. And, getting so involved in the village festivities in Cavendish took up a great deal of time and there wasn't a thing he hated about any of it. But, he did believe they were forgetting to enjoy some quality time together. They'd only been in Cornwall a couple of days but they were already unwinding and enjoying a change of scene.

Beth motioned ahead. 'That may be the sign for the Sanctuary. The map here says there's a turn-off.'

He braked. A small wooden sign led them to the left. He turned and crested a hill. The pair of them gawped and James pulled over. 'My word, what a stunning view.'

They climbed out of the car. James put on his straw hat and reached into the glove compartment for his binoculars. They leaned against the bonnet and took in the vista in front of them. Under a canopy of blue, the sea glistened cobalt and turquoise. Gulls squawked high above them, gliding on the thermals and the occasional black head of a seal popped up in the ocean below. The road leading down to the Sanctuary was a mass of colour. Hedgerows were filled with cow parsley, foxglove, hemp and stitchwort. A herd of cows mooed in the adjacent field and gently strolled toward them.

James wrapped an arm around Beth. 'I hope the rain that's coming doesn't last long.'

Beth hoped so too. 'That's one difference between here and the Riviera. You can rely on the weather a little more in the South of France.'

'I understand why artists love to paint down here. The air does seem clearer, doesn't it?'

'It's as if God has given your eyes a spring clean.'

Many artists flocked to this part of Cornwall where a group of prominent painters had begun an art society after the Great War. It had seen resurgence in the 1950s after the Festival of Britain and was proving popular for painters and photographers.

Beth reminded James that GJ and Catherine had come to Cornwall for their honeymoon. GJ gave art lessons at Harrington's and was an accomplished artist himself. 'I guess he didn't see it at its best in December.'

'Probably not but I know he said he'd be coming back when the weather was better.'

A car-engine spluttered behind them. James turned to see Tristram pull in behind in a Morris Minor van. He got out and waved.

'Hello. Are you on your way to see us?'

'Yes. We stopped to admire the view.'

'It's beautiful isn't it? Before you get back in your car, do you want to see what we've just rescued?' He grinned at Beth and beckoned them over.

He led them to the back of the van where he opened the doors. The smell of raw fish made them grimace and they waited a few seconds to allow it to dissipate. A man in his late thirties was sitting there, scooping up water in a huge rubber box and pouring it over what was inside. 'Hans, this is Lord and Lady

Harrington. They're on their way to see us but I thought they'd like to have first viewing.'

'Yah, yah,' Hans waved them in.

James helped Beth into the van and they quietly approached the box where a small seal with huge black eyes gazed back. Beth held her hands to her mouth. 'Oh James. How perfectly gorgeous.'

Hans, a well-built man, offered the bucket to Beth, who took over the slopping of water. James had to admit, it was easy to fall in love with such a beautiful creature. Its soulful eyes stared at them and its whiskers twitched.

She wiped away a tear. 'Oh Tristram, Hans, is he going to be all right? What happened to him?'

'Yah, yah, he'll be fine. We feed him good and he swim again.'

Tristram gestured for them to get back onto the road. He shut the doors gently behind him. 'Someone called it in. He was on the beach in Bude and looking a little malnourished.'

'Is he very old?' asked James.

'Beyond the pup state because his

white fur's gone but only a few months I reckon. We'll get him back to the Sanctuary and take a look at him. Normally just needs a few nights there and some food and we set them on their way.'

Beth let out a sigh of relief. 'Oh thank heavens. Can we watch you unload him?'

'Of course. Why don't you get going? We'll be driving quite slowly so I'll meet you down there. Once we've got him comfortable, I'll spend some time with you.'

James negotiated the narrow opening to the Sanctuary and parked on an uneven plot of land alongside a couple of cars and some bicycles. A wooden sign, battered by the elements, welcomed them to the Polpennarth Sanctuary. The building ahead was a converted stable block that had been extended over the years and included an office, a gift shop and tea rooms. James steered Beth toward the entrance and up to a ticket window. A teenage girl in jeans and a jumper greeted them.

'Hello, welcome to the Polpennarth

Sanctuary. Two adults is it?'

James had the right change and handed the money over. She gave them a sheet of paper displaying a hand-drawn map.

'It's pretty self-explanatory; just follow the arrows and you don't miss anything. There's a gift shop at the end and a small café — all donations gratefully received.'

Beth said they'd be sure to make a donation. They walked through to a paved area. Ahead of them was a huge pool with half a dozen seals frolicking and a few lounging on the rim. A large shed further along had a sign that simply said 'birds'. James checked the map. A handful of tourists were already making their way around and every so often a collective 'Ahh' could be heard. He steered her to the far end.

'Looks like we start down there and make our way back. They feed the seals in a little while and — oh look, Tristram's arrived.'

Tristram's van pulled up behind a No Entry sign but as soon as he saw them he motioned for them to join him. They dipped beneath the chained barrier and watched as he and Hans gently slid their precious cargo out. An older man appeared from the vet's office. He stood with his hands on his hips and then squatted down. After a brief inspection he suggested that the creature be placed in the nursery for a couple of days. He then returned to his office. Another helper came across and Tristram repeated the instructions and watched as the staff transferred the seal to the nursery area.

Beth asked what happened there.

'Exactly what the doctor ordered,' said Tristram watching the staffs' every move. 'We'll settle him down in the pool and make sure he's well fed. He's a young seal so our volunteers here will play some games with him and make him work for his food.'

'Games?' queried James.

'He's a young pup so we get him in the long pool that we have inside and he can use up some energy. They're like kids, they need to be active.'

'How many volunteers do you have?'

'Loads. They help with cleaning the pools, preparing the food, transport, working in the café and the gift shop. They lend their hand to anything that needs doing. We wouldn't be here if it wasn't for them.'

'But you're a paid member of the team,' said Beth.

Tristram explained there were four paid staff, including him. 'I'm the office manager but that also means getting out there and helping with rescues and releases. We have two qualified vets that work shifts and Hans does a bit of everything. He studied marine biology so he's handy to have on board. To be honest, we all dip in with everything if needs be.' He looked at his hands and winced. 'I know you've just arrived but it's my lunch break. I'll go and wash my hands and then do you fancy an hour up on the cliff there while I eat my sandwiches? I can get Mildred to cobble up a cuppa and some cake.'

Mildred, they discovered, was the lady who ran the café. She wrapped up two huge slices of moist Victoria sponge and prepared a flask of hot tea. They followed Tristram for about forty yards up a gradual incline and came to a natural clearing where the cliff-top fell away to reveal a small inaccessible cove with white sands and clear blue seas.

'How beautiful,' said Beth who helped Tristram spread out a tartan blanket they'd retrieved from the Austin. 'And you were born here?'

'Yes, Polpennarth born and bred. You can just see the end of the cove as you look across. This is a good walk to do. Polpennarth is just over there and if you walk further along here, you get to the next village. It's about five miles. Wouldn't live anywhere else. A bit bleak in the winter but even then, there's something magical about Cornwall. I know we're part of England but when you cross over the county line from Devon, I feel as if we're in a foreign country.'

James remarked that he knew they had their own flag and Celtic language. 'Can you speak Cornish?'

'It nearly died out but luckily a few people kept the tradition going. I can speak a little but it's difficult to have a conversation with the mirror,' he chuckled. 'But some schools are now teaching it so perhaps it'll make a comeback.'

'I certainly hope so; I do like traditions to continue.'

Beth explained to Tristram that they kept the local folklore and customs alive back in Cavendish so they were particularly interested in that side of things. 'It was quite fortunate that we booked our time away during such an exciting festival.'

'Yes, it's a wonderfully indulgent festival; celebrates all things Cornish really. Not just the legends, but the food and drink too.'

James shielded his eyes and looked further up the coast. 'I say, is that a tin mine there?'

Tristram looked across. 'Yes. Derelict now, of course. Most of our ancestors were miners. There're about ten old mines around this area. Some of 'em moved inland to Camborne 'cos they had a sort of mini gold-rush 'cept it was tin and copper. When the tin ran out, a lot of 'em went over to California for the proper gold rush. One of my ancestors went to South Africa thinking he could seek his fortune.'

'And did he?'

'Not to boast about, no.'

Beth asked if they could go down the mines and Tristram shook his head. 'No, 'fraid not. They're incredibly dangerous now. We've had a few people who've gone to explore and been caught up in rock falls. Most of 'em are boarded up. Only a couple open round here; South Crofty up at Camborne and Geevor; otherwise they're all shut down. Hans has explored one further up the coast. He loves going potholing so he knows what he's doing.'

'Is Hans German?'

'Yes, he was a prisoner of war. There was a camp further up the coast toward Devon and Hans helped out on the farm. He lived on a farm in Germany but his family were all killed so he stayed on here.'

'How sad,' said Beth adding that there were no real winners in war.

'Not for ordinary people,' Tristram put

in. 'We were delighted to get him here. He's passionate about this place and he could earn much more if he went abroad but he loves it here.'

'That's fortunate for you. Make sure you don't let him fall down any potholes.'

He turned to Beth. 'Don't you go exploring! Only have to step on a dodgy area and you could disappear.'

Beth shuddered and assured him she wouldn't be exploring anything underground. 'I'm sure you're pleased that mining is no longer a working option.'

'You're not wrong there. Mining and fishing were the predominant jobs a hundred years ago. Now it's fishing and tourism.' He pointed to the cliff-tops. 'Look over there, Razorbills.'

They looked across to the cliff tops where around twenty black birds with downy white breasts had taken off.

James listened as Tristram spoke passionately about the many different birds and animals that inhabited the area. He knew their habits and mannerisms; the seasons they came and went and could even identify some individual birds by certain markings. His empathy with the animal kingdom was evident and he didn't let a living creature suffer when they came to the Sanctuary.

'You know, it's a wonderful thing, to rescue a helpless soul and then be able to release it back to the wild. When you first get them, you can see the fear in their eyes but once they get used to you, it's as if they can see you're trying to help. They stay wary, of course, but providing we're gentle and patient, they seem to understand.'

'You must get awfully attached to them,' said Beth. 'Doesn't it upset you when you release them?'

'Oh yes, very much so. Not so much the birds but the seals and dolphins, yes. You fall in love with them; like you do a dog. There are times when I've sat on this cliff top and almost cried. It's good to be able to help 'em but also sad that I'll never see them again.'

'Does Hilda share your compassion?' asked James, who couldn't imagine she would.

Tristram gave him a wry smile. 'She's

not as emotional as me. She understands that what I do is good but her empathy is a little tempered. She's been a little short with me when I get too wrapped up. Tells me I'm being too soft, but I can't help it. It's who I am.' He began tidying his things. 'I told her she's being too hard on those women whose husbands have gone missing.'

James exchanged a look with Beth. 'Oh? *Is* she being hard?'

Tristram explained that his wife was an assertive lady who didn't suffer fools gladly. 'She's always been like it. That's what I like about her but she does think that Evelyn and Debra are a couple of doormats. I think she forgets that we're not all the same. She means well, of course; she's trying to get them to come out of themselves.'

As they folded the blanket and made their way back to the Sanctuary, James asked Tristram if he'd any ideas about what had happened to Colm and Bevis.

'It's a mystery. The rumours have started, of course.'

Beth mentioned that they'd heard the

locals say the Knockers and Old Bogey were responsible. 'Is that what you believe?'

'Not really, no. I don't believe in myths and I don't believe in gossip. I'm sure there's an explanation but we haven't found it yet.'

'And what,' asked James, 'are your thoughts?'

'That mad old witch, Nibbin. Some say she's spirited them away to put a curse on them. Why, God only knows.' He let out a short laugh. 'Others say it's Jonah Quinn.'

'The restaurant owner?'

'That's the one. They say he moved from London to escape his past.'

Beth frowned. 'What past?'

He shrugged. 'There's mention that he attacked someone, quite viciously too. Man must have a temper on him. Don't know why he'd want to harm Colm and Bevis though.'

'Do you know them well?'

'Went to school with Colm but I don't really know them that well. We don't mix in the same circles really. They spend their wages down the pub; I spend mine on Hilda and the Sanctuary. Not my sort of people.'

'I heard that he and the landlord have a dispute over a recipe, is that right?'

'That's right. Been going on for years. Colm ain't got no proof but he reckons Bidevin's grandmother pinched the Fiske's recipe book. It all blows up every few years then settles down again. Others are talking about some author woman who upset the pair of them. I can't express an opinion on that. I've never seen her. She had quite a to-do with Colm though, I heard.' He swung open the door that led through to the pool and chuckled some more. 'Other busy-bodies say it's my Hilda.'

James and Beth gawped.

'My Hilda; can you believe it? I know she's a bit of a bossy boots but that's going a bit far. Some people 'ave nothing better to do.' He held out a hand. 'Well, I'd best be getting on. Have a good look around and if you can spare a donation, that'd be grand.'

They thanked him for his hospitality and joined the other tourists as they meandered through the Sanctuary. Along with the seals were otters, gulls and puffins — all being tended to by volunteers. Through the window, they witnessed the vet examining a herring gull and stood alongside other delighted visitors as the seals were given their lunchtime feed. In the gift shop, Beth purchased two furry seals for Luke and Mark.

She heaved a sigh. 'I wish I could find something for Stephen and Anne.'

'You look for gifts?' Hans approached them with a bottle of lemonade in his hand. He had bleach-blond hair cut short at the sides and wore shorts and a cotton shirt.

Beth told Hans about the Merryweathers' anniversary and he shrugged. 'I'm not so good on searching for gift. But St Ives, it is good town, yah? Old with good shop. You find something there.' He held his bottle up in farewell and made his way to the pool.

'I say, that's a good idea. We could visit the art galleries. We're bound to find a nice painting or sculpture they'd like.'

They linked arms as they walked toward the car and Beth queried the suspicions of the villagers. 'Jonah Quinn seemed like a very nice man. Do you think he has a past?'

'Everyone has a past, darling, it's trying to fathom it out though. Don't forget he seems to be averse to speaking with the police. But what about this dispute over the Cornish pasty recipe?'

'It's a motive.'

He screwed his face up. 'But to what purpose? What does kidnapping solve? It doesn't get rid of the dispute?'

'Mmm, that is a strange one. No ransom demand and no body. If they're being held, then why?'

'The only conclusion I've come to so far is that Colm and Bevis appear to be rather undesirable individuals who spend their time in the pub. But that may be the culture down here. The pub was full of fishermen when we went in. But that's not a reason to kidnap them. And what about this Kerry Sheppard woman — a few rumours are flying around about her. Is that simply people making assumptions?'

'I guess we'll find out a little more about her tonight. I hope that Stephen and Anne have convinced her to visit them later.'

They wandered toward the car. Above, were the first indications that rain might be arriving. The earlier wispy clouds were turning to heavy grey and, far out to sea, they saw driving rain falling on the ocean. He opened the passenger door for Beth and leant on the rim.

'You know who could find out a little about Jonah Quinn?'

'You're not going to involve George, are you? I don't think he'd thank you.'

'No, no. I was thinking about Bert. He has contacts all over and I'm sure he could dig up dirt on a city banker, don't you?'

She smiled. 'Where would you be, Mr Harrington, without a mystery to solve.'

'Where indeed, Mrs Harrington.'

He walked round to the driver's side and, in the distance, observed Tristram and Hans climbing into their van.

'Looks like they have another call on their hands.'

'They're very dedicated, aren't they? Did you see the way they handled that seal? It was as if it were made of china.'

James pulled away and began thinking about his plans. He would have to telephone Bert and find out more about Jonah; getting to know Kerry Sheppard would be enlightening and he wondered how approachable this Nibbin creature was. She seemed to crop up on everyone's list of suspects.

12

Colm tensed. His heart felt like a stampede.

Someone was here, he was certain. Whoever had taken him had gone. He'd been given water and half a pasty. He'd complained and received a smack across the face for his objections. But that person had gone. This was someone else. He was sure of it.

There it was again. A faint moan. He strained to listen and tried to yell but his words were stifled by the gag.

His eyes pricked. He hadn't cried since he was a kid; when he fell off the harbour wall and cut his knees open.

Now he wanted to weep. He wanted to go home. He wanted to feel the ocean breeze and watch the tumbling seas.

13

'Are you joking?'

James assured Bert he was doing nothing of the sort. After two phone calls; one to the market trader and one to the bookmaker, James had tracked him down to a pub in Brighton. He gave Bert a bite-sized version of events to date and emphasised that Bert 'knew' people and could find out if anything untoward had happened with Jonah Quinn.

'Listen, me old codger, if anyone's likely to know, it'll be that copper you mentioned earlier — Innes. He sounds like the sort of geezer who'll spill the beans; he thinks you're a big fish in the little old port of Polpenn'f. He wants to make a good impression.'

'I will take that into consideration but I don't want to get Innes in trouble. And, the said constable has already told this Inspector Wormstone I was asking questions.'

'Blimey, you got Jarvis Wormstone down there?'

James couldn't hide his disbelief. 'Bert, is there anyone you don't know?'

He heard the suggestive chuckle down the line. 'That's for me to know, mate. Look, I'll put a few feelers out this end and you give it a shot with that young copper. Do what you normally do — keep it general and slip in the odd question.'

'George mentioned that you may be coming down this way.'

'That's right, prob'ly tomorrow or the next day. There's racing on at Buckfastleigh so I'll jump on a bus from there.'

'And will we have the delightful Gladys here too?'

James grinned as he heard a groan. 'Jimmy boy, stop putting two and two together and making seven. I'll be on me tod. George gave me your number there, now let me get on with my pint. I'll let you know when I'm down.'

They said goodbye and James went upstairs to change. 'What does one wear for an evening in a caravan?'

Beth gave him a playful slap. 'Don't be

159

such a snob. Have you ever been in a caravan?'

'I don't think I have.'

Beth opted for Capri pants and a pale blue sweater. James put on a pair of cream trousers and chose a loose open-necked shirt and a sweater.

At the site, they parked alongside the Merryweathers' Austin 30 and managed to scamper inside as the heavens opened. The rain drummed on the roof but this only increased the sense of cosiness inside. The Merryweathers took them on a tour of the caravan. They began at the far end where one double bedroom spanned the width. It had a triple aspect and the back window looked across the countryside to the north. They then entered the kitchen which held a small cooker and a larder. This opened out to the lounge area with a dining table and another triple aspect. Seats were fitted to both sides and at the far end there was a panoramic view out to sea which, this evening, was obscured by the now vertical rain streaming down the windows.

'Good grief, look at that rain,' said

James peering out. He looked about. 'This is actually rather nice, isn't it?'

'Where do Luke and Mark sleep?' said Beth.

'Ah ha!' Stephen lifted up the cushions in the lounge area and slid a bench across. 'The s–same thing happens the other s–side so it makes up two single beds.'

'Ingenious.'

Anne clapped her hands together. 'Now, who's for tea? Or do you want something stronger? We have a bottle of white wine. I know it's raining but I've concocted a salad supper, I hope that's all right. I discovered a little butcher's shop up one of the side streets and I have home-made pork pies and some lovely cheese that I bought from the farm next door.'

An order for white wine was the unanimous decision. Stephen uncorked a bottle of Blue Nun.

Beth nudged Anne. 'Is Kerry Sheppard coming?'

'Oh yes,' her eyes sparkled, 'have you found anything else out?'

161

They went through their chat with Tristram and the rumours that were beginning to circulate. Stephen questioned each and every one.

'B–but Jonah seems s–such a nice man. And this Nibbin woman is simply an eccentric. And w–why would Kerry be kidnapping men? She spends a–all her time writing and researching.'

Anne tut-tutted him. 'How do you know any of them are what they seem? We don't know these people; they may all be psychopathic murderers.'

Stephen sighed to the heavens. 'I–I'm sure you're quite wrong.'

Beth joined Anne in the kitchen area and helped prepare the salad. 'James put a call through to Bert and he's finding out a little more about Jonah and his time in London. Did anything untoward happen at the beach today?'

The Merryweathers reported that the morning had gone by without a hitch. The sandcastle competition was a great success and the fairy parade finished about thirty minutes after James and Beth had gone.

Anne held up a tomato. 'We did witness an argument with that man Enoch and his wife.'

'Y–yes, a little unsavoury, especially as there were ch–children in the area.'

'How d'you mean?'

Stephen explained that Enoch had taken exception to something his wife had done or said. 'He was incredibly rude to her and I–I'm certain it wasn't w–warranted. Indeed, I know it wasn't warranted. Nothing like that is warranted.'

'A horrible man,' said Anne, 'no two ways about it.'

'Or perhaps,' said Beth, 'he has a lot on his plate at the moment.'

There was a knock. 'Hello?'

Anne quickly turned to open the door. 'Kerry, come in out of the rain.'

James turned to see an attractive lady with an olive complexion enter. She stood at around five feet six inches tall with thick dark brown hair that fell around her shoulders. She wore blue jeans, a red polka dot blouse and white plimsolls. He got up as Anne introduced them.

163

She made eye contact with them both and had a firm, no-nonsense handshake. 'So lovely to meet you.'

Beth reciprocated and added that they were particularly interested in the subject of her book. 'I'm sure Stephen and Anne have told you how we try and keep the local customs alive where we are.'

Kerry accepted a glass of wine and sat down opposite them. 'Yes, and it sounds like a place I must visit. I did some research on the bonfire societies in Sussex but it appears you do quite a lot in Cavendish. Anne mentioned that you have a scarecrow festival, is that right?'

'During the autumn,' said James and he went on to highlight a number of traditions they celebrated. 'You should certainly come and visit if you're in the area.'

Stephen topped the glasses up as Anne and Beth distributed plates of salad. The pork pies and cheese were displayed separately and Anne instructed them to simply help themselves to what they wanted. James looked out of the window.

'Where are Luke and Mark?'

'A few families and their children are in the little social club. They're playing board games — wet weather contingency plan. We thought they'd enjoy that more than sitting listening to us. The site owner's wife is a nursery school teacher. She organises things according to the weather.'

'Splendid,' said James as he helped himself to a pie. He cut into it, pleased to see the crisp pastry and the coating of aspic jelly inside. 'So, Kerry, you were here when all this business started with kidnappings?'

The writer groaned. 'I've had the police round, did you know?'

As one, they all stared at her.

'Yes, apparently, they viewed me as a suspicious person.'

'But why?' said Anne.

'I'm an independent woman with my own mind and I argued with the two men who have gone missing.'

James proffered the cheese platter. 'Question — what has being an independent woman have to do with anything?'

She looked pleased with his observation. 'Precisely. I do feel I've been transported back to before the war when I come down here. The general order of things in such remote places, cut off from society is that, as a woman, you must marry, have children and/or be a home-maker. If you are anything other than that, you are deemed odd. I've made it perfectly clear that I have no need of a husband; I hate the thought of having children; and men, no disrespect to either of you, are a nuisance around me.'

He couldn't help but laugh. 'I say, that's a little strong isn't it? Are we of no use to you whatsoever?'

She joined in with the laughter. 'I don't mean it to sound so harsh. I did have a someone a few years ago and what a trial it was! He was needy, wanting me to be with him all the time. I never got a chance to write.'

'P–perhaps you chose the wrong man.'

'No. I am simply not a social girl. I don't like people.' She gestured her hand. 'This is acceptable. I was asked if I would like to come; I am not confined to a specific time to leave, I don't have to wait for a companion to leave with me. I am my own woman.'

Beth sliced some cheese. 'And this approach of yours presumably has been communicated to the villagers.'

Kerry confirmed that it had. 'I make no bones about it. Those two fishermen were annoyingly bad-tempered in The Pilchard on my first evening here. They were saying inappropriate things about my appearance and I put them in the picture.'

'What sort of things?' asked Anne.

'Lewd, suggestive and completely unacceptable. This is because I entered the bar without a man. That Colm thought he was the leading stag in the herd and his little protégé, Bevis, brought up the rear. Some of the other fishermen joined in but, like I say, I put them in the picture. I told them they'd be sorry if they didn't stop.'

James raised his eyebrows and enquired what she had intended to do.

She gave him a shrug. 'I've no idea but I did say the wrong thing. It was the evening before the festival and I simply said that Old Bogey would get them. I know some of them believe in this rubbish and it worked. They went quite quiet.'

'And this led to the police coming to visit?'

'Yes.' She sipped her wine. 'Inspector Jarvis Wormstone visited. Told me I'd been mentioned as someone having an argument with the missing man.'

'And what did you say?'

'I agreed that I had. But if every man I'd had an argument with had gone missing, we'd be pretty short where the male population are concerned.' She cut into her tomato. 'I told him to search the caravan, search my car and go and speak with that weird woman, Nibbin. I sit on the cliff-tops with my dogs. I have a small typewriter and a notepad, I sit in a deckchair and write. She will have seen me.'

The conversation went directly to Nibbin and how strange the woman was. Anne asked Kerry if she'd spoken with her.

'She yelled at me yesterday. Something about poking my nose into village traditions. Apparently it's none of my business but it's hardly a private affair is it? Then she let out a cheer about me confronting Colm Fiske. She seems unbalanced.'

'Do you know exactly where she lives?' asked James.

'She heads off inland whenever I see her. The cliff-tops have no shelter so she must be further back. I'm down here to research the folklore not follow the mad woman. Why are you so interested in her?'

The question caught James off guard but he was quick to think of a reason. 'Some of these people often have a more in-depth knowledge of the customs. She may be someone who could give you an eccentric slant on things.'

Kerry dismissed it as unlikely. The conversation lulled and as Anne tidied up the plates she asked how the book was going.

The author fell into a resigned slouch. 'Oh it's fine. Hard work sometimes but you have to work through it.'

'And folklore is obviously an interest of yours.'

'No it's not. My publisher feels there is a need for this sort of thing and I'm not exactly rolling in pound notes, so here I am researching a subject that although interesting, is not something I'm passionate about.'

James sympathised and added that perhaps she would get her break one day. He added: 'So do you have any notions about what happened to these men?'

Kerry went through the people that she'd observed during the parades and surmised that most were tourists. 'The residents seem to either take part or wait for the parade to end up at the far field. I didn't actually know the names of the men who went missing until they disappeared. The tourists do touristy things, the residents are welcoming on the surface but don't like you to see what's beneath. They seem a reserved lot, wary of outsiders. But if you're asking if I saw anything then the answer's no. The newspapers report that no one saw any struggles. It is odd, I'll grant you. Certainly more interesting to write about.'

James asked where she originated from and learned that she lived in St David's in Wales. She didn't speak with a Welsh accent but, she explained, this was because she moved from Southend in Essex, several hundred miles to the east.

James baulked. 'That's quite a change.' He recalled that Southend was a favourite holiday destination for Londoners and was chock-a-block full with fish and chip shops, as well as having a beach, an exceptionally long pier and a recently opened airport.

'Hell-hole. As soon as I could, I left home and moved somewhere quiet and peaceful with no controlling father hovering over me.'

'Oh dear; you didn't get on with your father?'

'Stepfather. An idiot of the first degree but unaware of it. Bullish by looks and bullish by nature. What he said went and that was the end of it. If I'd have stayed there any longer, I would have put a knife in him.'

'Th–this would be the r–reason why you're so a–averse to the male population.'

She gave Stephen a curt nod. 'I think so, yes. I've seen many men like that and I'm not wasting time trying to find the one that breaks the mould.'

Beth was quick to state this was a somewhat narrow-minded approach. 'Don't you think you've simply been unlucky?'

Kerry began to gather her things. 'Perhaps, but I'm not wasting years of my life trying to find one that isn't. It's kind of you to invite me but there is no rest when you're a writer. Needs must.' She turned to James and Beth. 'It was good to meet you. Perhaps I may bump into you again if time permits me to cover your customs in Cavendish. I hope your residents there are not as improper as the fishermen of Polpennarth.'

James offered his hand adding they'd be delighted to see her.

Once the door had closed, they all

looked at one another. Anne broke the silence. 'She really is anti-men, isn't she?'

'I'll say,' said Beth. 'And she doesn't seem to have given relationships much of a go. I mean one failure is not the end of the world.'

'I–I feel that she is simply an independent woman in no n–need of company, male or f–female.'

James agreed. She was an independent lady set in her ways about her views on men. To have a controlling stepfather would have contributed to that and must have been awful, especially if her mother had loved this man. He wondered if she was an only child. During their discussion, she never mentioned any siblings, or any other family nearby. To uproot and take yourself as far away from home as possible might indicate a troubled childhood. Whatever it was, it had put Kerry Sheppard firmly in the camp of disliking company and being bothered with men in particular.

Colm clearly influenced Bevis in his thinking. Goading a single woman because of her independence was ignorant and ill-mannered. Was this simply a clash of backgrounds? Kerry loathed the fishermen for their outlook, hard-drinking and rudeness. It obviously touched a nerve. Had this riled Kerry Sheppard and forced her to resort to kidnap? If it had, how on earth did she manage it? And to what purpose? She said she wasn't rolling in pound notes but there'd been no ransom demand.

Anne interrupted his musings to ask what he was thinking about.

'I'm pretty sure that whoever kidnapped Colm and Bevis knew them. How else could no one have seen them disappear? If you're kidnapped by a stranger, you would put up one hell of a fight. They're local men, born and bred in Polpennarth; I would imagine that most villagers know them either by sight or through working and drinking with them.'

'W–what are you saying?'

'I'm saying that this is not an outsider. Kerry Sheppard has been targeted by villagers and the police because of her views and her lifestyle. Her attitude is not unusual to us, or anyone in our area, because we see it every day. Look at Elsie Taylor who runs the café. She's fiercely independent and as far as I know has never had a steady chap by her side. For all I know, she may have the same background as Kerry but we're comfortable with that and think nothing of it.'

'So,' said Anne, 'the way of life here is that women get married and become home-makers and mothers. A woman down here does not branch out on her own.'

'Except for Gretchen Kettel but I view her as unique. Perhaps she was married and is now widowed. The only reason the police have been to see Kerry is because she stood up for herself in The Pilchard. The fishermen didn't like that. They don't like a woman standing up to them.'

'She is certainly fiery,' said Beth. 'And she admitted that she'd have put a knife in her stepfather if she hadn't left.'

'But she did leave. And that was to save her own sanity. A chance argument with two local fishermen is not going to have the likes of Kerry Sheppard resorting to kidnap.'

'Sh–she said she was struggling to make ends meet.'

'But there's been no ransom demand. Why would she kidnap them; what is she going to do with them?'

They retreated into quiet reflection. James then tapped the table. 'These men have been targeted for a reason and it's not financial. Something historic; something that only a local would know. The trouble is, Kerry is right: it's difficult to get beneath the surface of such a small community.'

Beth added that a number of villagers thought that Hilda might be responsible. The Merryweathers looked on in horror.

James gave them more information about their conversation with Tristram. 'He found the whole thing quite amusing. As you mentioned before, darling, Hilda is similar to my sister but, for me, it's part of her bustling personality. I don't see why she would kidnap people. What would be her motive?' He grinned. 'I think, ladies, that this may be one for you.

Hilda, Evelyn and Debra belong to the WI. Why don't you take a leaf from the Snoop Sisters and get in there and do some delving. They have a meeting tomorrow night, don't they?'

'I–is there another parade tomorrow?'

Beth confirmed it was a free day. 'They resume the following day with the Knockers.'

Stephen gave James a despairing look. 'Jonah Quinn, Nibbin, Gretchen, Bidevin. Debra, Evelyn, Enoch. This isn't Cavendish. There are hundreds of v–villagers and the l–likelihood of finding the kidnapper is re–remote to say the least.'

James told him not to give up hope; that police in London must feel like that every day, especially with the thousands of people travelling in and out as well as living there. 'The game is afoot, as Sherlock Holmes once said. Let us not fall into despair, let us cast our net and see what comes to the surface.' He turned to Beth. 'You and I will hunt down PC Innes tomorrow and see what else he'll let slip. Later, you and Anne will attend the WI. And see if you can find out where this Nibbin woman lives.' He then addressed Stephen. 'When the ladies are gossiping with the women, we will ensconce ourselves in The Pilchard and await an old friend.'

'An o–old friend?'

Luke and Mark stumbled through the door.

'We've played all sorts of games,' said Luke and went on to enthuse about a number of board games including his favourite, Ludo.

'And we made two new friends. They're in the far caravan,' added Mark. He turned to James. 'And we played Snap and Happy Families.'

'Well that all sounds very exciting,' said James ruffling Mark's hair. He indicated that this was their cue to go. 'You'll be wanting to make these beds up, I should think.'

Stephen followed them to the door and pulled James back. 'An o–old friend?'

James gave him a sly wink and suggested that all good things would come to those who wait.

Back at the hotel, James stood by the

bay window. A light caught his eye. He snatched the binoculars. 'There it is again.'

Beth, who was sitting up in bed with a book, looked over the rim of her reading glasses. 'What?'

'That blasted light.' He leaned against the window and examined the cliff-tops. 'It's very intermittent.' He checked his watch. 'It seems to happen around this time every night.' He turned to Beth. 'Was there somewhere in the harbour that hired motor boats?'

Beth glared at him. 'If you think we're going on a boat in the middle of the night, you have another think coming. Perhaps it's a lighthouse.'

He dismissed the suggestion. 'There isn't one there. And anyway, a lighthouse is a permanent rotating light, it doesn't just pop up a signal at eleven. Annoying thing is I can't make out if it's on the cliff or just out to sea.'

'Well, instead of getting us into difficulty in the middle of the Atlantic, why don't you ask the locals what it is?'

He gave her a wry smile. 'Clever clogs.'

He climbed into bed and peered over her shoulder. 'What're you reading?'

'*Dr No* by Ian Fleming.'

'Good?'

'Surprisingly apt, sweetie. A fellow operative has gone missing and James Bond has gone to Jamaica to find out what's happened.'

'And what's happened?'

'I've just reached the part where Bond discovers that Dr No is working in an underground base on an island and is working with the Russians to sabotage a US base.'

James gazed out of the window and pondered on the Bond story. Was there something bigger going on here? Were those lights some sort of ship to shore message? He didn't know Morse code; perhaps he should jot it down and see if someone could translate. He admonished himself for being too imaginative.

But without a ransom demand, why else would Colm and Bevis disappear? There were no bodies; they had no reason to walk away; perhaps there was a bigger story behind this.

They turned out the light and snuggled in together. Beth fell asleep in his arms but James found it difficult to switch off from his thoughts. They had a full day ahead of them; perhaps he'd have more clarity this time the next day.

14

After breakfast the following morning, James retrieved a note that Desmond had slipped under the door. He opened it, read the contents then slipped it in his pocket with a degree of satisfaction. He wandered across to Beth who was fastening the button on her navy blue swing trousers. She adjusted the collar on her white cotton blouse. He stepped up behind her and gave her a hug.

'Are you ready to hunt down a police constable?'

She popped a lipstick and sunglasses into her handbag and confirmed that she was. 'But where does one hunt down a constable discreetly?'

'I've no idea. Let's hover around the police station and see if we can come up with a plan.'

They came out of their hotel and crossed the road. The sand on the beach was peppered with pieces of seaweed and driftwood from the previous night's storm. Although grey clouds scudded across the sky, the sun tried its hardest to pierce through them and reveal patches of blue. The forecast was that Polpennarth was in for another few days of warm sunshine.

With no parade scheduled, they examined the shops either side of the street. For such a small village, they discovered a surprising variety of stores catering to villagers and tourists. They saw Enoch enter the fisherman's bazaar, a shop made up of a number of market stalls selling fishing tackle, rope, jumpers and fishermen's smocks. Further along was a bakery where the smell of warm dough enticed them to look in the window. Wholemeal and white cottage loaves stood on the shelves along with a variety of rolls and scones.

James suggested they had yet to have a cream tea and suggested doing this when visiting St Ives. Across the street was a small bookstore that stocked a number of local authors as well as handy guides to the area. Up a side-street, Beth spotted the butcher's shop that Anne had mentioned.

Gretchen Kettel scurried out of her shop as they approached. 'Good morning, good morning,' she said with her customary chuckle. 'How are we today?'

'In excellent health,' said James.

'And how are you?' said Beth.

'Always well.' The old lady prised open the newspaper poster board and asked James if he would assist. He helped her insert the local paper's headlines. She fastened the board.

James stood back to read the *Polpennarth Weekly* headline. 'Colm Fiske and Bevis Allan — Where Are They?' He turned to Gretchen. 'Where indeed? Any ideas, Miss Kettel? You must hear quite a bit of gossip.'

She twitched with excitement. 'It's like *Dixon of Dock Green*, isn't it?'

James knew the television programme well. *Dixon of Dock Green* was a series he and Beth enjoyed about a certain Sergeant Dixon and his escapades as a London copper. He watched as Gretchen snatched a children's police helmet from her display and assumed the upright pose of Dixon.

'Evening all,' she said, using Dixon's famous opening catchphrase. 'Who is the kidnapper I hear you say? Some say Nibbin; some say Hilda; some say the Knockers. Can't go arresting people without evidence.' She clasped her hands together. 'It's lovely to have something to get your teeth into, isn't it?'

Beth's brow knitted together. 'Are you investigating this?'

She beckoned them into the shop. 'No, no, no. Me? Investigate? No. Doesn't surprise me they went missing though.'

James picked up the *Polpennarth Weekly* and felt for the right change. 'Why on earth do you say that?'

'Scratch beneath the surface and all sorts of things emerge. Not my place. Not my place.'

He and Beth glanced at one another and back to Gretchen who simply shrugged, chuckled and announced that she must get on. She accepted the money for the paper and chivvied them out. 'Don't quote me. Speak to Evelyn and

Debra. See why they lost their oomph, although I'm not sure they have now.' She closed the door behind them.

Out on the pavement, James turned to Beth. 'See why they lost their oomph? What's that supposed to mean?'

'I don't know but wasn't that a telling statement. *Scratch beneath the surface and all sorts of things emerge.* D'you think those wives are up to no good?'

'Hopefully we'll know more about that later. There's the police station; let's go and see if Innes is on duty.'

A polite enquiry established that PC Cardew Innes had one more hour of work to complete before going off shift. James checked his watch and suggested they had an ice cream and watch the world go by.

Settled with two cones of creamy vanilla ice cream, they sat on the promenade's stone wall and watched the families on the beach. The children screamed as they raced the tide streaming on to the beach; the Punch and Judy man was setting up his pitch and half a dozen donkeys were being led off the back of a lorry to offer rides for the day. Beth picked out one particular dad who'd been almost buried; just his head stuck out of the sand, causing his children to giggle uncontrollably.

Raised voices shifted their attention to the side, on the promenade, where Enoch faced a woman of a similar age.

The drama unfolding in front of them unsettled James. Enoch was a big hulk of a man with grey stubble and short grey hair. He towered over the lady James assumed to be his wife. No other woman would put up with his words. He understood Stephen's abhorrence of the man. The woman had obviously upset him in some way.

'Enough of your interfering, Edith. I've told you my decision and that's an end to it. I want nothing more said about it.'

Edith brought out a handkerchief.

'And don't turn those tears on; they cut nothing with me. She's made her bed so she can lie on it.'

'But Christine's our daughter.'

James' stomach flipped as Enoch closed in on his wife. He held his index finger an inch from her face. 'You so much as speak her name again and you'll rue the day.'

Beth sidled up closer to James. 'James, do you think we should intervene?'

He suggested they wait and observe. 'It's not our business darling and I'm loath to go wading into a quarrel between husband and wife.'

Enoch grabbed Edith's arm. 'Do you hear me?'

James gritted his teeth and leapt off the wall. 'I say, madam, is everything all right?' He stood firm as Enoch snarled at him. 'Is this man bothering you?'

Edith gave a hesitant smile and announced that she was quite fine. With her lips pursed, she strode away. Enoch glared and ordered him to keep his nose out of everyone's business. 'I've heard about you, asking questions.' Before James had a chance to react, the man had barged past him and begun walking in the opposite direction to his wife.

Beth dashed over. 'What a horrid man.'

James put his sunglasses on and watched Enoch stride into the distance. 'Charmless bully. I wonder what all that business is with the daughter.' Beth suggested that if she had any sense she'd have left home. He wrapped an arm around her. 'We're certainly seeing some interesting characters down here if nothing else.'

'Gretchen's right. Scratch beneath the surface. There are some tense people here for such a quaint village.'

'You're right, darling. Makes you wonder what on earth is going on behind closed doors.' They began a slow walk back toward the police station. 'I say, if that Edith lady is a member of the WI, you could perhaps hear what her story is.'

'Good idea. I'm looking forward to meeting everyone there.'

They saw PC Innes chatting to a tourist and giving directions. He looked up, waved and jogged across the road to meet them.

'Hello. Are you having a good time?'

James went through the normal pleasantries and Beth suggested tea and asked Innes if there was a good spot and would he like to join them.

The young man indicated that the best

place was up on the hill. 'There's a farm on top of the cliffs there, a little further along from the Sanctuary. They do bed and breakfast but have a great outlook. You can see from south to north Cornwall up there. They do cream teas if you're up for it. The bus is due in about half an hour and I'd like to get changed out of this uniform.'

James instructed Innes to get changed and he would collect the Austin Healey and they'd drive up.

'Crikey, are you giving me a lift?'

'It'll be a bit of a squeeze in the back but I'll have the roof down.'

The young PC looked as if all his Christmases had come at once. He thanked James and dashed off past the station and up a side street. Beth said she'd wait for Innes to return as James strode back to the hotel to collect the car.

* * *

The location of the farmhouse didn't disappoint. Perched one hundred yards from the cliff face, the views rendered them speechless. They were approximately 10 miles from Land's End and were able to scan the entire tip of Cornwall. To the south on one side was the nearest major town, Penzance. James could make out the harbour and about a mile further along was the imposing St Michael's Mount, a small island just off the coast where, during low tide, you could walk across a causeway to visit it. Some of the buildings on the mount had been there since the Norman Conquest and it was another destination they wanted to visit before leaving. The jagged coast line stretched into the distance. His gaze followed it around to the north where views of the ocean continued.

'My word, it's spectacular,' he said.

'And where is St Ives from here?' asked Beth.

Innes turned to face inland. 'About five miles that way. Once you get over the far crest, you can see it. Pretty little town; very hilly, but pretty.'

They seated themselves at a wrought iron table. To one side was a hand built open pagoda with white Clematis that provided a dappled shade. A menu card stated that cream teas were the speciality and all three put their order in. The large farmer's wife who took the order waddled into the kitchen. Five minutes later, they were presented with half a dozen home-made scones, home-made strawberry jam and a dish of thick Cornish clotted cream, made on the farm.

James sliced his scone in two and spread a generous helping of jam on each. With a spoon, he placed an equally generous dollop of clotted cream. Beth agitated the tea and let it rest for a couple of minutes. James leant in and took a bite. The flavours melted together like a dream. There was a subtle hint of vanilla in the scones that complemented the jam and cream.

He closed his eyes. 'Mmm. Now these are more like Granny's scones.'

Beth mirrored his delighted expression. 'Delicious.'

'Told you they were the best,' said Innes. 'Tourists always stick to the village and forget to hunt out what's off the beaten track. Some of the locals pop up here and get their jam from the farm.'

Beth poured the tea. 'How long have you been a policeman, Mr Innes?'

'Call me Cardew, please. Well, while I'm off duty, that is. About three years now. I started off helping dad collect the milk churns. This was one of the farms we'd stop off at; but it weren't for me. I've always liked the idea of being a copper; Bobbies on the beat, that sort of thing, you know, keep the community safe and all. So I thought I'd give it a shot. If I didn't like it, I could jack it in but you don't know unless you try, do you?'

James agreed and commented that one should never look back on life with regrets. He highlighted his dream of being a racing driver and the brief stint he had among the greats of the day. Cardew gave him his full attention, enthralled by this glimpse into another world.

The young man sat forward. 'I hope you don't mind me asking; but what's it like being a Lord and Lady? D'you get to meet the Queen and film stars?'

James exchanged a bemused smile with

Beth. 'It's not as glamorous as you may think Cardew.'

The pair of them commended the positives of their position and that yes, occasionally, their social circle brought them into the proximity of royals and film stars but the reality was they still needed to make a living. James found himself, for the umpteenth time over the last few years explaining that many titled individuals, although fortunate, could not rely on income alone. 'We have to work for it,' he said, explaining the set-up in Cavendish with their former home, Harrington's.

Cardew sipped his tea. 'What film stars have you met?'

Beth was quick to announce that she'd been introduced to Errol Flynn about ten years previously. 'He was a dream. I wanted to hug him.'

'And you, Lord Harrington?'

'He didn't do anything for me, I'm afraid.'

They laughed and chatted a little about films and television programmes. It transpired that Cardew had got his first television just the previous year. 'I love all the detective shows, especially *Murder Bag*'

'Probably because you love being a policeman,' James said, trying to steer the conversation. 'How are you getting on with all this kidnapping business? Are you any further forward?'

Cardew groaned. 'I don't feel we are but that Inspector Wormstone keeps going on about small steps.'

'Well, he's right. It's a little like a jigsaw puzzle. You put in one piece at a time and to begin with it looks a mess but slowly a picture begins to emerge.'

'Yeah, I s'pose you're right.'

Beth brought Cardew back to the question. 'You must be a little further forward; discounted some people and put others for more questioning.'

He brightened. 'Yes. Yes, we have.'

James stirred his tea and asked if he were able to share. 'In confidence, of course.'

He observed Cardew wrestle a little with his duty but he knew the young man felt privileged to be having tea with a real Lord and Lady. A title did come in handy in these situations. He didn't have to wait long.

'Well, we've discounted all the tourists. Inspector Wormstone reckons this is a local. He said this had to be planned and it has to be someone that knows the area and where to keep 'em. Also, he said that the victims appeared to have gone voluntarily; or thought they were, so they must know each other.'

'Anyone else discounted?'

'Lots of the villagers. The elderly and the children; those that have physical problems or who are small. Mr Atherton, the blind man, he's out of it. Colm and Bevis are big blokes; there's no way that a slight person could do this let alone a blind one. He reckons it's a man who's capable of looking after himself.'

James stopped him. 'But that makes no sense at all? You're discounting a whole group of people who could have everything to do with it. What about if it's two people working together? It could even be Gretchen Kettel if she had a gun. People don't argue if there's a revolver sticking in their ribs.'

Cardew sighed. 'I know. I thought the same but Wormstone's having none of it. Mind you, he's got the benefit of London policing up his sleeve. He's not stupid; he's handled kidnappings and murders in the city.'

Beth asked if Inspector Wormstone had a theory about the kidnapper. 'You know, like a personality trait or the age-range of such a person.'

'He may do. He's been speaking to some of his contacts in London. He only shares things with me when he's sure himself. He spoke about two kidnapping events he handled in the city and both were carried out by men.'

James felt the exasperation rise. 'So he's discounting all the women.'

Cardew gave James an incredulous stare. 'D'you think a woman is responsible for this?'

'I don't know but I don't think I'd be this quick to dismiss the idea.' He prepared another scone. 'And these incidents in London, did they involve a ransom demand? Because if they did, this is a completely different scenario. There is no ransom demand. Makes you wonder what the point of it is. Are you absolutely sure they've been kidnapped and not just run off?'

Cardew confirmed that they were confident about that. 'Colm had set his fishing nets up for the next day. Got his boat ready for an early shoot. Bevis was keen to get the market prices. It was one of the blokes' birthdays too and they were all going down The Pilchard to celebrate.'

'I understood that Colm had been thrown out of The Pilchard.'

The young man explained that Bidevin kicked Colm out several times a year. 'Along with a few others too. Colm gets loud and aggressive when he's had a few. He'd crossed the line again and Bid chucked him out. He'll let him back in. He has to. Colm and the fishermen keep him in business.'

'Does Bidevin like Colm?'

Innes pulled a face. 'He puts up with him. Colm gets lippy and he insulted Bid's mum a couple of years ago. And every so often, the business about the recipe comes up.'

James asked if Wormstone had discounted that.

'There's no substance to the allegation, nothing to suggest it's anything to do with that. But I know Bid gets fed up with him. He'll serve him and take his money but that's it.'

'Does Inspector Wormstone really have no idea?'

'At the moment, he's looking at the fishermen. There's about twenty of 'em and it's taking some time to sort the wheat from the chaff. They're very insular and they close ranks.'

'What motive would the fishermen have?'

Cardew hesitated and then leaned forward. 'Colm and Bevis were both in debt to a fisherman called Johnny Sepp. He's a Penzance man who runs poker games. They owed Johnny around forty pound each which is a lot of money for them. We've had the fishermen in for questioning and around half a dozen of them are part of this gambling ring.'

'Is Enoch involved?'

Cardew sat up with a start. 'Enoch

Pengilly? I don't think so, no. Why d'you ask?'

James waved the question aside. 'He's big enough to overpower the men that went missing and seems a pretty bad-tempered individual. Would he be owed money? Perhaps he lent money to Colm and Bevis.'

Beth added that this could be why Enoch was in such a bad mood.

Cardew said that Enoch was always in a bad mood. 'It's his way. But getting back to your thoughts, your Lordship, Enoch has a code of conduct in his life and it don't include gambling. He's as tight as they come so he wouldn't lend it either. We normally have a book open when we do the pancake race through the town and he won't even contribute to that so I can't imagine him betting on poker.'

'What does this Johnny Sepp have to say for himself?'

A shrug. 'Nothing. He has a strong alibi and he says he's set up a weekly pay back for the pair of them. He's adamant that he's stopped 'em both from playing until they've paid their debts.'

'How can he afford to do that?'

'He's a fisherman, your Lordship, but not in the sense of one fisherman and his boat. He owns a fleet of fishing boats and married well. We're trying to establish if Colm and Bevis owed some of their mates money.'

'But if this is to do with money, why hasn't there been a ransom demand?'

Beth restocked the tea pot with a jug of hot water. 'The villagers suspect Hilda Roscarrock. Why's that?'

'She's a strong, assertive woman who does occasionally say bad things about the men of the village.'

'Bad things?'

'Colm and Bevis are men's men; well, a number of men around here are. They speak their mind, can sometimes swear and be aggressive and Hilda puts them in their place. I've seen her stand up to Colm and Bevis a few times; when they're with their wives. And Enoch. Tears strips off of 'em.'

'Good Lord. Do they not retaliate? Enoch's wife appeared a little hesitant to contradict him when we came across them.'

'They're different outside the house though, aren't they?' He let out a laugh. 'Can you imagine Hilda kidnapping two beefy blokes — anyway, what would she do with them?'

'How many villagers own a car?'

'Ah, yes, that's another thing. The Inspector's discounted anyone without a car.'

Another stab of exasperation hit James. 'Why?'

'Well, they'd need a car, wouldn't they?'

'Not necessarily.' James went on to detail how a simple invitation for a pint could lure someone away. 'Do you have a pharmacy here with sleeping draughts or anything? They could have been drugged and be sitting in a cellar somewhere.'

Cardew assured him that the doctor and the pharmacist had been questioned and they'd taken stock of their supplies. 'Nothing is missing and the only people on sleeping pills are some of the women.'

James shifted in his chair. 'Do you

know which women?'

'Yeah, Debra Allan — she works in the pharmacy, Evelyn Fiske, Mrs Johnson up on the hill, Edith Pengilly. I think that's it.' He gave them an urgent look. 'Don't you be telling the Inspector I told you that.' He checked his watch. 'I'm going to take a meander back to the village.' He held his hands up. 'No, no, don't get up. It's only a couple of miles and all downhill too. Will we see you at the next parade?'

James confirmed they'd be there. 'Before you go, could you tell me if you have any information about Jonah Quinn's background?'

The young man thought for a second. 'Nothing. Why, do you know something?'

'No but I'll let you know if I do. By the way, are there any ships moored off the coast at the moment; or an island to the south there.'

'No islands, no. May be a ship waiting to get into Penzance or up to Plymouth. Why?'

'I noticed signals the last few nights; intermittent lights as if someone were sending a message.'

Cardew gave him a perplexed look and shrugged. 'No idea, I'm afraid. See you tomorrow.'

They watched as the young man sauntered away along the cliff-tops.

'This Inspector chap appears very quick to discount people, don't you think Beth.'

'I do. I know George said he's an excellent detective but do you think all that business with the murdered child affected him more than he's letting on? I'm not qualified in such matters but I'd be delving a little more into Hilda's history if the villagers are setting these rumours in motion. Gossip is a dreadful thing but sometimes they have an ounce of fact about them.'

'And why is he so quick to discount the women?'

Beth reminded him that Wormstone didn't appear to confirm things to Innes until he was sure. 'Perhaps he has evidence that suggests a man.'

'Perhaps. When you're at the WI tonight, see what you can glean from the women there. If the men were drugged, I could quite easily see how a woman would be responsibile.'

'A woman scorned?'

James turned to her. 'D'you know what, Beth, that's exactly what this appears to be. This isn't to do with money. If it was, the kidnapper would have demanded a ransom. We need to establish the underlying reason for those men going missing and a woman scorned is a good start.'

The farmer's wife appeared at the table. 'Everything all right?'

'The best scones I've had in a long time.'

'Heavenly,' Beth added. 'Your scones had a wonderful vanilla taste through them. I presume you use an extract of some kind.'

She offered to give them the recipe. 'I get lots of requests so I got a few printed off. Hold on a moment and I'll go and get one.'

When she returned, James asked the same question about the lights. Her reaction faltered before telling him that no, she didn't know what they'd be. But James had seen a flicker of alarm that unnerved him.

They took a slow drive across the hilltops toward Polpennarth. The skies had cleared completely and a warm breeze had replaced the slight chill from earlier. James breathed in the fresh sea air and looked back over the last two days. What was the matter with this village? Cryptic comments from Gretchen, volatile fishermen, fearful wives, an eccentric on the moors and strange lights out to sea. Most peculiar. He wondered whether fellow tourists had formed the same impression of the village. Probably not. They were simply enjoying a leisurely holiday and he couldn't imagine any of them asking questions about the local crime. He'd have to see what the night's enquiries would bring.

15

The WI gathered at seven o'clock and James strolled with Beth until they reached the meeting place. He pecked her on the cheek with a promise to meet her in a couple of hours. Checking his watch, he still had fifteen minutes before meeting Stephen so made his way along the harbour wall where he'd seen pleasure boats available for hire. He stopped half-way along where several craft were moored. A young lady, around seventeen, was securing the boats and closing the rental hut for the day.

'We're closed now. If you wanna hire a boat, you'll have to come back tomorrow.'

'Would you allow an excursion later this evening?'

Her brow knitted together. 'Tonight? What d'you wanna go out tonight for? Pitch dark out there and the current might catch you unawares. Anyway, we're closed. Closed at six o'clock and no-one's 'ere after that.'

'Sorry, what's your name?'

'Lisa.'

'Well, Lisa, I'm happy to pay double if you're happy to oblige. I'll be ten, fifteen minutes at the most. Good profit for you.'

'Double! You got more money than sense, you have. I'll do it for double, so long as you're not going out to sea. My dad'll knock me senseless if he finds out.'

'I'm literally poodling along the coastline, following the promenade. Be back before you know it. I'm used to sailing so I'm pretty sure I can handle one of these.'

She scrutinised him. 'Fifteen minutes you say.'

James nodded with a reassurance that he wouldn't leave the bay.

'What time?'

'Ten fifty-five.'

'That's a bit precise ain't it? What you gonna do?'

'Nothing for you to worry about. Your boat will be well looked after. This is about me satisfying my curiosity about something, that's all.'

'You pay me before you go out.'

James promised he would. To his relief, the girl agreed to the unusual request. Thank goodness the daughter had been left in charge. He had a feeling that her father would have been less inclined to do business.

★ ★ ★

A few minutes later, he met Stephen and they grabbed a bench on the terrace outside The Pilchard Inn. Luke and Mark were within sight playing on the swings in the small garden at the side. Their small dog, Radley, dozed by Stephen's feet, worn out by the boys' play. In front of them were three pints of local ale.

'C–come on, James, who are w–we expecting. You keep looking at your watch. W–will I know them?'

'You will. He should be here by now.'

As if awaiting his entrance, a familiar voice called out. 'Oi, oi.'

Stephen's jaw fell. 'Bert?'

Bert slapped him on the back and shook hands with James. 'The very man, vicar, the very man.' He sat down next to

James and grinned. 'I'm 'ere for the night.' He picked up his dimpled pint jug. 'What's this?'

James held his own up and announced that this was ale brewed in Polpennarth. 'Rather tasty too. Drink up and tell us all. I'm presuming from your message that you're not empty handed?'

'E–empty handed? What message?'

Stephen looked bewildered, so James enlightened him. 'I got in touch with Bert a couple of evenings ago and he left a message with the Simms to say he'd much to tell.'

Stephen looked at James, then Bert, and back to James. 'About what?'

Bert glanced behind him. The nearest occupied bench was some distance away. He shifted forward. 'Jonah Quinn.'

'Oh. Is there s–something to tell?'

'This Jonah Quinn bloke was a banker in the city of London; quite high up by all accounts.'

James interrupted him to ask where he was getting this information from. 'It's not hearsay is it?'

Bert baulked at the suggestion. 'My

source is someone who worked alongside him.'

'Good Lord, how on earth did you find him?'

'By being nosy, Jimmy boy. Anyway, never mind about that, the point is I gets talking to this bloke; goes by the name of Leslie Saunders. He worked with Jonah Quinn for about a year and he wasn't everyone's favourite person but this Saunders bloke got on with 'im all right.'

Stephen reminded James they already knew he didn't get on with his boss. Bert gestured for him to stop.

'They came to blows in the Olde Cheshire Cheese'.

'Th–the what?'

James explained that this was one of the oldest pubs in London. After the Great Fire in 1666, it had been one of the first to be rebuilt. 'It's full of nooks and crannies and is incredibly big once you get inside.'

'It was in one of those nooks and crannies that Jonah Quinn stabbed his boss.'

James stared in horror and mouthed

'*Stabbed his boss?*' back to his friend. 'Are you sure?'

'Sure as I'm sitting 'ere drinking this beer. It weren't a serious attack but Jonah had drunk too much and decided he'd had enough. He apparently lunged at him and caught him in the side. No organs damaged; just a lot o' blood.'

'Was he charged?' said James.

'No mate. Coppers gave 'im a ticking off. The boss didn't wanna press charges but it was on the understanding that Jonah leave.'

'D–do you know why they didn't get on?'

'Yeah. Jonah was seeing the boss's daughter. Things took a turn for the worse when he convinced her to take a bus ride with him.'

James didn't like the sound of where this was going. He felt increasingly uneasy as Bert detailed how Jonah and the young woman boarded a bus and she never went home that night.

'Stayed away three nights. The boss reported her missing and he blamed Jonah; accused him of kidnapping her.

The police went round to his digs but she weren't there.'

'Where was she?'

'She'd got the bus back home that day but decided to stay at a friend's place. She was a sulky girl who wanted to put her dad through it for not liking Jonah.'

James scratched his head and knew he must have looked puzzled. 'Are you saying this girl was quite young?'

His friend nodded. 'She was seventeen and this Jonah bloke was in his forties. Would that be right?'

Stephen confirmed that Jonah was certainly the wrong side of fifty now so what Bert said had made sense.

James went through it all again to make sure he'd understood. 'So Jonah has a fling with the boss's daughter who is young enough to be his own daughter. The boss makes life hell for Jonah who in turn gets drunk and stabs the boss. The boss drops charges providing Jonah clear off.'

'That's the gist of it, mate.'

'C–can I ask. Do you know w–what the

boss did to m–make life awkward for Jonah?'

'No pay rises for a start. They had two increases one year and Jonah didn't get one. He pulled him up on some shoddy work and demoted him so he then had a pay cut. This Saunders bloke reckoned that Jonah was a good worker so it didn't make sense to him.'

James supped his ale. 'It's all very interesting but it doesn't really put him in the frame for kidnapping these men.'

'I ain't finished yet.'

James raised his eyebrows. He and Stephen instinctively leant toward Bert.

'He also had a holiday romance. Bragged about it when he was still in the city. He'd come down 'ere for a recce; must have been about the time he was thinking o' moving down here.'

'A romance with whom?'

Bert felt in his pocket and brought out an old betting slip. 'I wrote the name down. Might not mean anything though.' He examined it. 'Evelyn. Evelyn Cline.'

James turned to Stephen. 'How long

has Evelyn Fiske been married d'you think?'

'I don't know. A few years.'

'Who's Evelyn Fiske?' asked Bert.

'The wife of Colm Fiske, the first man to be kidnapped.'

James twirled a sodden beer mat. 'I believe our Jonah is a bit of a lothario, don't you?'

'I–I wonder if he's romanced that Debra woman too?'

'We need to find out if Evelyn Cline and Evelyn Fiske are one and the same.'

'That should be pretty easy' said Bert drinking the last of his beer. 'Drink up, I'll go and find out.'

James looked on as Bert entered the bar and engaged Bidevin in some friendly banter. As the landlord pulled three pints, he spoke with Bert then appeared to show him directions. Bert held a hand up in thanks and emerged with their drinks.

'Evelyn Fiske, maiden name Cline, married ten years to Colm.'

'G–good grief.' Stephen insisted on knowing how he did it.

'I said I've got distant family in these

parts; name of Cline. Anyone of that name 'ere?'

James chuckled. How wonderful it was to have his friend here. Holidays were no doubt enjoyable with new places to discover, new acquaintances to make and fresh experiences to be had but having the Merryweathers and Bert here was an absolute joy. He came out of his musing and asked if Bert had any more news about Jarvis Wormstone.

'Not really. He was a good copper by all accounts. Thought things through — didn't just go blustering in. What's he been like down 'ere then?'

James went through the conversation that he and Beth had had with PC Innes earlier in the day and hinted that he felt Wormstone was overlooking vital information. 'He seems to be set in a certain direction and dismissing obvious lines of enquiry.'

'I'm sure he 'as a set way of working. He don't sound like the sort of bloke who'd dismiss things for no reason. And you ain't got access to what he's discovered so far. What's Jarvis think of Innes?'

He pulled a face. 'Not entirely sure. He's a big cheese from the city and Innes is only a couple of years into the job. Do you think he's playing his cards close to his chest?'

'Per'aps. Coppers come in all forms and Wormstone is up there with the best; like George.'

DCI George Lane was highly regarded in the Sussex Constabulary and this was indeed high praise from Bert. His cockney friend was a wheeler and dealer and the police were never high up in his estimations. But, in fairness to Bert, he recognised a decent detective when one came along. So far, Inspector Jarvis Wormstone was deemed an intelligent and fair policeman. Perhaps James was wrong to make judgements based on Innes' opinion.

'Bert, do you have any other snippets of information?'

'No mate. I like the sound of that Nibbin woman. You ought to track her down. Those types normally know more than you think. But you two have obviously got your teeth into it all.

217

Anything else to report?'

James said he didn't think so. The pattern so far was that the two men were involved in the fishing community and belonged to no clubs or shared hobbies. The only link was that their wives all attended the WI. 'There are some odd lights that have been flashing up the coast there. I've asked a couple of people about them and one gave me the impression she knew but wouldn't say.'

Bidevin appeared with a tea towel over his shoulder. He scanned the tables and collected up any empty glasses. When he reached them, James asked about the flashing lights out at sea and whether it meant anything.

The landlord stopped dead and narrowed his eyes at James. 'It means you're asking too many questions. Those lights . . . they only . . . ' He picked up the glasses. 'Go and speak with Andrew, the old bloke in the corner.' He strode off.

'I say, that was disconcerting.' James sat up and looked across to where Bidevin had pointed. A wiry old man with a tobacco stained beard sat gazing across the bay. He wore a Guernsey jumper and smoked a long clay pipe and looked like a character from a Dickens novel. James excused himself and threaded his way through the benches to speak with Andrew.

The old man puffed his pipe and his piercing blue eyes fell on James. 'Arr?'

'Hello, my name's James and Bidevin suggested I speak with you about some lights I keep seeing off the coast every night.'

'Arr.'

'He suggested you might know what they are. Thing is, I'm the only one who seems to see them.'

'No one else sees 'em you say?'

James pulled up an old beer barrel and sat down. 'Are you able to enlighten me?'

'We had strange lights out to sea from the end of the Great War. Said to be the ghosts of fishermen drowned after their boat was hit by a submarine. The lights, back then, were supposed to lure German boats to their doom but we ain't at war no more.'

'Are you telling me I'm seeing ghosts?'

'People who see mysterious lights have to be careful.'

'Careful of what?'

'Their own wellbeing. You're the man asking questions about Colm and Bevis?'

James assured him it was simple curiosity. 'I'm fascinated about how two grown men can just disappear. I don't mean any harm.'

Andrew chewed the tip of his pipe. 'Per'aps it's time to stop that. Those lights are luring you to danger. You back off, the lights'll disappear.' He placed the pipe in his mouth and returned his attention to the sea.

James returned to Bert and Stephen and recounted the conversation. Stephen's eyes opened wide with horror.

Bert chuckled. 'Bloody fairy stories. They're all bonkers down 'ere with all their folklore and ghost stories.' He tilted his head. 'I asked you before you left. You don't believe any of this cobblers, do you?'

James laughed at him but he felt uneasy about the ghost lights. 'The best way to put this to bed is to hire a boat and see for myself. I've already asked someone who is able to lend me a boat.'

He turned to Bert and asked if he would come. Stephen immediately objected and even Bert had reservations.

'Oi, why don't we get ourselves on the cliff-tops tonight with some binoculars and keep a look out — see if we can make out what it is.'

'Surely being on the sea would be better.'

'Not for me, it ain't. I 'ate boats and getting in one with you in the middle of the night ain't my idea of a good time. What'll Beth think about it? I can't imagine she's happy about you playing sleuth when you're s'posed to be on holiday.'

He and Stephen exchanged a wry smile prompting Bert to ask what was so funny.

'Beth and Anne, as we speak, are attending the WI meeting with strict instructions to instigate discreet investigations.' He looked across to the road to the old Seaman's Mission on the far side where the meeting was taking place and wondered how they were getting on.

16

Beth felt her shoulders relax as Hilda, the matriarch of the Polpennarth WI, gave her and Anne the warmest of welcomes. In her booming voice she announced that Lady Elizabeth Harrington and her friend Anne Merryweather were here on holiday and were keen to visit the local WI.

There were around fifteen women in the hall, including Gretchen, Evelyn, Debra, Edith and Vivian. Beth asked if any were missing.

Hilda explained there were some absentees. 'During the holiday season we dip in numbers. A few of ours run full board accommodation so it's difficult to get away. Once the holiday season's over, we swell to thirty. Now, we'll sing the anthem and then you'll be having tea.'

They gathered together and launched into 'Jerusalem' which Beth felt sounded a little tired with so few people singing. Following this, they were nudged toward a bench table at the side of the hall and introduced to three elderly ladies who prepared tea and offered out slices of sponge.

Hilda strode to the front and clapped her hands. 'As we have guests, I've divided the evening into two. It'll be nice for our guests to get to know us but we must also go through the hymn.'

One of the ladies leant toward Beth and Anne. 'We're singing 'Eternal Father' at a special fishermen's day next month.'

Hilda continued. 'We'll go through the hymn a couple of times now and have a break and continue later along with making plans for future evenings. Perhaps Lady Harrington and Mrs Merryweather could tell us a little about their WI and what they do.'

Beth and Anne said they'd be delighted. They were provided with song sheets and invited to join in with the group. Gretchen Kettel adjusted the stool by the piano and arranged the music. Her frame was so tiny that Beth felt she needed a smaller piano. She wondered how her fingers would stretch across the ivories. She hammered down hard on the keyboard and an off-key chord rang out.

Anne whispered in Beth's ear. 'Is it me or does that piano need tuning?'

Beth suppressed a smile and agreed. The women all stood and began to sing:

'Eternal Father, strong to save; whose arm hath bound the restless wave,
Who bidd'st the mighty ocean deep, its own appointed limits keep.
Oh hear us when we cry to Thee, for those in peril on the sea.'

As the hymn continued, Anne wiped a tear away. Beth turned to her. 'Oh Anne, what's the matter?'

'This hymn, it always makes me cry. It's so moving.'

Beth put an arm around her and squeezed her shoulders. 'It is a rousing hymn. I feel the same way with 'The Banks of Green Willow'; you know that one by George Butterworth. It reminds me of English meadows and a simpler world.' Tears welled in her eyes. 'Oh look at me, you've started me off.'

They lent their voices to the singing and, after two more renditions, Hilda clapped her hands and announced an early tea break.

Beth turned to Anne. 'Right, plan of action. Who shall we target first?'

'Let's do Evelyn. She's the first one we met; we could just ask her how she's coping.'

Beth looked across. 'We're in luck. She's teamed up with Debra, we can kill two birds with one stone.'

'We can't just swoop in with questions.'

'We won't. Let's find a common interest and steer the conversation. Come along.'

They wandered across to the ladies in question and pulled up two wooden chairs. For the next few minutes, the ladies chatted about fashions, food and the community in Polpennarth.

Beth heaved a satisfied sigh. They'd cast the net out; how long should she wait before tugging the imaginary rope? As they spoke, she observed the women. James had taught her that sitting back and watching a person's body language and mannerisms could speak volumes.

Evelyn appeared a little wary of letting her guard down. She was almost hunched and wrapped her arms close around her body. She clearly didn't trust strangers and Beth detected a reluctance to discuss her private life. That same fearful look they'd witnessed when first meeting her remained in her eyes and Beth wondered if there was a time when this woman hadn't been frightened. Did she live in fear? Was her upbringing an unhappy one? It struck her that she had the worries of the world on her shoulders.

As time went on, Debra became more animated — happy to chat and laugh which Beth suddenly felt uncomfortable with considering her husband had gone missing. And how different she seemed to the anxious wife searching for her husband the previous day. This looked like a woman devoid of concern. It was as if she'd been set free. Her eyes were bright, her smile ready and she came across as younger and more confident.

In a natural lull, Beth sat forward. 'And how are you coping at the moment? Are the police any further forward with their investigations?'

Evelyn retreated further into her shell and studied her hands. 'They've no idea. People have said he must have tripped over and fallen off a cliff or something but my Colm wouldn't do that.'

'They've drunk together before,' said Debra. 'I wonder if they're making our lives a misery out of spite. Prob'ly holed up with one of the fishermen.'

Evelyn shrank.

Anne sat up with a start. 'But surely they wouldn't do that. They're working men with responsibilities.'

Debra shrugged. 'Mine spends his money on drink and gambling. I get the bare necessities for food and he moans if I dish up rubbish. What else am I supposed to dish up if he don't give me enough money to get decent food? I've had to take a job at the pharmacy to make ends meet. It don't give me much more but it's something.'

Beth asked if she had spoken to the police. 'I understand they were asking if any drugs had gone missing, sleeping aids, that sort of thing.'

Debra stiffened. 'I didn't take 'em. And anyway, nothing's gone missing. My drugs are on prescription, I don't steal 'em.'

'Oh goodness, I wasn't suggesting that, Debra. Please forgive me.' But Beth had already noticed an invisible barrier return.

'Don't speak so open to strangers, Debra,' said Evelyn. 'It's not right and Bevis won't thank you for talking about your habits. You know what he's like.'

Beth tilted her head. 'What is he like, Debra?'

Debra's bravado slipped. She fiddled with her wedding ring. 'He's a good man. Don't mind what I say. Don't you repeat any of this back to anyone. I don't want him knowing I spoke out of turn.'

'We wouldn't dream of it, would we Anne?'

'Certainly not. I'm a vicar's wife, I have to keep confidences all the time. I've seen similar expressions from other women in your position.'

The ladies glared.

'I mean that your husbands are proud men and don't like their lives discussed with strangers. That's understandable. The women that chat to me simply see me as another female to share their troubles with. It goes no further.'

Evelyn remained quiet but Debra rubbed her forearms and pursed her lips. 'You couldn't be further from the truth. There's nothing — '

Beth closed her eyes in frustration as Hilda blustered her way in. 'Having a lovely evening ladies?'

Evelyn forced a smile and made an excuse to move on. Debra asked Anne to forgive her outburst; that she had a lot of worry with Bevis being gone. She squeezed Anne's hand in apology and followed Evelyn.

Hilda sat down. 'Bearing up well, those two, don't you think?'

Beth praised them, stating she'd be in no position to visit her WI so soon if James had been abducted. 'I'd be sick with worry. If I did attend, I'm not so sure that I could be as happy as Debra; she seems almost pleased that he's gone.'

'But,' Anne put in, 'Evelyn looks terribly anxious.' She shifted forward in her chair. 'I get the impression things were not good between her and Colm.'

Hilda lowered her voice and explained that many marriages down here were not always a bed of roses. 'People muddle by. Life is tough down here, especially if you're connected to the fishing industry. The men are proper men, don't suffer fools gladly. They work long hours, three hundred and sixty five days a year; all weathers. The women have got to support them, nurse them, be there for them whatever the circumstances. It's not a life for everyone.'

Beth gave an understanding nod. It must be hard. She and James had already spoken about this. A bleak, stormy day in December would be horrific. Wives seeing their husbands go fishing and steering their boats into waves as tall as the cottages they lived in; in danger of being washed overboard and lost at sea. *For those in peril on the sea.* It certainly was a poignant hymn and brought home the dangers those men faced every day. She wondered whether she could be a fisherman's wife and answered the question before coming to the end of it. No. A man coming home from dragging in nets would be a weary, bad-tempered man wanting food, drink and a roaring fire. She could imagine any wife in that position becoming almost servile.

She stumbled out of her thoughts and heard Anne ask Hilda how she and Tristram met.

Hilda, dressed in a plain skirt and blouse, looked up to recollect her thoughts. 'We went to school together. He was the year above me but I always had a soft spot for him. He reminded me of Tintin with his blond hair and little quiff at the front. It hasn't changed since the day I met him although, of course, the sun has bleached his hair even whiter; but even that suits him.'

'You seem very different to Tristram if you don't mind me saying,' said Beth.

Hilda whooped. 'You mean he's kind, thoughtful and wouldn't hurt the smallest fly if it landed on you and I'm loud, clumsy and would hit you if I thought it'd do you some good?' She laughed again. 'If that's what you mean then, yes, we are different.'

Beth joined in with a chuckle. 'I guess that's what I mean. But you're well suited.'

'We like our own company. That's our secret — our independence. Tris is at his happiest up at the Sanctuary, rescuing things, helping the helpless, roaming the cliff-tops, tending to poorly birds. A proper Dr Doolittle, that's Tris. I'm wrapped up with the WI and baking.'

'So did you snare Tristram or was it the other way around.'

'Funnily enough, the other way around. I didn't think I stood a chance with him. He always had a glamorous girl on his arm but do you know who I reminded him of?'

Beth and Anne waited for her answer.

'It's going to sound unflattering but I reminded him of his grandmother.' Another bellow went up to the rafters. 'I punched him on the arm when he told me why he'd asked me out. I told him, I'm not your grandma, I never will be and you can take a running jump.'

Beth chuckled. 'But he persisted. I guess his grandma had similar traits to you.'

'Exactly. I was thinking he thought I looked like an eighty year old hag — like my grandma, but he was looking at the person inside. Stupid of me to have made such a meal out of it.'

Anne commented that grandparents tended to be a child's favourite people. 'Our two love staying with mine and Stephen's parents.'

Hilda agreed. 'He spent most of his time with his grandmother. His parents split up when he was ten and he and his mum stopped with her. I believe she was a strong and assertive lady who kept them safe. They stayed with her. And, of course, I'm also in that category — like to make sure people are safe. Never quite sure whether that's a good or bad thing.' She slapped her knees and got up. 'Excuse me but I need to get song sheets for the next rehearsal.'

'Before you go,' said Beth, 'I couldn't help but think about the comment you made when you were with Evelyn the day we met you.'

Hilda's brow knitted together.

'You said to her that things were looking up.'

A momentary loss of composure was quickly replaced by a smile and a shrug. 'Did I? I say the oddest things sometimes. Tris always tells me off for speaking before thinking. Come along ladies, we must get on.'

'Are you singing another hymn?'

'We're doing a song that's a little out of season. 'Halantow'. It's a Cornish folk song that we normally sing on 1st May but it's all about summer coming and lends itself to a lot of harmonies. When we've done that, would you mind giving us a little talk about what you do at the Cavendish WI?'

As she strode off, Beth caught the eye of Edith Pengilly. The lady approached with a cup and saucer in her hand and sat down opposite them. Almost immediately, she placed a hand on Beth's knee and apologised for her husband's behaviour earlier that day.

'Enoch gets bad-tempered occasionally. He don't mean nothing by it.'

'That's quite all right, Mrs Pengilly. James and I were a little concerned. I'm not used to seeing a husband behave that way toward his wife. Not in public at least.'

Edith shifted in her chair and pulled her chin in. 'Like I say, he don't mean nothing by it. It's just his way. No need for your husband to have got involved.'

'I'm sure he wouldn't have done if he'd known. I'm sorry if that offended you; he was only doing what he thought was right.'

'Very chivalrous, I'm sure.'

Anne exaggerated her cheerfulness and enquired about Enoch. 'He's a fisherman too, is he?'

Edith explained that he'd fished since he was ten and was now in his sixtieth year. 'God willing, he'll keep coming home safe. I'd be lost without my Enoch.' She gestured to the area where Evelyn and Debra stood. 'I don't know how they're managing.'

'Perhaps they're putting on a brave

face,' said Beth, although silently she felt Debra couldn't have cared less about the missing Bevis. 'It's strange that nothing's been heard from them. Do the villagers have any idea about what's happened?'

Edith drew herself in. Beth saw this was a subject Edith didn't want to broach and, to lighten the mood, highlighted the rumour about the Knockers and Spriggans.

She shrugged. 'Someone has those men. If it is the Knockers, they need to hand them back. They're working men. Those wives haven't two ha'pennies to rub together. The fisherman's co-operative are helping them but it won't last for long.'

Anne asked how long Edith had been married and they discovered she'd recently celebrated her 40th wedding anniversary.

'And do you have children?'

After a moment of reflection, Edith said: 'A daughter.' She looked to the floor. 'Don't see much of her now. Left home and moved to Devon.'

Beth said that surely that was no distance. 'It's only the next county along.'

Edith blinked two or three times.

'She's busy with her own friends.' She put her cup and saucer down, clasped her hands together and looked up with a smile. 'So are you joining us for the next parade?'

They confirmed they would definitely be there and expressed how much they were enjoying seeing the customs celebrated in another county. Edith wished them well as Hilda beckoned the group together again.

Song-sheets were given out and 'Halantow' was sung with great gusto. Beth and Anne were sure they wouldn't know the song but, once they began, they remembered Bob Tanner, who ran their local folk club, singing this regularly. They lent their harmonies to the chorus:

'Hal-an-tow, jolly rumbalow, We were up long before the day-o
To welcome in the summer, to welcome in the May-o.
The summer is a-coming and the winter's gone away-o.'

A feeling of elation washed over Beth. She turned to Anne. 'We should start a choir in Cavendish. I can't believe we don't have one. I find this so inspiring.'

'Me too. Why don't we organise it when we get back? I'm sure there are plenty of people who'd love to join.'

Hilda invited Beth and Anne to the front where they spoke about the Cavendish WI and the varied activities they had. They swapped ideas and suggestions and on the whole, each side felt they'd benefited from knowing what the other club did. Beth certainly came away with some thoughts of her own that had nothing to do with the WI. She looked forward to sharing them with James.

Anne linked arms with her. 'Come on, Beth, let's join the men and see if anyone has made any discoveries.'

17

James ordered five portions of chips at Vic and Flora's and once again they witnessed some intensive nagging from Flora. He pulled a face at Stephen, as if to say 'poor man'. Stephen said he'd wait for the chips so James went outside and joined Beth, Anne and Bert at one of the outside tables.

The sun had gone down and, although the hot fryer provided some warmth around the doorway, one needed a jumper or cardigan. A toot from a passing van made them look up. It was Tristram and Hans who had slowed down to wave and shout hello. They waved back and watched them swerve around the corner and disappear.

Luke had fallen asleep on Anne's lap and Mark dozed in James' arms.

The ladies questioned Bert about his romance with Gladys. He insisted they weren't a couple. 'She's a lady friend, that's all. Nothing more. We met up after a number of years and we're back in that footing. There ain't no romance.'

Beth and Anne giggled like schoolgirls meeting a film star. Bert told them to change the subject and asked Beth if she was all right with her husband becoming a midnight sailor.

Beth glared at James. 'A midnight sailor? Where're you going?'

James, in turn, glared at Bert and shifted uncomfortably. 'I thought I'd find out a little more about those lights.'

'Over my dead body. In the middle of the night? Have you gone mad? You can't even sail.'

'I don't need to sail. There's a motor boat moored up down there that I've managed to hire. All I have to do is point and go.'

Stephen arrived with the chips. 'Flora is nagging Vic for overdoing the chips again.'

Bert smothered his in salt and vinegar and tasted one. 'Don't know why, they're lovely. Crisp on the outside, fluffy on the inside. That's how you want yer chips.' He turned in his chair, held a chip up on his wooden fork and shouted across to Vic. 'Lovely chips, mate.'

Vic gave him a broad smile. Flora rolled her eyes and pushed Vic further down the line to wrap a fish.

Before James had a chance to argue his case about the boat, Tristram reappeared. 'Hello all. Thought I'd grab a fish supper to take home. I take it the WI have wound up for the night.'

Anne asked him to thank Hilda for inviting them. 'We had a lovely evening. It was so kind of her to let us come.'

Another burst of nagging made Tristram turn. James tugged at his sleeve.

'Are they always like that?'

He shifted on his feet. 'I don't think they'll ever be anything other than that.' He went inside and picked up two portions of fish and chips.

Vic wrapped them in newspaper and handed them over. As he passed their table he asked James if they were going to the next parade.

'Of course. Have the police arrested your wife yet?' James said with a beaming smile.

Tristram joined in the banter. 'Not yet. I've packed her bags just in case she needs to make a quick getaway.' He leant in. 'The police took Hans in earlier though.'

'Good lord, what on earth for?'

He squatted down and explained that he thought they would. 'Hans is even softer than I am where the animals are concerned. A couple of seals got caught up in Colm's nets last week and Hans was livid. Colm put 'em back in the sea but they washed up injured.'

'And what did Hans do exactly?'

'Punched him good and hard.'

'Oh d–dear, was that a–absolutely necessary?'

Tristram grimaced and said he didn't think so. 'Colm respects the sea. If they pull in a seal or a dolphin he releases it. He says he didn't do it on purpose. Colm took Hans on as a fisherman for a while but he had to let him go.'

James asked why.

'All manner of things. He's a good biologist but I gather he's not a good fisherman. Spent a lot of time being sea-sick and studying the ocean. And Colm wasn't tolerant of Hans' background either.'

Tristram went on to explain that Colm's father had been killed in a German prisoner of war camp. He held his hands up. 'I know you shouldn't lump everyone together but Colm is the sort of man that does.'

'A great shame,' said James. 'Hans seems a decent chap.'

Beth remarked that Hans didn't seem the violent type.

'You've only said hello to him, your Ladyship. He's a temper on him. Don't see it often but it's there.'

James asked if Hans ever had a run in with Bevis. Tristram was reluctant to go into details but suggested that Hans wasn't keen on some of the people in the industry. 'He knows they have to make a living but he doesn't think they respect the other creatures in the sea.'

Beth sympathised. 'It must be difficult when you work with injured animals all the time.'

'You're right. You have to take a step

back otherwise it'll consume you.'

She sat up expectantly. 'And how is our seal doing?'

'He's eating and looking a lot happier. Why don't you come and visit him again before you go?'

Beth revealed they had every intention of doing so and invited Anne to come along. 'You'll fall in love with him.'

'I say, Tristram' James put in, 'are you dressing up for the Knockers procession?'

'Yes I am. Most of the residents get involved in this one. It's a popular day. Knockers are the darkest characters and we love to scare the tourists half to death; but there's lots of dancing and music too. You'll enjoy it.' He held his wrapped fish supper up. 'I'd best get home before this goes cold.' He went on his way.

'Who's that?' said Bert.

James, Beth and the Merryweathers updated Bert on all the locals they'd met to date and Anne and Beth described their evening at the Women's Institute and how pleasant everyone was. Anne added that they'd been asked to speak and mentioned the fishermen's service the WI was proposing to put on.

'It really was a lovely evening.'

James peered down to see Mark was asleep in his arms. He lowered his voice. 'And, Beth, did you put your powers into play?'

Anne turned to face Beth. 'What powers?'

'James told me to observe; that people give a lot away by the way they hold themselves.'

'D–did you get that from Mr P–Patel?'

James confirmed they had. Kushal Patel was a man he'd met in the spring of the previous year when working on the untimely death of an elderly villager. He worked for the government and debriefed spies on their return to the UK and assisted with psychiatric assessments for trauma. His knowledge and wisdom was endless and James knew he'd only touched the surface when discussing such things with him.

Kushal was unique in that he took the best of Western psychology and incorporated it with the mystic Eastern philosophy and the culture he'd been brought up with. But, little tips and suggestions had served James well and he found himself observing more and more. He gestured for Beth to tell all.

Beth expressed her personal thoughts. 'I have to say that I found it difficult. I pushed a little too much I think — when I was asking questions. Anyway, Evelyn still had that haunted look about her and it's my opinion that this is something that's been with her for some years; not just the last few days. The woman doesn't appear to have anything to smile about in spite of Hilda's jolly hockey sticks attitude. She was careful with what she'd say, almost as if something would happen if she said the wrong thing.

'And then Debra was a surprise package compared to when we saw her yesterday. No more the concerned wife worried about her husband. She was incredibly chatty, bright and confident.'

'And,' Anne added, 'suggested that Colm and Bevis had probably got drunk and were hiding out of spite.'

The five of them looked at one another in astonishment. James nudged his chips away. 'You didn't manage to establish what Evelyn's back story was I suppose?'

'Sorry, sweetie, no. Evelyn wasn't about to divulge information about herself to strangers.'

'Did you speak with anyone else?'

Anne went through their conversation with Edith. 'She apologised for her husband's behaviour toward you this morning.'

'The apology should come from him. I didn't take to him at all.'

Beth reminded them that although Enoch was clearly the boss in the house, Edith didn't seem to mind. 'She more or less expected it and stuck up for him.' She turned to Anne. 'That was a little odd about her daughter though, don't you think?'

'Oooh, yes. She lives in Devon and they never see her even though she's just in the next county. Beth told her it was only a short distance but she evaded the subject.'

'She also looked a little upset. I wonder if she left under a cloud.'

'P–perhaps the ogre of E–Enoch

suppressed her young spirit. Youngsters these days want a bit of fr–freedom and I would imagine Enoch being strict beyond r–reason.'

James turned to Bert who was dipping into everyone's leftover chips. 'You're very quiet, Bert.'

'Listening, Jimmy-boy, always listening.'

'And what do you surmise by our mutterings?'

'Still thinking. You're not the only one who observes, mate.' His suggestive laugh set everyone off.

Stephen suggested to Anne that they ought to head back. 'Luke and Mark are both in dreamland.'

James gently transferred Mark across to Stephen and they bade them goodnight with plans to meet for the next procession. They had a free day the next day. The Merryweathers had pre-booked a coach trip and the next parade was taking place the day after. James checked his watch and looked out to sea. Beth sat forward.

'Now, what's all this about hiring a boat?'

'The light out to sea appears around eleven o'clock every night. They're not on the horizon, they're off the coast. It could have something to do with those kidnappings or it might just be fishermen.'

'Or,' Bert added with a spooky voice, 'it could be the ghosts of ancient mariners to warn you of danger ahead.'

Beth sat up with a start. 'Ghostly mariners?'

Bert enlightened her about the earlier conversation in the pub.

She turned to James. 'Are you really going out there?'

James said he would take the boat out for fifteen minutes. 'I made a few enquiries earlier today about who hires boats out and I have access to a nifty launch. I made out I could sail and managed to convince the girl of my expertise.'

When learning that Bert would not set foot inside such a small launch, she insisted on going with him.

'Absolutely not.'

'Don't be ridiculous, James. You don't know the first thing about boats or shipping lanes. The currents could be dangerous and you may get swept out to sea. The wind is picking up even while we were sitting here; God knows what it's like out of the harbour.'

'I'm going a hundred yards offshore at the most. I'm not going beyond the bay. If you want to watch from the cliff-tops with Bert, be my guest.'

Beth pursed her lips. 'You either study the lights from the cliff or I go with you. Better still, we go back to the room for a nightcap.'

Bert wrapped the leftover chips and slammed the table lightly with the palm of his hand. 'You two need your heads banging together. You're on 'oliday.' He poked a finger at James. 'You're like a dog with a bone. Those lights are prob'ly just fishermen.'

'I don't believe they are.'

His friend got up. 'Right. We all go. Come on.'

'I thought you weren't going to set foot on a boat.'

'I don't 'ave much choice, do I? I'm not letting you and Beth go on your own.'

They made arrangements to meet ten minutes later at the harbour. It gave him and Beth time to change into something warmer. They both had woolly jumpers for the cold evenings and changed into trousers and plimsolls. Bert had donned his trademark flat cap and a large sweater.

At the harbour, Lisa handed the keys of her motor boat over to James and instructed him how to turn the engine on, how to steer and slow down.

'There's some spare petrol in the jerry can there. You be careful. And don't you be any longer than you said. Fifteen minutes.'

James handed Lisa some cash and promised they'd be back promptly.

'You be careful and wear your life-jackets. It's getting choppy out there. I'll wait 'ere.'

With their life-jackets on, they stepped into the boat, struggling to keep their balance. It was a copy of a classic Hacker Craft, with varnished wood and two bench seats. James instructed Bert and Beth to sit on either side of the rear bench. James slipped into the front and got his bearings on where the controls were.

The engine fired up and Lisa untied the rope and threw it to the back of the launch. James gently pushed the throttle out and they pottered along. An anxious feeling ran through him as they passed the harbour walls. He pushed the throttle down further and the throaty engine responded.

The lights of Polpennarth were now behind them. In front was darkness — the welcoming blue seas of daytime had turned inky black. A chilly wind picked up and the sea slapped the boat. He turned the wheel and followed the coastline. The coloured lights along the promenade gave him some sort of indication of where they were in relation to the town and how far out they'd gone.

Bert shifted forward. 'These lights, were they in a sequence, like Morse code or something?'

James shouted against the noise of the engine. 'I don't think so. It was all pretty vague but very clear.'

'Are you sure there's no island 'ere?'

'Not according to the locals and it's certainly not visible from the shore if there is one.'

Beth squeezed his shoulder. 'There's our hotel. We must be close.'

James pulled back on the throttle and they drifted on the tide. He stared out to sea and then checked his watch. 'It's two minutes to eleven. Keep your eyes peeled.'

The chill of the evening seeped into his bones as the wind picked up. Constant waves bounced them from side to side, lapping the side of the launch as if to urge them to return. James suddenly had misgivings. They weren't far out but what if they capsized; what if they sprang a leak? He realised his mouth was dry.

Beth hugged herself. 'I don't see anything and it's gone eleven.'

Bert shifted in his seat and looked toward the shore. 'What's that there?'

James turned and followed Bert's pointing finger. Up on the cliff-tops, a light made its way along. It was intermittent. 'It looks like someone with a lantern or something. Someone strolling along the footpath perhaps.'

'At this time of night? What's up there?'

'A couple of farms. The farmhouse café and the Sanctuary's a bit further along but they're both closed.'

Beth scrunched up to stay warm. 'It may be the farmer looking for lost livestock.'

James looked out to sea. Was it signalling to anyone? In front of him, nothing but murky blackness. A thin layer of cloud obscured the stars. He told Bert and Beth to hold on as he turned and opened up the throttle. Beth insisted he slow down.

Bert tapped him on the shoulder. 'They're gone. Whoever was up there has either switched their light off or gone inside.'

'But I'm sure all the buildings are further along,' said James explaining that they'd driven that route earlier. The closest house was the farm where they'd had a cream tea. He pulled back on the throttle. They could see the harbour lights about a mile ahead of them. The sea rocked them back and forth.

'James,' said Beth, 'I'm really getting quite chilled. It's gone eleven and we've seen nothing except someone with a lantern. It'll be a farmer or someone walking their dog. They do have some sheep up there. Can we please go back; this seems a wasted exercise.'

He agreed that it had been a foolhardy decision and fidgeted to get comfortable in the driving seat. As he went to push the throttle Bert shouted. 'Watch out!'

Beth screamed. James squeezed his eyes shut and instinctively ducked as the roar of a huge speedboat passed by. He waited for the impact, the collision that would reduce their boat to splinters. The speedboat veered and sped into the night. They grabbed the sides as the following wake tipped the boat violently.

Beth put her hand on her chest and took a deep breath.

'Bloody Nora,' said Bert. 'That was close.'

James pushed down on the throttle and headed for the harbour. As they entered, the safety of the surrounding walls provided a welcome calm and they breathed a sigh of relief when the vacant mooring came into view. Lisa caught the rope from Bert and secured it to the rusty iron ring cemented to wall. James helped Beth onto dry land.

Bert joined them and asked Lisa if she saw a speedboat go by. The young girl shook her head and pointed to her hut. 'I was in there, listening to the radio.'

'Lisa,' said James, 'is there someone here that owns a speedboat? A pretty classy vessel with a lot of engine?'

She pulled a disinterested face and shrugged. 'I've gotta go, it's getting late.'

He returned the keys and life jackets to her and gave Beth's shoulders a squeeze. 'Come on, let's get you home. I think we've all had about enough tonight. Where are you staying Bert?'

'The bed and breakfast in Pier Road. But I'm up to the races tomorrow morning so I prob'ly won't see you.'

James slapped him on the back and thanked him for being there. 'I do appreciate it Bert; I always feel as if you have my back covered.'

Bert gave Beth a hug and told her to

keep her husband in line. 'I'll see you back in Cavendish and don't do anything else stupid. Get back to being on 'oliday.'

They parted company and as they wandered back to the hotel James apologised for hiring the boat and risking their lives. 'It was senseless. I should have listened to you. I don't even know what I gained from it.'

'Ordinarily, I'd agree but that boat must have seen us. It had a search light on it. I saw it in the distance and it turned toward us. It was intentional.'

He stopped and faced her. 'Are you absolutely sure?'

She nodded.

'Perhaps Bidevin was right. I'm asking too many questions and someone has become tired of it.'

'This isn't a game James. We could have been killed out there.'

'No darling. That boat could have sliced us in two but it didn't. It was there to scare us off.'

'Well it worked. Let's *be* scared off and get on with our holiday.'

When they arrived at the hotel they saw

that Desmond was still up. He put his pen down. 'Ah hello. We've just had Gretchen on the telephone with the latest.'

'Oh?' said James.

'Yes, seems Enoch Pengilly's gone missing.'

18

James paced the bedroom floor, itching to learn more about Enoch's disappearance. The near head-on collision the previous night meant he owed it to Beth to revert to holiday mode. But, while she was washing and styling her hair, he decided to make enquiries about one thing. With the excuse of wanting to pick up a couple of leaflets, he trotted down the stairs to reception where Vivian was dusting the worktop.

'Off somewhere nice?'

'Yes, St Ives. It looks a quaint little place and we wanted to look at some of the art galleries.'

'Lovely.'

He picked up a leaflet about St Michael's Mount and gave her a sideways glance. 'I say, do you know anyone that drives a large, powerful speedboat. White, with quite a long bow to her.'

'That'll be Johnny Sepp. He's got a

fishing fleet in Penzance and St Ives.'

Desmond came through from the back office. 'Nice boat. He saved for years to buy her. Only brings it out on high days and holidays.'

'Or,' added Vivian, 'if he wants to impress someone.'

James leant on the counter. 'He doesn't take it out at night?'

'I wouldn't have thought so.'

Desmond's brows knitted together. 'I don't think anyone goes out at night unless it's the fishermen; certainly not in a speedboat — could do it some damage depending on the current. There's a rocky line running along the sea-bed and it'd rip the hull out depending on the tide. Can't say someone like Johnny Sepp would want that.'

James thanked him and returned to their room to pick up his car keys. He brought the Austin round to the front of the building to pick up Beth. He jumped out and squeezed her shoulders. 'Are you all right, darling?'

She hugged him tight and assured him she was. 'I won't be going out on any

260

boats for a little while though.' She got into the car. 'Let's go and have a relaxing morning.'

He closed the door and jogged round to the driver's side, wondering all the time whether Johnny Sepp would be in St Ives.

Fluffy white clouds hung in the blue sky as the Austin climbed the hill away from Polpennarth. There was a contented silence between them; each lost in their thoughts. They'd gone through a mixture of emotions on what had been a busy day but one that had almost ended in disaster. James found it difficult to push the event from his mind and struggled to focus on the good things, the reason they were here; a holiday, cream teas, exploring new places, the vibrant Legends festival and the delight in sharing the Merryweathers' anniversary celebrations.

The car crested the hill and dipped into the next valley. James lightly tapped the brake pedal. He repeated the action and frowned. He sped up the next incline. As they reached the peak, the rooftops of St Ives appeared in the distance. The whole town appeared to cling to steep hills that swept down to the harbour.

The road dipped again. He dipped the brake pedal and went down through the gears quickly. Beth looked at him. 'Is there something wrong?'

'The brakes are a little spongy.' He crested the next hill slowly and again went down the gears as the hill dipped. It was a steep decline and families were making their way down toward the harbour and beaches. He noticed Beth grip the leather strap on the door.

He slipped down into second gear; the engine screamed in defiance. James watched the speedometer. Twenty-five . . . twenty . . . fifteen. He used what oil was left in the brake line and pumped the pedal quickly until it was floored. He pulled on the handbrake and the Austin came to a gentle stop.

He let his shoulders relax, rested his head back and let out a nervous laugh. 'That was a little unnerving.'

'Didn't you get this serviced recently?'

James assured her that he did. He jumped out of the car and opened the bonnet. Peering down through the pipes, he noticed oil dripping from the brake line. He got down on his knees, rolled onto his back and peered at the underside of the engine. His stomach lurched; the brake line had been snipped. He examined it as closely as he could. It hadn't been cut right through, just nicked. Had he driven over rough ground and caught it? He waved that idea away. If he had, the wire around the nick would be grazed. No, this was a clean cut. Intentional.

He clambered back to his feet and rubbed the dust from his hands. Looking past Beth, he saw a telephone box.

'Darling, I'll ring the RAC and see if they can send someone out. It looks like the brake-line has come loose and I don't have the tools to fix it. I don't mind doing a rough and ready repair on most things, but not the brakes. Why don't you hop on a bus and I'll meet you down in the harbour.'

Beth accepted this without question. She perused the small guide in her hand. 'I'll hover around the Coffee Cup café at eleven o'clock. Hopefully you'll have arrived by then.'

James checked his watch. That gave him over an hour. 'If I'm there before, I'll scout around and try and find you.' He pecked her on the cheek and watched her walk toward the bus stop. He turned and made his way to the phone box.

The mechanic from the Royal Automobile Club arrived within twenty minutes and had James on his way shortly after. He'd still fifteen minutes before meeting Beth so he parked by the railway station, wandered through the cobbled streets and knocked on the harbour master's door.

'I say, is Johnny Sepp here?'

'He's around, yeah.' The man spoke with a pipe in his mouth. He joined James at the door. 'That's him there. The man in the oilskin trousers with the crew cut.'

James strode up to Johnny Sepp. He stood around four inches taller than James and clearly worked a physical job. A powerfully built individual with a steely look. His short hair was bleached by the sun and, although he was around forty years of age, his skin was dry and weather-beaten giving the appearance of someone much older.

'Mr Sepp?'

Johnny met his gaze and narrowed his eyes. 'Do I know you?'

'You should do; you damn near ran me down with that boat of yours last night.'

'Ah.'

'Is that all you have to say? You could've killed us.'

'I could have. But I didn't.'

'If you wanted to warn us off about something, you only had to say.'

'I got nothing to warn you off about. I was asked to swing by.'

James gawped. 'Someone asked you to do this?'

Johnny bent down and picked up the end of a rope and began looping it around his elbow. 'I got a note under my door early in the evening. Typed it was. Said if I took the speedbird out last night and did a high speed pass to scare you, I'd get ten pound. They said it was a joke and you'd see the funny side.'

'A joke!'

He shrugged. 'That's what it said and

265

ten pound is ten pound. And they paid up. That's a pound a minute. Won't get that sort of money every day.' He stopped winding the rope. 'It wasn't a joke I take it?'

James confirmed it most certainly wasn't. 'My wife was beside herself. Was it you who tampered with my car?'

He straightened up. 'Now hold on a minute. I don't tamper with things. I don't know anything about your car and I wouldn't put anyone in danger unnecessarily.' He held a hand out. 'I'm sorry about the boat thing. You've obviously rubbed someone up the wrong way. What you been doing?'

James muttered under his breath. 'Asking too many questions.'

Johnny tilted his head in confusion and James let it go. His instinct told him this man was telling the truth. He accepted the apology and wandered back toward the shops that lined the harbour. He gritted his teeth. First he'd been scared off at sea; now his brake-line had been cut. Someone is intent on having him back off. He caught Beth waving in the distance and his worries disappeared. She looked stunning in a canary yellow dress with thin shoulder straps. She'd caught the sun over the last couple of days and this complemented the outfit. He held a hand up and walked toward her.

They passed a pleasant hour in the village of St Ives and were delighted to find a beautiful painting by a local artist for the Merryweathers' anniversary present. It depicted the view looking across Polpennarth and out to sea. As they sat with a milky coffee on the cobbles outside the Coffee Cup café, the town rose above them on the hillside. The layout was higgledy-piggledy with cottages, apartments and houses jostling for space from the top of the hill right down to the harbour which was surrounded by several sandy beaches.

The tide was as far out as it could go and many families had made their way to Porthminster beach just around the corner from the harbour. Out to the distance, on a small island, was Godrevy lighthouse built on a stone reef. They could just make out white, foamy waves, splashing on the rocks there.

Pleasure cruisers rested on the sand waiting for the sea to bring them back to life and fishermen, at the end of the harbour wall, prepared their nets for the next trip. The smell of fish, chips and seaweed mingled and gulls sat on wooden posts waiting for discarded crumbs of batter or Cornish pasty. They squawked encouragement and pounced once the tiniest morsel dropped.

Beth closed her eyes and faced the sun. 'What time are we meeting Stephen and Anne tomorrow?'

'There are two parades for the Knockers. One is a family thing that Luke and Mark are going to and there's a later one; an after-dark affair. It starts at ten o'clock. We're meeting outside The Pilchard Inn at nine thirty. Stephen had showed initiative and asked Bidevin to put by some pasties for us. He's wrapping them up so we can eat them as the parade goes by. I'm rather looking forward to it.'

'Mmm, me too. It's a good festival, isn't it? Perhaps we could do something like this in Cavendish. Do we have many Sussex legends?'

'Not as many as Cornwall. I'll have to do some research but, yes, if we've half a dozen we could certainly incorporate that into our year.'

She checked her watch. 'I'm a little concerned.'

James turned, reached across and squeezed her hand. She'd had a couple of scares and he knew he'd crossed the line. 'Tell me.'

'You've not mentioned the kidnappings today. Not once. You're either hiding something and doing things behind my back or what happened last night has scared you into dropping it. Which is it?'

James studied her until she shifted uncomfortably and asked why he was staring. 'Because you are too perceptible for your own good.'

She waited.

The waitress came to collect their cups and he requested another two coffees. He settled back in his chair. 'The RAC chap came and fixed the car but I also made another telephone call. To Inspector Wormstone.'

'About last night?'

'Darling, what happened last night could have killed us. This business of investigating the kidnappings is a selfish act and one I should never have begun. I mean, good grief, Polpennarth has a population of around three hundred. How could I possibly get to the bottom of this? I don't know these people. They're not going to confide in me, are they? It's a closed community.' He stroked her cheek. 'I've arranged to meet Wormstone at the little cream tea place we went to yesterday at three o'clock. I'm going to let him know everything we've found out and spend the next few days enjoying this holiday.'

Beth held his hand to her mouth and kissed it. 'I'm glad. I can't believe I'm hearing it, but I'm glad.'

James settled back as the second coffee arrived. He felt a weight lift from his shoulders. Much as he loved a good mystery, it wasn't fair on Beth or the Merryweathers to act so irresponsibly.

He'd stop asking questions and word would get out that he was simply a tourist. And word spread quickly in such a small community. Whoever he had annoyed would stop targeting them and let them enjoy the rest of their break.

After lunch, they drove back to the south coast and parked in the small village of Marazion, a community that consisted of very little. It did, however, serve as a good staging post for visiting St Michael's Mount. When the tide was out, it revealed a causeway that connected the island to Marazion, just along from the larger town of Penzance. It was a gusty afternoon and a number of children were flying kites on the wide expanse of sand. Families tucked into picnics and some braved a swim in the chilly English Channel.

James and Beth trod a careful path along the slippery causeway. It was a rocky, cobbled walkway worn away by the ocean and littered with puddles and slimy moss. They entered the tiny harbour to see a row of white-washed terraced houses and a gift shop. The main house with its arched windows and castle turrets loomed above them. James read the pamphlet he'd picked up and told Beth it had been in the same family for centuries.

'Similar to Harrington's then.'

'Except they've been here since the 11th century and we Harringtons from around the 17th. There's a priory here and apparently this is where the first beacon was lit to warn of the coming of the Spanish Armada.'

They spent an enjoyable hour exploring the gardens and strolling around the harbour. A quick peek at the tidal times indicated they needed to return if they wanted to walk back along the causeway. They opted to meander back and visit the small pub opposite. It had a long walled terrace overlooking the Mount and afforded views all the way along to Penzance.

They ordered a half of mild each and took in the panoramic view until a familiar face approached. 'Afternoon.'

James held a hand out. 'Jonah, how lovely to see you. Do you want to join us?'

'Just for a few minutes. I'm meeting someone but I saw you here and thought I'd come over.'

Beth moved her handbag. 'Are you being a tourist?'

Jonah sat next to her and explained that he was only open in the evenings. 'Once I've got the food in, there's not much more to do. I'm actually going into Newlyn to pick up some fish there.'

Newlyn was a fishing community that James had heard of. It had a bigger fish market than Polpennarth and was also another area renowned for artists.

'Fish doesn't take long to prepare. The simpler the better so I haven't got to spend loads of time in the kitchen. So, yes, I suppose you could say I'm being a tourist. Sometimes you don't realise what's on your doorstep.'

Beth agreed and explained that they rarely visited the sights in London. 'We only do that if people come and visit us from further afield. I guess it's the same for everyone.'

'It was the same when I lived in London. I had the Tower of London just

down the road and never went there
once.'

James asked if he spent much time
exploring Cornwall before moving there.

'Yes, I came down here two or three
times a year for about three years. There
were some things that happened at work
that caused me to re-evaluate my
position; well, my life really. Work
concerns, love interests, that sort of thing.
It all went downhill for me and the best
thing I could do was walk away from it.'

James sipped his mild. This was clearly
the business Bert had dug up with the
attack on his boss and the likely affair
with the boss's daughter. He placed his
drink down. 'And have you been successful in looking for love down here?'

'Not really.'

Beth slipped her sunglasses down and
to James' bemusement flirted with the
restaurant owner. 'Surely you must have
had a holiday romance. Everyone has those.'

Jonah shifted in his seat. 'I've had one
or two yes.'

'Anyone we know?'

He cleared his throat. 'You don't know

her. We had a bit of a fling when I was looking for a place down here. Nice girl but by the time I'd got back she was married.' He played with a beer mat. 'She was engaged when I met her so I knew it wouldn't come to anything.'

Beth frowned. 'That's running a risk in such a small community.'

Jonah agreed that it was, adding that he felt awkward whenever the couple were in his vicinity. 'They don't come into the restaurant. Can't afford it but I steer clear of the husband.'

James asked if the husband had found out.

'He never said anything to me. He had no proof. Ev — .' He stopped himself. 'She wouldn't have said anything, I'm sure. He had a suspicion but that was it. Avoids me when he can and isn't the friendliest person in the world when we do have to speak.'

'And the single ladies here are a little sparse, aren't they?'

'I'm not an angel, Lord Harrington, and I've had one or two one-night stands with married ladies.'

Beth gawped. He held a palm up.

'Some of the fishermen's wives see me as a trendy gentleman from London. I told you I was called a beatnik when I first arrived. I was seen as exotic, well-read and worldly. It attracted naive women and I can't deny that I took advantage of that.'

As he and Beth spoke, James pondered the man's history. He'd nearly let it slip that Evelyn wouldn't admit to untoward behaviour. This man Bevis, although not a fisherman, was away sometimes at the markets. He wondered if Debra Allan was also a conquest of Jonah's. Were things getting a little uncomfortable for Jonah Quinn? Had Colm and Bevis discovered his roaming ways and challenged him? It would certainly give Jonah a reason for wanting to deal with them. He had a violent streak — that was already proven. That fearful look that Evelyn and Debra had — was it because they knew the truth was about to surface?

Jonah checked his watch. 'I'd best get on. Enjoy the rest of your day.'

James watched him walk toward his

van. He turned to Beth. 'What did you make of him?'

Beth described him as a rogue but could quite see how young, lonely wives would have their heads turned by him. 'He is a handsome man and clearly has an eye for the ladies. It's obvious that it was Evelyn he was talking about.'

'Yes, he nearly let that slip, didn't he? I was wondering if he'd snared young Debra too.'

'It wouldn't surprise me. He seems to know when the menfolk are away. Are you going to let the Inspector know about this?'

'Of course. He may already know but I've a feeling that Bert was able to delve much deeper into Quinn's life than any policeman could.'

They watched as Jonah did a three-point turn and then gaped, open-mouthed, as he pulled away.

James met Beth's astonished look. 'Did you see who got in the passenger seat?'

'Yes,' said Beth, 'Debra Allan.'

James watched the van disappear. No wonder Debra had perked up.

19

The farm on the cliff-tops was open to the elements and there was quite a breeze blowing in from the ocean. The sea had turned from a mill pond to a constant motion and even at this height, they heard the splash of waves on the shoreline below. Inspector Wormstone arrived shortly after them and they made themselves comfortable in the garden. Beth suggested the table by the fence which was a natural suntrap, shielding them from the worst of the breeze.

James ordered cream tea for three and studied Wormstone as he made himself comfortable. He could imagine him in the London force. He dressed in a dark suit, a white shirt and a black tie. He had a felt trilby that wasn't worn in the heat but he carried it with him. Even in this weather, the man kept his jacket on. His shoes were polished and he had an educated look about him. He made some small talk with Beth about holidays and asked what her favourite destination was.

'Usually the last place I visited, Inspector. Polpennarth is exquisite and we've been so lucky with the weather. But if you were to ask me to put everything in the mix, I think that Zermatt, in Switzerland, is high on my list.'

'Winter or summer?'

'Winter.'

'You ski?'

'Not terribly well, I never seem to progress further than the gentle slopes but the whole ambience of a Swiss village is appealing. Have you travelled, Inspector?'

Wormstone hadn't travelled as much as he'd have liked. But he did enjoy his annual breaks and tended to opt for walking holidays. 'I've travelled the length and breadth of the United Kingdom; from the highlands of Scotland to the cliff-tops of Cornwall. I fancy the idea of skiing but I think I'd be an accident waiting to happen.'

Beth poured the tea and James held up

the plate of scones for the Inspector to take one.

'This is good of you,' he said. 'I wasn't expecting a cream tea.' He cut the scone in half and scrutinised James. 'And you paid for dinner the other night. Could be deemed as suspicious but I assume you have me here for a reason, Lord Harrington.'

James allowed a quick smile. 'I do, Inspector, and I haven't been entirely honest with you.'

The Inspector frowned and his eyes darted from James to Beth and back again. 'You're not confessing to kidnapping, are you?'

James laughed. 'Good Lord, no.'

'I was joking.' He layered his scone with jam and cream. 'So what do you want to divulge?'

'I'm a bit of an amateur sleuth and — '

'So I've heard.'

Beth sat up with a start. 'How did you know that?'

'The locals talk. I understand you've been, how can I put it, interested in the crimes committed but the questions you ask are not the sort a tourist would think of. Your questions have been considered; as if you're trying to establish motive and opportunity.'

'I was trying to do that, yes.'

'Was? Do I take it you're no longer pursuing enquiries?'

James crossed his legs and gave the inspector a brief background to his hobby. The crimes he'd helped solve and his friendship with DCI Lane. Wormstone was delighted to hear about George and for a while the conversation turned toward their time together in the Yard. Wormstone confirmed what James already knew; that George was one of the best detectives he'd come across and a gentleman too.

'We've walked off the trail, your Lordship. I asked you to confirm that you're not looking into things anymore.'

'I'm not. We had two threats against us over the last twenty four hours and I don't intend to get us killed.'

He felt Beth's eyes bore into him. 'Two? When was . . . oh, the brakes.'

James manoeuvred his chair closer and

held her hand. 'Inspector, last night we were almost mown down by a man paid to frighten us and this morning I discovered the brake-line on the Austin had been tampered with. I feel fortunate to be sitting here at the moment.'

Wormstone held a palm up. 'Right, let's go back. This is the result of things you know. An attempt made because of the questions you've been asking. Tell me what you know and give me the finale later.' He reached inside his pocket for a notepad and pencil. 'Who did you speak to, what did you ask?'

They listed their contacts in the order they met them: Desmond and Vivian, Gretchen Kettel, Bidevin, Evelyn and Hilda, PC Innes, Jonah Quinn, Tristram, Hans, Debra, Vic and Flora, Kerry Sheppard, Enoch and Edith.

James assured him he hadn't been intrusive with his questions; that he'd simply slipped the odd enquiry in here and there. Beth added that she'd met several members of the WI but had only asked questions of the people on their list.

Wormstone finished listing the names.

'Right, now, what do you think about all these people?'

'Our hosts are a delightful couple from Torquay who I believe have nothing to do with this. Viv's a bit of a gossip and Desmond is a normal chap making a living.'

The Inspector glanced at his list. 'Gretchen Kettel.' He looked up. 'I think we can cross her off the list, don't you?'

'Not so quickly, Inspector,' said Beth. 'When we saw her recently, we mentioned the kidnapping and she hinted that Colm and Bevis were bad men.'

'You're right, darling. We asked her what she meant and she said something about Evelyn and Debra having lost their oomph and we were to look into that.'

'And did you? Look into why they'd lost their oomph?'

'That may come out later in our thinking. Can you hold fire on that one?'

The Inspector took a sip of his tea and moved on. 'Bidevin. Thoughts?'

'You know he threw Colm out of the pub recently; and there is some bad blood over the ownership of their Cornish pasty recipe.'

'A frequent occurrence from what I hear. Colm is definitely in the bad books. He has no proof about this recipe business.'

'He appears a thoroughly nice chap but he did warn me off.' James topped up their teas. 'I wanted to ask him about the lights I'd seen off shore.'

'Lights?'

James realised he'd overlooked that part of the story. He gave the Inspector an account of the lights he'd seen at eleven o'clock every night. 'They were difficult to see but I believe they were just off shore.'

'Go on.'

He outlined the story about the ghosts of fisherman and how they lured people who saw them to some kind of unpleasantness.

'And that was him warning you off?'

'No, not exactly. I'd asked what it meant and Bidevin said it means you're asking too many questions.'

Wormstone raised his eyebrows and

jotted a few notes down. 'And what did you make of Evelyn Fiske?'

'A frightened woman,' said Beth. 'There's something deep-rooted there. I do feel she has a story, Inspector. That fear isn't a reaction to a kidnapping. It's something ingrained.'

'I know what you mean. A bit of a nervous sparrow, so to speak. What did you make of Hilda?'

James and Beth pitched in with alternating descriptions: assertive, bossy, forthright, organised. They said she could appear unsympathetic but added that they felt she had an underlying sensitivity.

James elaborated on the sympathy side. 'She's stuck by those women, Evelyn and Debra, like a protective mother hen. But she said something rather odd when I first observed her with Evelyn. She'd brought her a drink and said something about things looking up for her.'

'And,' Beth put in, 'she described Bevis as a fool and told Debra she was probably better off without him.'

'The rumour mill is that she has something to do with these kidnappings.

Are you able to let on?'

'Divulging information is just the one-way format, your Lordship.'

They signalled their understanding.

'That brings us to Jonah Quinn,' said Wormstone.

Beth sat up with a start. 'Now he is interesting. Did you know he stabbed his boss when he worked in London?'

Wormstone sat back and observed the pair of them. 'Now how on earth did you find that out?'

'You mean you know?' said James.

'I'm a policeman, with links to the Yard. It only takes a phone call to find these things out. How did you find out?'

'I have a friend who appears to know everyone; he put out a few feelers.' He leant forward. 'He did find out a little snippet that you may not know about.'

The Inspector waited.

'When he decided to move down this way, he spent a holiday down here looking for a place to live.'

'And?'

'Turns out he had a bit of a fling with

the current Mrs Fiske, although it was before she married. We bumped into him earlier.' He went through their conversation. 'And young Debra hopped in the van before he drove off. Perhaps he's carried on with Debra and Edith too, although I can't quite see him with the latter.'

For once, James was pleased to see that he'd enlightened the Inspector. Beth added that Debra, although fearful initially, appeared to have a spring in her step. 'Perhaps that's the oomph that Gretchen spoke of.'

'That is interesting.' He flipped a page over on his notepad and scribbled.

'And,' continued James, 'Jonah thought Kerry Sheppard had something to do with the kidnappings.'

Wormstone appeared to ignore this and checked the list again.

'Tristram.'

Beth melted. 'Adorable. A man with such sensitivity and kindness. It almost flows from him. When he was showing us that seal he looked positively gentle and loving.'

'I say, steady on Beth, he's not Cary Grant.'

'He doesn't have to be; he's beautiful on the inside. He showed us around the seal sanctuary and we had lunch with him up on the cliff-top. His whole life seems to revolve around the Sanctuary. I see him more as an animal man, not a people person. I can see him kidnapping seals to keep them safe but I can't imagine he gives two hoots about people.'

'Have you interviewed him, Inspector? Does he have a blot on his perfect landscape?' The look he received reminded him that questioning was a one-way process. 'Who's next?'

'Hans.'

'Ah yes. Haven't had much to do with him but Tris did say that he'd had a run in with Colm about his fishing methods. There is some animosity there.'

The Inspector agreed and said that Hans had had quite a quarrel with both Colm and Bevis. 'Pretty passionate on animal cruelty. He and Tristram. Can't see that it would warrant kidnapping though.' He studied his list. 'Debra Allan.'

Beth again sat up with a start. 'Now there's someone who is interesting. Whereas Evelyn is frightened of her own shadow, Debra is now having a wonderful time. She certainly let her guard down last night.'

'In what way?'

'Forgetting Anne and I were there. Do you remember, darling, when we first saw Debra? Inspector, you were there too. She had that same look as Evelyn; scared and fearful. Well, last night I saw a different woman. She struck a more confident pose, not hunched up and defensive. It was as if someone had taken shackles off of tethered horse. It wasn't until I asked what sort of man her husband was that she retreated a little.'

The Inspector made no comment and moved on. 'Vic and Flora. What did you make of them?'

James considered Vic to be under the thumb. 'I don't know how he puts up with it. Vic do this, Vic do that. Even when he does it, it's wrong. Odd isn't it, the way people rub along together.'

Wormstone moved them along to

Kerry Sheppard. James explained that they'd had supper with her and the Merryweathers a couple of evenings previously and she was certainly a unique individual.

'Have you met her, Inspector?'

He bowed his head slowly but kept his thoughts to himself. James bit back his annoyance. He had hoped Wormstone would be a little more talkative than this. He clearly had his own opinions about these people but they would remain unspoken.

Beth described Kerry as an independent and strong-minded woman. 'I admire her. I think the locals here have something against women like that and I understand why. This is an entirely different community to the one we're used to. Women have their place here. But I heard nothing to suggest that she's a suspect, unless being anti-men is a crime.'

The last couple to consider was Edith and Enoch: they detailed the number of observations they'd made of the pair arguing in public. James outlined how he intervened when they were on the promenade the previous day. 'I did fear that he might actually hit her.'

'Oh,' Beth exclaimed putting her hands to her mouth. 'Do you think he would have?'

Wormstone shrugged and said 'It happens.' Beth gave him a horrified look and expressed her surprise at his flippant comment.

'I don't mean to be flippant. It's a fact of life, I'm afraid. I see it down here and I saw it in London. There are certain men, like Enoch, old school who want their women to remain in their place and if they step out of line they get a slap. That's all I'm saying. I don't agree with it, I'm just telling it like it is.'

James couldn't imagine living under such circumstances. Striking a woman was cowardly and disgraceful in his book. The Inspector checked his watch and indicated that he should be going.

'Your insight into these individuals is interesting and I'll be following up on one or two. I believe you've reached your finale.'

'The climax of our story, yes.' James

reiterated his concerns over the lights he'd seen out at sea, the myth of the ghostly fisherman and his desire to establish exactly what he was looking at. 'Although we saw no lights out to sea, my instinct tells me the lights on the cliff top are significant.'

Beth added her horror at being almost rammed by Mr Sepp's boat and asked what on earth he thought was funny about such an action.

'He had the grace to apologise,' James said. 'He did look genuinely shocked that he'd also been set up.' He described the problem he had with the Austin Healey. 'The line had most certainly been snipped. The cut was far too clean for it to be anything else. It could have been nasty though.'

'Lucky you know how to handle your car. You've had experience with racing I understand.'

James didn't need to know how the Inspector knew that. They'd only been here a few days and once a snippet of information was given to someone, it was a certainty that the rest of the village would know soon after.

'And you're certain this Johnny Sepp was telling the truth?'

'Yes, yes, absolutely. Unless he studied drama, I can't imagine someone reacting the way he did.'

Wormstone put his notepad and pen back in his pocket with an expression of deep thought. 'You've rattled someone's cage that's for sure. If you hear of anything else, you'll let me know.'

Beth shuddered. 'We are now tourists. We're not asking any more questions or seeking out witnesses. You'll see us at the parade tomorrow night and we won't be gallivanting off into the middle of the Atlantic.'

He asked the pair of them what their overview was of the situation. 'If you've helped George Lane out in the past, he must value what you have to say so come on, out with it.'

James prepared his second scone. 'I can understand why Hilda is rumoured to be involved. Beth said the WI is a small club, they've recently started and there are only a few members. Three of them have now had their husbands kidnapped. Hilda is not only a mother hen fussing around them but she appears to be convincing the wives to take something positive from this. That advice is fine after a few months, but a few days? I'd say that was unusual. I'd focus some attention on that WI lot. Everyone keeps pooh-poohing the idea that Hilda is involved but it wouldn't surprise me if she was.'

Beth agreed. 'I found it all a little peculiar last night; I didn't expect Evelyn and Debra to be there. I've said it to James and I'll tell you. There's something those women aren't divulging. And now Enoch's missing. The men have fish in common. Two catch them and one trades them. But that could mean you're looking at the fishermen. A lot of those men that mix with Enoch aren't the most ingratiating people.' She turned to James. 'And what about Jonah Quinn?'

James scratched his head. 'I can't fathom a motive though. There's no ransom demand so something else is being played out here. If these men are being held captive, someone must be feeding them, keeping them safe. Have you done a thorough search, Inspector?'

Wormstone flinched at the suggestion and advised them that they'd done a number of house to house enquiries, searching cliff-tops and caves and checked to see if people were buying extra food and had come to a dead end.

'Well, I'm stumped, I really am. Perhaps it's someone with a grudge against fish,' James said with a grin. 'I say, Inspector, will you see what those lights are?'

'I'll get the coastguard to keep a look out. Enjoy your time at the festival tomorrow.'

'Oh and Inspector, I know I'm asking questions but did you speak with that woman they call Nibbin?'

'Yes sir, I did.' He picked up his hat, bade them goodbye and walked to the car.

'Blast. Damned infuriating man. He doesn't give anything away, does he? I wonder what those lights were on the cliff top.'

Beth shot him a 'you dare' look. He

held his hands up and promised not to pry. As they finished the rest of the cream tea he made a mental note that it wouldn't hurt to have a walk up the foot path from the harbour. It was a public footpath after all. Perhaps they could have a stroll along the cliff path and they might bump into that Nibbin woman.

20

The sun was already melting into the sea as the Knockers parade began. James, Beth and the Merryweathers stood among the crowds lining the route and munched on Bidevin's warm Cornish pasties. It was the right sort of night for them, too. A chilly wind was blowing in off the sea so a hot filling of beef and potato set them up well for the evening ahead.

James rose on tip-toe to see what was happening. This was a much more sombre affair to the other parades. The people taking part each carried a lantern and dressed in dark costumes. Bidevin seemed to be the leader of the procession and, as with the previous characters, he fitted the image well. He wore a dark green felt pointed hat, a leather jerkin and brown shoes. His bushy beard suited the image and the villagers behind him had adopted similar costumes. Most of them carried a spade or a pickaxe. Those without a lantern brandished two pieces of wood waiting for their cue to use them.

Bidevin held his spade high and bellowed out:

'We are the Cornish Knockers, we live in the deep, dank mines.
We spy and hide from the miners and make sure they treat us fine.
All the time they feed us, we're happy, like today, But trick us and you'll hear us knock on the other side of the clay.
We'll take you to the darkness, take you down below,
It's black as night, you'll be a fright, and your death will be mighty slow.'

'G–gracious,' said Stephen, 'that all sounds a l–little ominous.'

Those holding bits of wood began knocking out a rhythm and an accordion player slipped in beside Bidevin. It was another slow, mesmeric tune and the landlord trod a slow step along the high street. The men and women following him gave out a low, continuous hum.

James felt Beth snuggle closer. 'This is creepy. Was the earlier one like this?'

Anne said the afternoon parade was more for the families. 'Luke and Mark loved it. I'm not sure they'd like this. It's like the beginning of one of those Hammer horror films. It's terribly menacing, isn't it?'

James studied the parade. There were around a hundred people there, wearing costumes and swinging lanterns. It was a spectacular sight and the haunting melody seemed to weave its way into everyone's soul. He spotted Jonah Quinn, Hilda, Tristram and Hans; further back PC Innes brought up the rear in his role as constable.

Beth suddenly roared with laughter and those around them followed. Skipping around Innes was Gretchen Kettel. Everything she wore was far too big for her and she struggled to stay on her feet in makeshift boots. Her felt hat was at an odd angle and she carried a children's tin bucket and spade. James laughed along with the crowds. She was certainly a bundle of fun; almost childlike in her enthusiasm. As the parade passed by, the music began to quicken.

Bidevin bellowed out:

'The Knockers are coming to get you, they'll take you into the black,
They'll hide you till you're skin and bones and you'll never find your way back.'

Beth put her hand on her chest. 'I'm not sure I like that sentiment.'

Anne agreed and Stephen instinctively drew her close. Across the road, Vic and Flora had closed the shop and stood to watch the parade go by. Mr Atherton, the blind man they'd seen earlier that week, also took it all in. James wondered what it must feel like; to miss out on the visual aspect of something so spectacular.

They slipped in behind the procession and made their way along the road. Residents who lived along the street, opened their top windows and waved. The haunting atmosphere lifted as Bidevin and his fellow Knockers waved and shouted out a greeting.

In twenty minutes, the Knockers and the following crowd had made their way to the top of the high street and into the park where the fairground was in full swing. The mood lifted as the crowds dispersed to the various stalls and rides.

The lights of the merry-go-round shone bright; its automated organ belting out old fairground classics. Alongside were bumper cars, the Waltzer and the Merry Mixer, each with its own musical accompaniment. People queued up for the coconut shy, strong-man machine and firing range. A stream of music hit the senses over the speakers; Fats Domino, Elvis, Chuck Berry and Buddy Holly. Beth and Anne jigged to the music as they walked around the fair. They each grabbed candyfloss and hopped onto the merry-go-round to catch a ride on the prancing ponies.

Stephen tried his hand at the strong man competition and swung a huge hammer onto a metal plate. The indicator reached half way. James didn't fare much better. They turned their attention to the shooting gallery where Anne won a rubber duck.

In the middle of the park, the organisers had set up a makeshift dance floor and a skiffle band were pounding out 'Pick a Bale of Cotton', linking straight into 'Rock Island Line'. Beth and Anne couldn't help but dance on the spot. James could understand why there was such frenzy around this rock and roll music. It was foot-tapping and catchy. The band launched into Razzle Dazzle and James felt Beth tug his sleeve.

'Oh come on darling. I can't stand here while this is playing.'

He rolled his eyes at Stephen and Anne and allowed himself to be dragged onto the dance floor. The darkness of the parade was well and truly behind them as he and Beth jived alongside the off-duty Knockers and day-trippers. He swung Beth around by the waist, skipped and twirled to the beat. Stephen and Anne joined them as the band continued with 'See You Later Alligator'. They danced for well over an hour under a canopy of stars until, after 'Jailhouse Rock', the lead singer brought the music to a stop and announced, in a breathless voice, that they needed to recharge their batteries.

The crowd applauded and concerned dancers asked if they were coming back. The singer checked his watch and assured them they had another half an hour of performing to come.

Beth led them staggering off the dance floor and let out an exhausted sigh. 'Oh I can't remember when we jived for so long.'

'Me too,' said Anne fanning herself. 'I'm completely out of breath. Are we staying for the last half an hour?'

'I–I'm happy too.'

'Of course,' said James who asked if everyone was as thirsty as he was. He rolled his sleeves up. Over the course of the last hour, they had discarded jackets, sweaters and cardigans. Beth and Anne had even slipped off their sandals. He and Stephen soon emerged from the beer tent with four glasses of shandy. 'If you can't drink it all, ladies, I'm sure that Stephen and I can help out.'

No sooner had they quenched their

thirst than the music started again. There was no let-up on the band's energy and the last half an hour was a string of hits from the previous two years. They ended the session with a dance called The Stroll which was a new one on James. Keen to try it out, they lined up, ladies in one line, gents in the other and simply strolled through their steps. At midnight, the band thanked their audience and turned the equipment off.

James took a breath. 'My word, that was an evening and a half, wasn't it?'

Beth picked up her sandals. 'I can't put these on. My feet are so sore, I need to soak them. Can you carry me darling?'

He gave her a stern look. 'No dear, you'll have to stagger along with the rest of us.'

They collected their things and made their way out of the park, carried along by a happy and still singing crowd. Stephen and Anne arrived at their car. They said their goodbyes with a promise to meet James and Beth at eleven the next morning for a walk along the cliff-tops.

James held Beth's hand and they

strolled toward the hotel. The crowds thinned out as couples and families headed for their accommodation. When they reached the harbour, they saw PC Innes talking to a dishevelled Vic Chenery and taking some notes. Hilda patted the shop owner's hand.

'Everything all right, Innes?' James said as they approached.

Vic appeared pale and confused. He shivered even though he wore a thick sweater. Beth joined Hilda and rubbed his back. 'What on earth has happened?'

'My Flora's disappeared.'

21

At breakfast, after a disturbed night's sleep, James dipped his toast in his soft-boiled egg and held it up.

'My theory that this links to the WI is well and truly shot out of the water. Flora wasn't a member, was she?'

Beth mirrored James' thoughts. 'Poor Vic looked distraught. I know they're always bickering but he dotes on her.'

'It's most odd. I don't understand why there's been no ransom demand or any communication from whoever's doing it.'

She reminded him they were out of it now. 'We made a good show of being tourists last night. Not that we were putting on an act but let's keep it that way.'

Desmond popped his head round the door. 'Ah, Mrs Merryweather is on the phone asking for one of you.'

Beth dabbed her lips with a napkin and followed Desmond out to reception where she picked up the receiver. Two minutes later she returned to James. 'Luke and Mark have a stomach upset — probably too many ice creams and sweets but she's going to stay with them at the caravan. Stephen's happy to meet up as planned but I've agreed to spend the morning with Anne to keep her company — do you mind?'

'Not in the least. It'll be nice to spend some time with Stephen. Vivian's making up a flask of tea to keep us going.'

Although disappointed that it wasn't the four of them, it did give him the chance to observe the cliff-top but he reminded himself that this was simply observation and not involvement.

After dropping Beth off with Anne, he and Stephen drove to the small car park at the end of the village that heralded the start of the cliff-top path. He opened up a map and they decided to cover the first five miles to the next cove and catch a bus back.

'I've a small flask but hopefully there'll be a pub or tearoom there for some liquid sustenance.'

He packed the map away, draped a camera around his neck and the pair of them made a start. The first few hundred yards saw them go up a gradual incline that, by half-way, made them realise they were not as fit as they thought they were. They stopped for a breather and spent a couple of minutes admiring the scenery. It was a blustery, yet balmy day and the sea streamed into the shore like white stallions racing to the finish line.

On the cliff-top itself, several people had the same idea as them and were heading toward the next cove with maps and cameras in hand. The only two trees left on the hill had been shaped by the wind, both curving at an alarming angle, the tips of the trees almost within touching distance of the ground they stood on.

Stephen undid his rucksack and got out his camera. Together they took a couple of snaps looking back to Polpennarth.

'A–are you snapping as a tourist or an investigator?'

James grinned and assured him that he was now a tourist. They'd updated the

Merryweathers on their escapades the previous day and Stephen was delighted to learn that James was going to stop delving. Solving a mystery in a strange town was entirely different to within one's own community. 'A–at least around Cavendish, y–you can cross most of the residents off of y–your list. Here, we don't know who's who.'

They continued walking and chatted about all manner of things, from children to retirement; cooking and restaurants; films and television and, finally, friendship. James pondered on their own friendship. Stephen was a modern vicar who delivered his sermons in a different way, one that brought most of Cavendish to church every Sunday. He remembered the first sermon he'd delivered, the way he roamed up and down the aisle, rarely staying in the pulpit, being animated and putting in some humour. Perhaps it was his short stint as an army clergyman that made him so unique.

In turn, James was no ordinary Lord; preferring to drop the title where he could and step back a little from the class system. He knew he had the best of both worlds, able to enter the realms of the elite and use his status or leave it behind if it suited.

It worked for them and it worked for both couples and he knew their friendship would be a long-standing one.

They'd covered about a mile when they saw a lady, distressed, sitting on the grass about fifty yards back from the cliff edge. James followed Stephen as they quickened their pace toward her, suggesting on the way that she might have twisted an ankle or something. It was only when they got closer they realised who it was.

'Good Lord,' said James rushing to her side.

Flora Chenery sat there, bedraggled and confused. Her hair was windblown and tangled, her complexion grey and eyes red-rimmed. She flung herself at James and wrapped her arms around him. 'I kept waving. No one saw me.'

He held her close. Stephen opened James' rucksack and brought out the flask and a plastic mug.

James gently pulled her arms away.

'Here, we have some tea. Come on, drink this, it'll do you good.'

She accepted the mug as if it were gold dust and sipped the drink. She closed her eyes and sighed. 'Oh that's lovely.'

Stephen brought out a Kit-Kat chocolate bar. 'I–I have a couple of these. Take them, get some sugar into you.'

She'd clearly not eaten for some time. Her fingers trembled as she tried to take off the wrapper. Stephen helped her. James, meanwhile, untied the jumper that was around his waist.

'Here, it'll be two sizes too big for you but it'll keep you warm.'

Flora let James manoeuvre her arms into the sleeves and popped the jumper on as if he were dressing a small child. 'Good Lord, Flora, you look all in. Have you been out here all night?'

'I don't know. Whoever took me came back and let me go; put me here.'

'You don't know who did this?'

She shook her head. 'I don't remember anything really. I watched the parade. Vic went back to open the shop and — yes, I heard a sound, someone behind me.' She closed her eyes, trying to remember. 'I thought it was just the crowds. Then I felt something on my neck.' She rubbed the area. 'Then I felt incredibly sleepy.'

James asked her to tilt her head. It was faint but there was a small pinprick on her neck. He asked Stephen to take a look. Neither of them spoke but they each knew what they'd seen. Someone had injected Flora Chenery.

'Do you know where you were kept?'

She wrapped her hands around the plastic mug of tea. 'No, no, I don't, I was in such a daze. It felt like a cave. It was very cold. I was blindfolded. He guided me along.'

'He?'

She shrugged. 'He, she, I don't know. Whoever it was didn't talk.'

Stephen squatted down. 'W–were you on your own in this cave?'

'Yes. No.' She met Stephen's gaze. 'At first I thought I was but I didn't feel alone. I felt as if someone else was in the cave.'

'Did this person walk you here?' asked James.

'I don't know. I slept. I woke up here just a while ago.'

'Apart from feeling a little groggy, how are you?'

She managed a brief smile but hadn't the energy to reply. James encouraged her to drink her tea. He and Stephen got to their feet. 'Stephen, do you want to stay here with her and I'll dash back and alert the authorities.'

'Of course.'

He opened up his map to see exactly where they were. Scanning the area, he noticed a dirt track that must lead to a farm or some outbuilding. An ambulance could get up there easily. He marked their location with a pencil. 'Right, I shouldn't be long, we're only about a mile from Polpennarth and it's all downhill.'

His long stride and intermittent jog meant he was back at the car park in a few minutes where he was grateful to see a telephone box. He swung the door open and picked up the receiver. It was heavy and cold and, thankfully, in working order. He dialled 999 and cursed the emergency services for using a number that took so long to dial. A woman answered.

'Which service please?'

James requested ambulance and police. He gave a brief overview of things and examined his map to give the best possible co-ordinates. 'There is a dirt track running along there so I think vehicles can access it.'

The woman assured James that the correct personnel had been requested. He put the receiver down and rang the operator.

'Ah, can you put me through to the Polpennarth police station please.'

With the right change inserted, James was connected to Inspector Wormstone. He gave a bite-sized version to the Inspector. From the noise in the background, James had caused him to jump from his seat.

'Are you heading back there?' he asked.

'Yes, Stephen's with her.'

'I'll see you there.'

'Pick me up. I'm at the car park at the base of the cliff. I can't do that hill a second time around.'

He rang off. Ten minutes later, James, Wormstone and Innes arrived. Innes knew the dirt track James spoke of and explained that the farmer used it occasionally. The ambulance and police had just arrived and were attending to Flora. Their diagnosis was that she was suffering from shock and exhaustion.

The Inspector asked quick questions that simply required a yes or no answer. Although she could give him no clues, he ordered the county police over. There were two policemen who had answered the call and Wormstone advised them this related to the kidnappings. With that, he had their full attention.

'She's not given us much but has given us an indication that she was in a cave. Any thoughts? You know this area better than I do.'

The men chatted amongst themselves and came up with three possible locations.

'Right, I'll clear it with your superiors, but I want all available men looking at these caves. Get the coastguard out, divers, whatever it takes. I want a thorough search of this coastline.'

The ambulance man handed James his jumper back and threw a huge blanket around Flora as he led her to his vehicle. Flora looked back and mouthed her thanks to him and Stephen.

The ambulance left, the two constables sped off and Innes waited by the Inspector's car. Wormstone turned to them. 'I wonder why he let her go?'

'I know I'm not supposed to be concerning myself with this but I'd be happy to think about it. If I fathom something out, I'll let you know.'

The Inspector was happy to accommodate that, thanked them for looking after Flora and told them to enjoy the rest of their morning. In less than a minute, Innes and Wormstone had driven off in the direction of Polpennarth.

Stephen let out a big sigh. 'W–well, that was an e–eventful hour wasn't it? Wh–where do you think she'd been?'

James steered Stephen back on the footpath and they carried on with their walk. He remarked that he hoped the police search came to something and

316

they'd find one of the caves occupied. When he and Beth had been looking at the smuggling boltholes during the previous year they'd found an amazing cave that took them some way back into the cliffs. Unfortunately, as the tide turned, it had put them in a dangerous position and threatened to sweep them out to sea. But large caves existed and it would be an ideal hiding place. If that was the case, then the kidnapper would have to have access to a boat. Did that put Johnny Sepp back on the suspect list? How accessible were these caves? It seemed an awful lot of trouble to hide someone. And still that same question nagged at him — to what purpose?

'To r–repeat the Inspector's questions, why do you think he I–let her go?'

'Yes, I wondered that.'

'Another one taken in plain sight. Whoever's doing this is making g–good use of this festival.'

'If it is a cave, that may explain the lights I've seen.'

Stephen pulled James back. 'L–look.'

James stood fascinated as he watched

the lady known as Nibbin prance and skip in a circle, waving two large feathers in her hand. She was about fifty yards away and behind her was what he assumed to be her house, although it was the most unusual dwelling he'd ever seen. It appeared to be made of layers of mud moulded into a large mound and shielded with sheets of old tarpaulin. She wore what he could only describe as a dress of rags that reached her ankles and had tied a saucepan to her head.

Stephen stood rooted to the spot. 'Y–you want to speak to her, don't you?'

James grinned. 'Rather.'

22

He heard Stephen groan as they made a tentative approach. Nibbin appeared oblivious to the outside world and continued dancing and shouting. At first he thought these were the ramblings of a lonely woman but as he listened, he realised this was something quite different. She chanted in a raspy voice.

'Treat those who are good with goodness; treat those who are not good with goodness. Thus goodness is attained. Be honest to those who are honest; be honest to those who are not honest. Thus honesty is attained.'

James answered Stephen's quizzical look. 'If my memory is correct, I believe this is ancient philosophy; a quotation from Lao Tzu.'

Stephen shrugged with an 'if you say so' expression and they continued watching Nibbin hop and spin.

'The measure of a man — ' She

stopped, mid-stoop. Her gaze bored into them. 'Psh, psh,' she muttered as if swatting them away. Her gaze eventually fell on James. 'The measure of a man . . .'

James felt pleased with himself as he remembered the quote exactly. 'The measure of a man is what he does with power. Plato, I believe.'

To his surprise, Nibbin stood up straight, broke into a broad smile and put her hands on her hips. 'There are two things a person should never be angry at.' She tilted her head and narrowed her eyes at him.

'Ah, this is Plato, too. What they can help and what they cannot. Is that correct?'

'Very good. Tea?'

James accepted for the pair of them and they followed her into her den, having to duck through a low-framed opening secured by driftwood. The dwelling was built against a slope in the ground and Nibbin had smeared mud and peat across the walls in the way that he imagined Celtic people had done thousands of years ago. He was quietly impressed. This was an abode shielded from driving rain, cool in the summer and snug in the winter.

'I say, this is rather cosy.'

As Nibbin collected an old tin kettle, Stephen nudged him toward one of the sloping walls. James stepped forward to see old newspaper cuttings from the local paper stuck there, showing various stories of the mad woman of the moor. One showed a large photograph of Nibbin with two angel wings strapped to her back. He turned to the woman.

'Correct me if I'm wrong but you don't strike me as the mad woman of the moor.'

Nibbin, a lady he put in her mid-sixties, raised an eyebrow and lit the camping gas stove. Stephen helped her manoeuvre some old cushions for them to sit on.

'Is that something you do purposely?'

She gestured for them to sit. 'That's for you to find out. Where would the British be without an eccentric or two? Have to keep that tradition alive.'

Stephen chuckled. 'Y–you mean you

live out here p–pretending to be mad?'

'Oh I am mad.' She spooned tea into a brown Betty teapot and set three chipped cups and saucers in front of them. While waiting for the water to boil, she told them about her father who used to be a lecturer and her uncle was a scientist in the armed forces who went AWOL. She spoke in a matter of fact way as if all families had the same background.

'And your mother?'

'She *was* wacky. Put in an asylum. Died years ago.'

'B–but this is a pretence, isn't it?'

The water boiled and Nibbin filled the tea pot. 'Dad climbed off the merry-go-round; had a breakdown. Never recovered. He and Uncle built this place. They raided dustbins and tips picking up old blankets and tarpaulin. Made this a home from home. Dad died when I was twenty three. Uncle lived here. He tunnelled through that little gap — built another place. He died. I use it now. It's a two-room squat and I love it.'

James peered through to see a mattress and some blankets. 'Good Lord.'

'He was Nobbin. I was Nibbin.'

'I–I beg your pardon?'

'Uncle devoured Cornish folklore, created two mischievous piskies and made up stories about them. Nibbin and Nobbin.'

James was beginning to understand this woman. 'And you prefer people to see you as Nibbin, the mischievous piskie?'

'Perceptive of you, Mr . . . ?'

James apologised and introduced himself and Stephen. 'We're on holiday.'

Nibbin pulled over the only armchair in the cave, a moth-eaten affair that James was glad he hadn't been offered. She explained she only had the one chair for a reason. 'No one visits. They think I'll gobble them up. And to be honest, I don't like visitors. Happy for them to think I'm some sort of cannibal.'

Stephen noticed a certificate propped up on the side. 'Philosophy? You d–did a degree?'

'Mmm.' She looked at James. 'You studied?'

'I did, but not philosophy. I take a passing interest in philosophical quotes.

They fascinate me. Where did you study?'

'Cambridge. You?'

'Oxford.' He accepted his tea. 'Do any of the villagers come and see you?'

'Two. Gretchen brings essentials and books. Bidevin brings pasties.' She reached across for a long clay pipe and filled it with tobacco. 'Not just on holiday, are you.'

James took this as a statement rather than a question. He exchanged a bashful look with Stephen and explained that he'd taken an interest in the disappearances in the village. Stephen added more detail about James' hobby in crime and how he'd helped to solve a number of mysteries back in Cavendish.

'H–he's really rather good. Even George, the DCI up there, consults him n–now and again.'

She drew on her pipe and untied the saucepan on her head. 'Proper little Sherlock. You say you *had* been looking into the mystery. You've stopped. Why?'

James splayed his hands. 'Nibbin, there are a few hundred residents plus tourists here. I couldn't begin to fathom out who kidnapped those men or why. I don't know these people from Adam.' He added that the two attempts on his life were a sure way to get him to step back.

'Gretchen said you've rattled the cage of one particular resident.'

He sat up with a start. 'Really? Who?'

'Hilda Roscarrock.'

Stephen remarked that Hilda appeared to react in an odd way around the wives of the men who were missing. He went through their observations about how sympathetic she was, yet how she hinted that things would now be better. His eyes darted from James to Nibbin. 'Y–you don't think she's killed th–them do you?'

Nibbin concentrated on stirring her tea. James thought she'd make a good poker player. Not even a twitch of a response.

'Nibbin, you're in the village a lot. You must have seen something?'

'I didn't see the men disappear.'

'You don't believe it's Knockers or Old Bogey.'

Nibbin snorted. 'I'm offended you'd suggest it. Nonsense. You shouldn't give up though. If someone wanted you dead, you'd be dead by now.'

James frowned. 'Do you know who's responsible? Is it Hilda? I thought it might be Jonah. He had affairs with the wives.'

She tutted and told him not to bother with Jonah. 'Fancies himself as Casanova and had his fingers burnt. Seeks his women along the coast; not so close to home. Hilda knows those wives better than you think.'

Stephen asked if the missing men had anything in common.

She kept quiet for some time and then took their half-drunk cups of tea away. 'I don't like people. People make life complicated. Gretchen and Bidevin visit but don't stay. They know not to stay. But I have to live alongside them, I can't be involved. I don't know who's involved. But if you find these men, I do know what to tell them. You may not understand it but they should.' She met James' eyes. 'You'll be able to explain it when the time comes.'

She flung some scraps of paper and

pencil at him. 'Write it down.'

James frowned at Stephen then picked the paper up.

'Tell Colm Fiske: *it's easy to be angry, but to be angry with the right person, to the right degree, at the right time, for the right purpose and in the right way — that's not easy.*'

James jotted it down and remembered the quote, an abbreviated version by Aristotle.

'Tell Bevis Allan: *if there's such a thing as a good marriage, it's because it resembles friendship.*'

Stephen held a hand up with a look of triumph. 'Ah, I've quoted that one myself, that's Michel de Montaigne.'

'To that stubborn stick in the mud, ngilly: *No man should bring the world who's unwilling to just the end in their nature and*

Nibbld and explained to back to Plato. 'And know we found her here.'

'Mistake. The

kidnapper didn't do their homework. I'd like you to go now please.'

He gritted his teeth. She clearly knew more about the victims. He understood her reluctance to spill the beans but why not say something now? He expressed his disappointment that she wouldn't divulge more information. 'These men are suffering and every day that goes by could lead them to danger. They may be dying of thirst.'

She appeared unconcerned and mumbled: 'A little hardship won't do 'em any harm. I've had enough questions. Give me my home back and don't visit again. I have to live here. I can't have the locals seeing you here.'

They climbed to their feet and she bundled them through the opening. James squinted as the daylight hit h eyes. She called out after him. 'We d have a killer here. Someone's tr right a wrong. The men won't sp the women are frightened of

She disappeared.

They went on their wa than ever. The next

spent firing questions at each other. Should James continue to investigate? What were all these quotes about? What did Nibbin mean about someone trying to right a wrong?

'Confound that blasted woman,' James blurted and waved the scraps of paper. 'I'd rather she'd have said nothing then bombard us with all this cryptic nonsense.'

Ahead of them was an ice-cream van and a number of walkers had flocked toward it probably, James thought, because the vans were such a curiosity. James had seen a few in London just a couple of months before and was astounded to see one all the way down here. They'd made their mark in the United States and the novelty had now spread across the Atlantic. They joined the queue and, on reaching the front, asked for two ice-cream cornets.

'I say,' said James to the vendor. 'This is rather natty, isn't it?'

The owner explained that he was one of the first to own a van. 'I've had it on the road for two months now. It's really taking off and I thought I'd drive it down to where the tourists are.'

'S–sensible man.'

James asked if he always parked there and learned that the vendor based himself in Penzance but came up to this spot because of its coastal walk. 'According to the guides, this is one of the most picturesque walks in these parts so it's good business, especially on a day like this.'

'You don't keep it parked up here at night?'

He received an astonished look. 'No mate. The tourists disappear back to the bed and breakfast places about five for dinner. I pack up and head back to Penzance and set up there. Why?'

James explained about the lights he'd seen on the cliff-tops at night. 'I wondered if that was you.'

He pulled a face to indicate it wasn't and suggested it might have been a late night walker with a torch. He politely asked them to move as the queue behind them had begun to build. James apologised and they stepped to one side.

'Oh look,' said Stephen. 'There's an old t–tin mine over there. Shall we take a look? I wouldn't mind a few photographs of that.'

Savouring the cool ice cream they wandered across to the desolate mine. The chimney stood tall and was in danger of crumbling although there appeared to be enough moss growing up one side to keep it standing. Alongside was an immense building that would have housed the huge steam engines used to power the machinery needed underground. This particular building looked a forlorn sight and they tried to imagine what it must have looked like in its day. They looked further up the coastline and saw a number of tall chimneys dotted along the cliff-tops.

Strolling around the building Stephen explored the areas that were not fenced off. They found huge steel rivets that would have helped secure the steam engines. In the corner, a dented tin mug lay in the dust. They climbed back out onto the grass where James realised they were near the entrance. It had a splintered door in place and, on the ground, some rusty railway lines almost buried in the earth. James gently kicked the rails.

'These must be the tramlines that led the wagons down. It must have been a noisy and dusty environment.'

Stephen agreed. He checked his watch. 'I–I think we ought to give that next village a miss. It's a–almost lunchtime.'

'Yes, you're right. Shall we pop into The Pilchard and pick up some pasties?'

'Good idea.'

As Stephen walked away, James' curiosity got the better of him and he tried the door. He pulled it open and did a double-take. Everything about this mine was ancient, rusted and crumbling. Why, then, was there a new door hidden behind an old one, with a brand new padlock on it? A piece of paper fluttered on the ground. He reached down to pick it up.

'Polpennarth Council — Mine in Danger of Collapse

— Please Keep Clear'

James guessed some inquisitive tourists had got themselves into a spot of bother and they'd had to lock the entrance. He pushed the dilapidated door back where a glint caught his eye. He squatted down and pulled back a slab of stone.

A lantern!

A new lantern, gleaming in the sunshine.

He turned it over in his hands. The cogs and wheels spun in his head. This was the light he'd seen from the boat. It must have been.

A fragment of the Knockers' rhyme came to mind. He quietly repeated the parts he remembered. 'We are the Cornish Knockers, we live in the deep, dank mines. We'll take you to the darkness, take you down below. It's black as night, you'll be a fright, and your death will be mighty slow.'

Stephen called out to him. He replaced the lantern under the stone and jogged over to let him know what he'd found. His friend looked back toward the mine and then at James.

'I–I know that look. Y–you're going to investigate again, aren't you?'

Beth's assertion about simply having a

holiday flashed like a neon sign in his head. He nudged Stephen forward. 'It may be nothing. That old door's had it; the council have fitted a new one. I just don't understand why there's a lantern there.'

He was loath to return to investigating, especially after promising Beth that he wouldn't. The discussion with Nibbin had been a frustrating but enlightening one. She was telling them to look for the simple explanation. Most crimes were committed because of something simple; an argument, someone slighted, jealousy. This would be the same. A small community where gossip was rife and someone had been slighted or felt aggrieved in some way.

James strode out. 'Come along, Stephen. Let's get those pasties, I could eat a horse.'

23

They'd ensconced themselves around the small dining table in the Merryweathers' caravan and eaten their pasties. Outside, they could hear the boys playing ball with Radley and assurances that they were now feeling much better.

Beth glowered at James. 'You're not serious.'

James had gone through the morning's events in great detail, describing finding Flora, their meeting with Nibbin and her odd words of wisdom; but Beth was finding it difficult to fathom.

'Why on earth would you believe a rambling woman who lives on a hill? How does she know you won't get killed?'

Anne agreed. 'She sounds unhinged and could be involved herself. She could be leading you into a trap. Look at what happened to you both these last two days. We could be arranging your funerals.'

Stephen assured their wives that

Nibbin was probably the most sensible and intelligent person who lived there. 'She doesn't b–believe in all that Knockers nonsense and is in–incredibly well read and intelligent. She went to Cambridge and h–has a degree in Philosophy.'

'But that means nothing, Stephen, if she's unstable.'

James asked Beth to hear him out and enlarged on Stephen's description. With some persuasion, he convinced Beth that Nibbin was not mad, just someone who loved to play the part but was actually profoundly observant. He repeated the quotes she'd insisted he impart to the men when they were found and that they were to look at the obvious. 'She said someone was righting a wrong.'

Beth gazed at him and he returned it with an earnest look, determined not to break eye contact. It felt like a contest. The first to look away would lose the argument.

Beth closed her eyes. 'Oh, all right. But we think this through and we don't do anything dangerous or untoward.'

James nodded his understanding. 'Anything we come up with will be given straight to Wormstone and Innes.'

Anne repeated Nibbin's statement that James had mentioned earlier about the men not speaking of it and the women being frightened of it. 'That's significant, don't you think? It's almost like a riddle. And you said she thinks it won't do those men any harm to be kidnapped a while longer. Why?'

James wiped his hands on a napkin. 'You're right. The police have been looking to see what these men have in common, as in clubs or interests. But they don't have anything like that. The men won't speak of it; the women are frightened of it. Beth, Anne, take us through what you observed with the wives at the WI.'

'Well,' said Beth, 'Hilda's a matriarchal figure. She has no children of her own but her attitude to the women in the WI is more often than not like a matron than an equal.'

Anne expanded. 'She's pushy and assertive and she's been particularly protective of Evelyn and Debra and I would imagine Edith now that Enoch's disappeared.' She chewed her lip. 'What if she is the kidnapper? She's been a suspect all of this time and everyone's dismissed it.'

James asked them to be more specific. 'What struck you most about Evelyn? Answer now,' he clicked his fingers, 'don't think about it. Beth, go with your instinct.'

'She's frightened.'

'Anne?'

'Yes, jumpy, frightened of her own shadow.'

'Why? What causes fear? What causes someone to have such a haunted look? Discard the fact her husband is missing; I think we've already decided this is deep-rooted.'

Anne sat forward. 'If I was that frightened, it would be either a phobia or that a particular person frightened me.'

Beth added: 'What about a fear of crowds or open spaces? She seems uncomfortable around people.'

'No,' said Stephen. 'She m–made her way to the WI without an es–escort. If she had agoraphobia, she wouldn't have made it to the fr–front step.'

'And,' said James, 'a fear of crowds doesn't tally. We've seen her at the parade, at the pub and mixing with villagers on the green. No, I think this is a person. She's terrified of a person and I believe it's her husband. There are snippets of conversation that suggest that. Look at the way she answered Hilda when we first met them at The Pilchard. She was wary about doing anything in case Colm found out.'

'But that doesn't explain Debra. She's positively radiant.'

'Debra's a different person with different reactions. When we first saw her at the fairground, she had that same fearful look.'

Anne slapped the table. 'And now she is full of the joys of spring.'

'B–because her bully of a husband is not there dominating pr–proceedings. How enlightening.'

'And,' said James, 'she said something at the fairground that I thought was odd and having had this discussion now makes sense. She said *he's done bad things too*, do you remember, darling?'

'Yes, yes, I do.'

'She thinks she's bad because Bevis doesn't let up on her but he's not an angel himself because of the way he is.' He held a finger up to emphasise his statement. 'And Nibbin did give us a clue. These quotes, they're to do with tolerance, patience and respect.'

Beth clasped her hands together. 'Sweetie, that's it. We know that Enoch is a domineering figure; we've witnessed it enough times. And what about Gretchen telling us that the girls have lost their oomph. Debra's found hers since Bevin went missing.'

James stomach did a mild flip as things settled into place. 'And remember what Hilda said about things being better for these women. She knows they're bullied. The fact their husbands are missing means exactly that. They can live without fear.'

'Wh–what about Flora though? We've witnessed her bullying her husband. Why was she let go?'

James reminded them to think about what they'd observed with Enoch. Although they hadn't met Colm or Bevis, the way the villagers had described them confirmed they were of the same mould as the old fisherman, their treatment of their respective wives was both domineering and officious; like a sergeant major drilling raw recruits, wearing them down. 'The slightest thing they do wrong, they pounce on it and drag them down, taking every bit of confidence from them.'

Stephen added that Debra had only been married a couple of years and that perhaps Bevis hadn't had time to do that. 'That's why Debra's f–found her oomph. Evelyn, remember, h–has been with Colm for ten years.'

Beth brought them back to the point that this didn't explain Flora.

'But don't you see darling. Observing Vic in that fish and chip shop; he wasn't downtrodden or lacking confidence. He doesn't have a look of fear or wariness about him. He looks on his wife with fondness; it's the way they are. He lets her nag him, it's her way. I would imagine that if he needed to stand up for himself he would.'

'So Flora was a mistake.'

'That's what Nibbin said. Look how distraught Vic was when he found she was missing. That's not the behaviour of someone suffering from abuse. That's someone who is truly worried about the person they love.'

Stephen held a finger up. 'A–and who was in the vicinity when you saw Vic?'

The group chorused. 'Hilda.'

'I wonder,' said Beth, 'if Hilda is working with Debra or Evelyn? Debra could be ecstatic because she's found a way to rid herself of a bully. Evelyn could be fearful because she's breaking the law.'

'A–and Debra has access to the pharmacy. She could have built up a supply of d–drugs from her own prescription.'

Something about that statement nagged at James but he couldn't think why.

'Perhaps Hilda and Debra are working together,' said Anne. 'We should follow them. At a distance, see what they get up to and where they go.'

Beth admired her enthusiasm but encouraged James to go to the police. 'You promised to take a step back and not get involved.'

James rested his elbows on the table. She was right, of course. The business with the boat and the brake cable was no idle threat. Someone wanted them to keep their noses out. Nibbin knew about the bullying but she couldn't say. Although living on the fringe of the village, she had to live in the community and so she refused to be drawn out. She was ostracised enough — being accused of betrayal might affect the visits of the few villagers who did befriend her.

'Beth, we're observing, nothing more. We'll observe in the village, see where they go, who they talk to, notice if there's anything unusual. We need to establish if Hilda is working alone or with those women. I'd hate for Wormstone to arrest them all as a result of our opinion.'

'D–do you think Edith is caught up in this?'

They fell silent. That a pensioner would be involved in such a thing appeared inconceivable. Anne dismissed the idea altogether, Beth tilted her head from side to side, unable to commit herself and Stephen asked James if he'd caught the recent release *Too Many Crooks* where an elderly wife took over the running of a gang to get revenge on her husband.

James chuckled. 'Are you suggesting that Edith is a master criminal?'

Stephen gave him a bashful look. 'P–probably not.'

'So, sweetie, what are you suggesting we do?'

'I suggest that Stephen and Anne tag on to Debra Allan. She's pleased as punch and may do something untoward; slip up because of her carefree attitude. We, darling, will pick up Hilda's trail.' He met Stephen's gaze. 'Have you plans?'

Stephen looked at Anne who explained that she and Beth had already been invited to a sewing hour. 'The WI need to make some more bunting for their next festival and they're having a get together this afternoon and asked if we'd like to attend.'

'We thanked them and said no,' said Beth, 'but I think we should change our minds. I know that Debra and Evelyn will be there and I can't imagine Hilda won't be although she didn't mention it. We can watch and observe. See if we come up with anything.'

Stephen explained that he and the children were going fishing. 'I d–don't want to let them down.'

'Nor should you,' said James. 'Anne, why don't you do the sewing hour with Debra and Evelyn. Don't put yourself in an awkward position, just observe. Beth, let's you and I tag Hilda and see where she goes. If she attends this sewing thing, you could join up with Anne there. We'll meet at The Pilchard to swap notes at six o'clock. If we have something to go on, we'll head straight to the police station.' He turned to Beth. 'Does that mollify your concerns, darling?'

Beth scrutinised him and eventually conceded. 'Yes, I'm happy with that.'

'D–don't forget it's our anniversary

tomorrow,' Stephen added. 'W–we are still eating out aren't we?'

James assured him that a table was booked at The Sardine and hell or high water would not drag them away.

With their afternoon plans in place, James and Beth drove back to Polpennarth to seek out Hilda Roscarrick.

24

James steered Beth towards the fish and chip shop. 'Let's have a cup of tea and enquire after Flora. If we sit outside we can pick up Hilda if she's about. Does she work?'

'I believe she works part-time in the bakery, three mornings a week, so her afternoons are free. Whether she has other jobs, I don't know. We'll just have to cross our fingers she makes an appearance.'

They entered the fish and chip shop. The lunch-time trade had been and gone and Vic stood behind the counter with a broad smile on his face.

'Ah, Lord and Lady Harrington, how lovely to see you. I understand I've you to thank for helping my wife.'

James waved the thanks aside and asked after Flora.

'She's upstairs in our sitting room. I've made her a nice cup of tea and got a fresh cream cake as a treat. I've told her she's not to think about coming down here for a few days yet.'

'Quite right. Does she remember anything about last night?'

'Only that a Knocker came out of the shadows. If it weren't so horrific, I'd have laughed. Fair put the wind up our Flora, I can tell you.'

'And she doesn't recollect who it could be.'

'No, nothing.'

Beth asked if Inspector Wormstone had called. 'They often ask the strangest of questions about smells and textures.'

Vic confirmed that those sorts of enquiries had been made. 'She doesn't remember anything much. I'd only been gone a few minutes. I'd left her by the roadside to come back here. She was stopping on to watch the rest of the parade. She was standing alongside Mr Atherton.'

'Mr Atherton?'

'The blind man. You've probably seen him walking around. Local man, always comes along to these things even though he can't get much out of it. I mean, it's a very visual thing, isn't it?'

James agreed and ordered tea. They wished Vic well and made themselves comfortable outside. The area was a few feet back from the main road and a couple of ice cream vendors pushed their carts past. Across the road was the main promenade and then the beach. They'd been fortunate with the weather; the sun was warm, the sky blue with wisps of clouds waiting to be burned away by the heat.

As he studied the tourists, he wondered how many of the men here worked in the city. Suits had given way to light slacks or shorts. Their wives and girlfriends wore pretty cotton frocks and sunhats. Further along, fishermen gathered and helped one another with their nets.

He lit a cigarette. 'That blind man, Mr Atherton. I wonder if he's worth speaking with.'

Beth reached in her handbag and brought out her sunglasses. 'Do you think he has information?'

'Just something that Vic said. He doesn't see anything of the parade but he probably enjoys it in other ways. They say that if you lose one sense, your others are heightened.'

'That's true. He may have heard something that no one else would notice.'

'Or some sort of aroma; a perfume perhaps.'

Beth announced that Hilda wore a version of Youth Dew. 'Estée Lauder sells a concentrated bath oil with that fragrance. I smelt it on her the other day.'

'Well our man Atherton must be able to distinguish between a perfume and an aftershave. We'll watch out for him but Hilda's our priority.'

They were able to enjoy their tea at leisure. It was approximately twenty minutes later, when they felt they either had to leave or buy more tea that they spotted Hilda. She was striding toward the harbour, thankfully oblivious of their presence across the road.

James helped Beth up. 'Come on.'

For the next few minutes, they strolled arm in arm with one eye on the shop displays and the other on Hilda. The woman popped in and out of the butchers and purchased a magazine at Gretchen's. She studied a scrap of paper and headed toward the grocers. Ticking off items as she emerged from each shop, she placed them in her shopping basket and continued on.

James held Beth back. 'We're getting too close. Hang back a bit.'

Hilda waved to another lady that Beth recognised. 'She's from the WI. I can't remember her name but she served me tea.'

They studied some local pottery for a couple of minutes until Hilda bade her friend goodbye and continued on her way. She crossed the road and made her way up the hill.

'I think she's going home,' said Beth. 'I'm sure she said their cottage is up here.'

As Hilda went up the hill, they spotted Tristram coming down. He waved at his wife. James nudged Beth into a doorway and they watched from inside a gift store.

As Tristram reached his wife, he and Hilda chatted for a while and he poked about inside her shopping basket. He took some of the shopping from her. Hilda went inside and quickly returned to Tristram minus her basket. She checked her watch.

'Do you think they have an appointment or something?'

'Perhaps,' said Beth. 'They look as if they're on a schedule.'

'Here she comes.'

As the pair walked toward them, James and Beth wandered around the gift shop and waited until they'd passed. Outside, they watched them walk alongside the harbour wall on the promenade.

'I say, if they're taking that cliff path, we'll be spotted a mile off.'

'Let's see. Come on.'

It was mid-afternoon and the sun had notched the temperature up a couple more degrees. James took off his straw hat and fanned himself with it. Beth pulled him back. 'They've stopped.'

Ahead of them, Hilda and Tristram chatted. She gestured to a side street and Tristram toward the cliff-top. He pecked her on the cheek and they went their separate ways. As she crossed the road, he called: 'I'll see you in a couple of hours.'

Hilda went up the side-street, knocked on a wooden door and entered the house.

'That's where the WI women are meeting,' said Beth. 'What shall we do now?'

James brought out his wallet. 'Listen, go in there and set up shop with Anne. I'll grab a paper and make myself comfortable here. If she leaves, I'll follow her. What time do you have?'

'Three o'clock.'

'I'll meet you here at five if not before. If it looks like she's going to stay the distance, I may go for a wander. If she does anything untoward, go to Wormstone.'

'Well if I'm not here at five, it means I'm bored and I've gone back to the hotel.'

He brought her close to him and kissed her forehead. 'Good luck. Don't do anything dangerous.'

She gave him a knowing look. 'You need to follow your own advice. Remember, you're observing only. I hate the thought of Hilda being responsible for this. She should take a leaf out of

Tristram's book and rescue cute seals and cuddle them to death.'

They parted and James studied the paperback books on a twirling display stand. Out of the corner of his eye, he noticed Mr Atherton, the blind man, attempting to cross the road. He bounded over.

'I say, do you want a hand?' James allowed Atherton to feel his arm and the sleeve of his shirt.

Atherton sniffed. 'My name's Atherton. And you're Lord Harrington.'

'Good Lord, how on earth did you know that?'

He snorted. 'No one round 'ere talks like you do for a start. That's a quality cotton shirt so you're not poor and that aftershave, I clocked that the first day you were here when you were speaking with Cardew. What's it called? I like to know in case I smell it again. Helps me identify people.'

'It's called Sportsman. My wife purchased a bottle when she was last in London.'

'All you get round here is sweat or Old

Spice. And you're wearing a fetching straw hat.'

James stood back. 'Now how could you possibly know that?'

Atherton chuckled. 'I passed you in the street just now. You told your wife you were glad you brought your hat. I presumed you were wearing it and that it was straw. Anything else in this weather would be a little warm. Prob'ly a Panama style, am I right?'

'You are. Do you model yourself on Sherlock Holmes?'

'I do not, although I have someone who reads Conan Doyle to me. A splendid writer and an ingenious character.' Atherton bowed as if receiving an ovation from an audience. 'I may not have my sight but my other senses are firing on all cylinders. Speaking of which, you have the Austin Healey, don't you?'

They spoke for a couple of minutes about cars and how Atherton could pinpoint the type of engine and vehicle once he'd heard it a few times. James peered over the man's shoulder and noticed Tristram heading toward the cliff path, en route, he presumed, to another rescue.

'Mr Atherton, you were standing by Flora Chenery when she was taken, weren't you?'

'Oh yes.'

'Was there something that came to mind?'

He chuckled. 'You doing a bit of sleuthing yourself are you?'

James insisted he was merely interested. 'The kidnappings do intrigue me but that's all.'

'Not what I've heard. But, yes, I heard a couple of things. Flora'd been chatting to me for a while and her voice faded a little. I didn't put any store by it 'coz it was noisy. I knew she hadn't moved on because I could feel her close so I thought something had caught her eye. I felt her arm move up and then she stepped back. I thought it was funny that she didn't say cheerio. She normally does.'

James reiterated his offer to help Atherton across the road. As they reached the other side, Atherton said, 'I heard a van too.'

'A van?'

'Yeah, it's used by the seal sanctuary. Tristram and Hans use it a lot but it must have been someone else because they were in the parade.'

'Are you absolutely sure?'

'I heard them go by — chatting they were about setting out to rescue something.'

'Was that before or after you heard the van?'

'Before, why?'

James asked if Inspector Wormstone had asked him any questions.

Atherton said that he hadn't; that he'd spoken to a police woman who hadn't been terribly specific with her questions and more fascinated by his Braille books. 'D'you think it's important then? It's not either of them. Tristram and Hans wouldn't hurt a fly.'

James thanked him and said he had to be on his way. That's what had troubled him about Hilda and Debra. How would they know how to mix a drug and inject it? Tristram and Hans had access to the vet's facilities and the training to mix a compound to drug the men. He'd told them they did everything at the sanctuary. He turned to cross the road. Hans, driving the sanctuary van, drove by in the direction of the cliff-top and waved. Perhaps he was wrong but instinct told James to quicken his pace.

25

Although he wanted to stride out purposely, James opted to ramble up the slope to avoid getting too close to Tristram. A number of walkers passed him and signalled a hello. He remained easily out of sight and began to think back on his time up here earlier in the day with Stephen.

He recalled how they'd discovered Flora, shaken by her ordeal, the old tin mine with the hidden lantern and the brand new padlock. And Mr Atherton was adamant the van he heard belonged to the seal sanctuary.

Was Tristram or Hans really involved? Both came across as gentle men, reluctant to harm the smallest of animals. But then Tristram had told them about Hans' run-in with Colm which sounded like quite an altercation. Plus the humiliation of being sacked.

Both were strapping lads, capable of

manhandling a dead weight; were they in it together? They were both heading in this direction. Or perhaps they were simply doing their job; rescuing a stricken creature. Had he got it all wrong?

As the path levelled out, the tall chimney came into view. Ramblers continued hiking along the main footpath. James stood and watched. Tristram had veered off the track and was heading toward the mine. He swallowed hard and checked his watch. Half past three. He reminded himself that he was to observe only and report back to Wormstone.

He scanned the area; it was daytime, people were about. There wouldn't be any danger, not with so many tourists here. The ice cream van was up ahead and he wandered across and ordered a choc-ice. The vendor remembered him from that morning and joked that he must like it here.

James half-smiled, all the while keeping an eye on the mine. 'It's a lovely view. I thought I'd take some more photographs.' He held his camera up as if to prove his statement. 'Do you see many people going toward the mine there?'

'Not really. One or two are like you, take pictures, but they're mainly walkers or tourists come out for the walk. Jonah Quinn strides along here when he's not open and that odd woman with the saucepan on her head is always charging about upsetting the customers.'

'What about people from the sanctuary? I hear they're up here rescuing birds and suchlike.'

'Oh yes, that Tristram, he was hanging off the cliffs a few days ago rescuing some puffins. Nice bloke. Yes, he's up here a few times and that mate of his, Hans. The cliffs just along there are home to hundreds of birds. There you go — one Choc Ice.'

He paid for his ice cream and loitered for twenty minutes. Some walkers vacated a wooden bench and he sat down to admire the scenery, all the while keeping the mine in sight. After forty minutes, he checked his watch and wondered if Tristram had simply walked back to the village another way. He hoped that he had. He liked Tristram and didn't want to think of him being responsible for this crime. And there was no sign of the van. Had Hans picked him up and continued on?

He pushed himself up and decided to return the way he came. Packing the camera in his rucksack, he took one last look at the mine and stopped.

Tristram had appeared.

James sat back down and looked out to sea. He waited a full minute before turning. When he did, Tristram had joined the path and was heading back to the village. The bag he'd been carrying was gone.

James got up and strolled across to the mine. He swung open the old door and put his ear against the new one. He heard nothing. But a mine is deep. If the men were down there, they could be anywhere. He held the padlock in his hands. Bert had shown him how he picked locks some time ago. He hadn't taken much notice because it appalled him that his friend would think that it was a task he'd require. Little did he know that it was to come in handy all these years later. Back then, Bert had used a hair clip. Beth used them all the time. He checked his rucksack to see if he had anything like that but he hadn't. Time was pressing. If the men were in there, they would need help and possibly a medical team.

He shrugged the rucksack back on and half-jogged back to Polpennarth where he discovered Beth eating some cockles in vinegar. She held the plate up for him and he took a couple.

'Hilda is still in that house. I said I needed some fresh air and came out. I was going to finish these and go back to the hotel. You were a long time; Tristram went past a little while ago. He waved as he went by.'

James sat beside her and gave her a wary look.

'What's the matter?'

'Not here. You'll never be able to hide your surprise. Come on.' He led her further along the promenade toward their hotel. When they'd reached a quiet area he signalled for her to remain quiet. 'Tristram is our man.'

Beth's jaw dropped and her eyes

searched for an explanation. They leaned on the railing and looked toward the beach. James went through his conversation with Atherton and where Tristram had led him.

'It all makes sense, Beth.'

'It doesn't to me.'

'Nibbin suggested this was to do with behaviour. The simple fact of the matter is that Tristram hates anything to be hurt. Not just animals.'

'Exactly. So why put those men through all of this?'

'Because of what those men are, Beth.'

Realisation struck her. 'Of course. Because they abuse their wives.'

'I think Hilda's been chatting about her WI women and how a few of them are treated by their husbands. We're assuming it's her because she's rather forthright and we can imagine her doing it, albeit with the best of intentions, although that doesn't excuse it. This business about him hating animals being hurt doesn't just run to seals. I believe it runs to people too. It's incensed him so much that he feels he has to do something about it. You remember

Hilda told you that his parents split up and that he then lived with his mother and grandmother.'

'You're thinking they separated because his father abused them?'

'Exactly.'

'But what on earth is he solving by kidnapping them?'

James shrugged. 'I don't know. Giving those women some respite?'

'Or teaching those men a lesson. We should go straight to Wormstone although he's not there at the moment. He drove out of the village about ten minutes ago.'

James chewed his lip. Beth glared at him, reminding him again of his promise to simply observe.

'Beth, I want to get into that mine now. Do you have a hair pin?'

She frowned at him as he explained why. She opened her handbag and brought out a couple with another reminder that he shouldn't be getting involved.

James gave her hand a reassuring squeeze. 'He's not likely to go back up there so soon. I think that's the light we

365

saw when we were out on the boat. He goes there during the day and last thing at night. I'm going to get the car and drive up that dirt track where the ambulance went. If you see Tristram heading toward that coastal path again, go straight to PC Innes and tell him to get up there.'

Beth clasped his hand. 'I'm getting Innes regardless.' She dragged him across to the grocery store.

'Where are we going?'

'You have a torch in the car. Those men could be dying of thirst. The least you can do is take some lemonade or something.'

He stopped and pulled her around. 'You mean you don't mind me putting myself in danger?'

'Of course I mind. But your saving grace is that you didn't talk me out of going straight to the police. They may even get there before you.'

With ample supplies of soft drinks and chocolate bars James gave her hand a reassuring squeeze. 'I'll see Innes up there.' He crossed the road and headed toward the hotel to pick the car up.

* ★ ★ ★

A brisk five-minute walk saw Beth arrive at the police station a little flustered. It was a converted terraced house with a blue light above the doorway. She stepped into the hallway which served as the reception area where there were two wooden chairs for visitors and a narrow desk with no one behind it. She rang the small bell on the side several times and studied the posters on the wall.

They displayed various images: photographs of missing cats, a reward for a stolen bicycle and an advert for the Cornish legends festival. Further along, in a locked display case were photographs of Colm Fiske, Bevis Allan and Enoch Pengilly. She moved closer.

Colm had an old-fashioned look about him, as if he belonged in the 1930s. He smoked a pipe, had two days of stubble and wore a black Greek fisherman's hat. He looked every inch the man that people spoke of — a man's man who stood no nonsense.

Alongside, the picture of Bevis showed

a much younger individual. This appeared to be a picture taken on a holiday and showed a fresh-faced man with thick dark hair combed back. He wore a white T-shirt and a jacket with the collar up. Beth leant in. He was trying to be something he wasn't and she felt a little sorry for him. He idolised the moody celebrities of the day and she imagined he not only dressed to copy the style but took on the persona as well. Colm Fiske had a natural moodiness about him and if Bevis saw him as a role model, he would likely try to change his personality to match him.

She was familiar with the arrogance of Enoch and the image staring back at her from the picture was of a hard, stubborn man with wispy hair, white stubble and a face aged and weathered by the sea.

'Can I help you?'

Beth turned and acknowledged the young policewoman who stood behind the desk. Her uniform was pristine and its buttons gleamed. She held up a mug. 'Just went to get some tea.'

'I wondered if I could speak with PC Innes?'

'You can, Miss, but not for an hour.'

Beth clenched her handbag. 'Oh dear.'

'Anything I can help with?'

'Do you know where he goes for his lunch?'

The young woman said that he normally walked to the end of the harbour wall. 'He takes his sandwiches and watches the boats going in and out.' Her brow knitted together. 'Are you all right, Miss?'

Beth did her best to breathe calmly as she asked if there was anyone else in the building and when would Inspector Wormstone be back.

'Only me in the building and the Inspector's popped across to Penzance.'

'Are you allowed to close the police station and come with me?'

She looked horrified and told her it was against orders to lock the police station. Beth stemmed her rising panic and told her not to worry. 'I'll catch up with PC Innes on my way back to the hotel.'

When she left the building, she ran.

26

James wedged open the dilapidated wooden door and turned the padlock on the new entrance toward him. He opened up the hair pin and widened it slightly as Bert had shown him. Poking the two ends into the lock he fiddled back and forth with no clue as to whether he was doing this right or not.

He muttered the odd damn and blast and after two minutes he let the padlock fall from his hands. He then admonished himself for being an idiot as a new idea sprang to mind. He dashed over to the Austin and opened the boot where he knew he had a few basic tools. He grabbed a hammer and returned to his mission with fresh purpose. After a few wayward swings, the hammer came down and the padlock broke. He unclipped it and threw it to one side.

Jamming the door open with a large rock, he picked up the unlit lantern and entered the tunnel. Even after a few yards, darkness descended. He switched his torch on and examined the lie of the land. Ahead was one tunnel with a gradual slope down. The remnants of tramlines were visible and fallen rubble looked to make exploring difficult. He made a start and, after about twenty yards, he came across a lift cage and grimaced. After heaving a resigned sigh, he reached across to the buttons that operated and pressed a couple. To his utter relief, the electrics didn't respond. He let a silent phew; the last thing he wanted was to descend further.

He continued gingerly on the downward slope, careful not to trip on stones and rocks scattering his path. After covering around fifty yards, he turned. The entrance was out of sight although he could see a speck of daylight from the open door. Looking ahead he found himself cursing again as the tunnel gave him a choice of direction — left or straight on. The torch's beam swung down both avenues. There was nothing to indicate which way to go. He continued forward, stopped, aimed his torch to the ground and relaxed as he observed footprints and evidence of stones being cleared away. He continued straight on.

It was cool here and the quiet was disconcerting. Darkness held no fear for him but underground tunnels were not somewhere he'd willingly go. And this darkness was something he'd not experienced before. This was black; as black as coal. He recalled his father once going potholing around the caves in Cheddar Gorge in Somerset. Although he was happy to explore the opening of the caves, he left his father to descend into the depths, preferring instead to take in the views above ground.

He shone his torch on his watch. He'd been down here ten minutes and guessed he'd covered a couple of hundred yards. He stopped and listened. Kushal Patel had once told him that in order to listen, you must slow your heart beat and now he understood why. In such complete silence, there was nothing; no resonance, no echo. Every sound bombarding him was internal; blood rushing, heart pumping and tinny sounds in his ears that he'd never noticed before. He breathed slowly and consciously ordered himself to relax and calm down. It took around a minute to do so but he noticed the difference.

Remembering his conversation with Mr Atherton and calling on different senses, he switched off his torch and listened. He remained still and silent. His breathing became shallow. The coolness of the mine sent goose bumps across him. He didn't think you could smell dryness but, at this moment, that's the thought that came to mind. Ancient air with nowhere to go.

Then a shuffle.

His eyes shot open and his heart leapt from the starting line. He swallowed hard. It was a short distance away but he'd heard it. His breathing quickened. What if it was an animal? Do animals live in old tin mines? He shook the thought from his head. Tristram wasn't here. He had nothing to lose by shouting out. He switched his torch on.

'Hello?'

The greeting echoed down the tunnel.

A muffled shout came back. James screwed up his face as if it would make him hear better.

'Hello?'

Louder now and more than one person. Feeling assured, he continued on. The muffled shouts were closer now.

'Don't worry, I'm coming!'

James' pulse raced and a sense of purpose swept over him followed by a rush of adrenalin. In two minutes, he'd entered a natural opening and ahead of him were Colm, Bevis and Enoch. He swept the torch beam across them and they glanced away from the brightness. They sat on the floor with their hands and feet tied. All were gagged by thick cotton rags. Their eyes expressed so many emotions it was difficult to gauge what they were feeling; fear, relief, exhaustion. Colm, in particular, appeared drained. The air smelt stale, of body odour and rotten food.

He squatted down, took some matches from his pocket and lit the lantern. The cave was a large one with two tunnels threading off. To one side there appeared to be a recent roof collapse. Above, he glimpsed several cracks and fissures. A sense of urgency now took over as he shrugged off his rucksack and took out a Swiss army knife. Levering free the biggest blade, he shuffled along and cut the bindings around their ankles.

'Lean forward.' He sliced through the ties on their wrists. They loosened their own gags.

Colm's eyes welled. His thanks came out in a sigh as he massaged his wrists and legs. Bevis simply closed his eyes and rested his head back on the wall. Enoch stared straight ahead and showed little in the way of emotion. James brought out the bottles of lemonade and watched as they gulped the liquid down as if their life depended on it. He then threw them each a Mars bar.

'Here, get that down you. I'm afraid I didn't have the forethought to get pasties.'

The comment lightened the mood for Colm. He'd just enough energy to smile but ripped open the Mars bar and took a huge bite from it.

Bevis turned his head toward him. 'Are you the police?'

'No, I'm afraid not but the police are on their way. I thought they'd be here by now but not to worry. You know who's responsible for this?'

'Tristram,' Colm replied wearily.

'He wanted to teach us a lesson,' said Bevis who looked, to James, like a small child next to his companions. 'Teach us we were wrong.' He glanced across to Colm. 'And we were wrong.'

James sat on a large rock. 'Wrong about what?'

The three men exchanged a wary look between them.

Bevis sniffed back his tears. 'Wrong about how-about how we treat — '

'How you treat your wives.' James finished the sentence as a statement more than a question.

Enoch was breathing heavily. 'It's our way. It's nothing to do with Tristram and his do-gooding ways. Who's he to tell us what to do? What goes on between a man and wife is nothing to do with anyone else.'

James noticed blood seeping through the hem of Colm's trousers. 'You're hurt.'

'That bloody roof collapsed yesterday. Some stones just caught me on the ankle.'

Enoch shifted and winced as he did so. 'We should get out of here.' He sank back. 'I 'aven't got the energy.'

James told them to sit tight. 'Let the lemonade and chocolate get into your system. It'll give you a lift. Five minutes won't make any difference.' He looked at the rocks structure above and sent up a silent prayer that it would hold. He studied their faces and frowned. They had slight bruising and red marks across their cheeks. 'Did Tristram do this?'

Bevis explained that Tristram was doing to them what they did to their wives. He sniffed back his tears as he spoke. 'At first he didn't speak. Kept our blindfolds on, but when he gave us a drink, we asked who it was and why he was doing it? Then he took the blindfolds off. He told us to see how we liked it; that they're women that love us and look after us and why do we do that to someone we love?'

Enoch snorted and looked away. The man was set in his ways and James wondered if he would ever change in the way that Tristram would like him to. He guessed he probably wouldn't. Out of the three wives affected, Edith was the only one who had reacted with genuine horror that her beloved companion was in danger. Enoch was right: it was their way and where he and Edith were concerned, nothing was likely to change.

'If you're not the police,' said Bevis, 'who are you?'

'My name's James Harrington. I'm on holiday here with some friends and stumbled across this mystery. It's simply luck that I worked out a few clues.'

'Is Debra all right?'

James ran his hands through his hair. How on earth does he answer that? That Debra now loves her life as an unshackled woman and was enjoying a freedom that Bevis doesn't give her? 'She's bearing up,' he said with a degree of guilt.

Colm rubbed his ankles and asked James how Evelyn was. He couldn't make eye contact and James knew he was scared to receive an answer. He remembered the quotes Nibbin had given him and her assertion that it wouldn't do the men any harm to be in the mine. The fear he'd seen in Evelyn's eyes prompted him to be more truthful.

'Colm, your wife is terrified of you.' He looked at Bevis. 'When you first went missing, Debra was beside herself and not for the right reasons. She was fearful she was meeting you in the wrong place. Frightened out of her wits that if she was late, what the consequences would be. I presume that anything that isn't quite right will result in a slap or some verbal abuse; a late dinner, a flippant comment perhaps?'

Colm and Bevis had the grace to look away. Admitting guilt was a difficult thing to do and these two struggled. They stared at their feet, shifted about and lowered their gaze; classic signs of shame and remorse where James was concerned. Enoch simply stared and gave nothing away.

James rooted around in his rucksack and found some more chocolate. He handed it to the men. 'I was told that when you were found I was to tell you something and now I understand why.'

'Told by who?' said Colm.

'That's by the way. The message is more important than the messenger.' James was loathed to reveal Nibbin's identity. The meaning of these quotes would be lost in derogatory comments about the hermit.

He turned to Enoch. 'Enoch, the message for you is that no man should bring children into the world who's unwilling to persevere to the end in their nature and education.'

Enoch turned away. James detected the first signs of vulnerability. Tears formed in the man's eyes.

'I believe that you and Edith have a solid marriage, Enoch. I don't agree one iota with treating the woman you love with anything but kindness and respect. You, on the other hand, are a man with an entirely different background to me. You work hard, you put your life on the line each time you go to sea. You expect those around you to toe the line. Edith does that. She loves you for who and what you are. She even tolerates your moods. But she cannot forgive you for driving your daughter away. It is your temper, isn't it, that drove her away?'

The old man barely acknowledged him. He stared at the ground.

'You're a man of few words, Enoch, and I don't expect you to expand on your history. Like you say, it isn't my business. But I think Tristram was trying to get you to understand why she left. It was you that drove her away. Tristram never knew his father. He drove them away and Tristram, I think, regrets a missing father.'

The man remained still.

'Talk to her, Enoch. Bring her back into your lives. She's a woman, making her way in the world. I'm sure she'd love to include her parents in that.'

James studied him. How he wished Kushal was here. He'd be much better at this sort of thing.

Bevis finished his second chocolate bar and was beginning to look a little brighter. His expression was one of trepidation as he asked James: 'Did this person have a message for me?'

'Yes, although if my memory serves me well, it's not the full quote. This person clearly observed you and Debra and gave me an extract. But, yes, the message is, if there is such a thing as a good marriage, it is because it resembles friendship.'

Bevis caught his breath and nodded. 'Whoever told you that is right. Me and Debs were good friends when we met. We did everything together.'

The silence was a thoughtful one that James didn't break. He'd learned that silence was a good thing; people gave consideration to things before speaking and this was exactly what Bevis was doing now. The young man gave him an earnest look.

'I thought that's what men did? I saw Colm and some of the others. They told me that to get respect, you 'ave to show who's in charge. Deb had started in the WI and that Hilda woman was telling her to keep her independence. She didn't always have dinner on the table, she was late getting stuff done and always had things to do in the village. Colm said he wouldn't stand for that.'

'And do you like what you've become?'

His shoulders slumped. 'Tristram dished it out to us. I got scared when he came down here.' He looked a beaten man. 'This is how my Debs feels, in'it?'

James closed his eyes. 'It's how she did feel, yes. I'm afraid that you going missing has seen a change in her. I believe you may see a different Debra when you go back. The one that you fell in love with I would imagine. You're going to have to convince her that you've changed.'

Bevis begged James for reassurance that she would believe him. 'I think the world of her, I can't live without her. She's everything to me, I want to have kids with her.'

James held up a hand. 'You need to be telling her that, not me.'

Colm had retreated into his own world; a world of reflection. He threw the sweet wrapper on the floor. 'I've lost Evelyn. She'll never forgive me. I can't help being the way I am. I can't change.'

James went across and sat next to him.

He handed Colm a piece of paper. 'This is what I was told to tell you. I wrote it down because I knew I wouldn't remember it. I was given a shortened version. It's a quote from an ancient philosopher. I looked it up — this is the full text.'

Colm's calloused hands took it. 'Anybody can become angry — that is easy, but to be angry with the right person and to the right degree and at the right time and for the right purpose, and in the right way — that is not within everybody's power and is not easy.' He looked at James and shrugged his shoulders. 'I don't understand. I'm not an educated man, what does this mean?'

'Colm, if you really want to change, you can. You have to want to, though.'

The man listened.

'If you want to keep Evelyn, you have to work at it. You're going to have to consciously remind yourself, every day, to be patient, tolerant and respectful. If you have a battle to fight, fight it with the right person. Were you happy to have Tristram abuse you for the slightest misdemeanour?'

A shake of the head.

'Then remember that's how Evelyn feels and still feels when she's around you. She's terrified of you — even now, she's worried that you'll take this out on her.'

Colm grabbed James' arm. 'But it's not her fault, it's Tristram's.'

James peeled away his grip. 'You must take responsibility for your actions. Do you want a companion who's scared of you or one that's allowed to laugh alongside you? Someone that you look forward to seeing at the end of the day; a woman who loves you, who looks after your every need and would do anything for you?'

James checked his watch. Where on earth were the police? He'd enjoyed being the ancient philosopher and prayed to God that some of it had sunk in but he had nothing more to add. Who was he to tell people how to run their lives? Bevis, who he believed would learn something from this, asked him if he were married.

'Yes, I am. Her name's Beth and she's not only my wife but my best friend. I could never commit myself to someone for the rest of my life who wasn't my friend.'

Although he was weary, James felt that he was getting through to Bevis and in some respects, Colm. The unacceptable kidnappings by Tristram had served a purpose. What a shame that Kushal wasn't here. Not only could he have helped these men but he was sure that Tristram needed guidance too. Although he seemed so happy and carefree, it was clear that his experience as a child had stayed with him. His ears pricked. Footsteps. He didn't realise how tense he was until that moment. He turned to welcome the police.

But his delight was soon shattered when he looked up to see Tristram.

27

Bevis backed against the wall, his feet scrambling to push him further than he could. Colm edged away. Enoch remained silent and still.

James pushed himself up and rubbed the dust from his hands. His heart was in his mouth as he spoke. 'Ah Tristram, I was just beginning to wonder what your plans were?'

Tristram's angry glare darted from James to the three men. He scowled at the loose bindings and empty bottles. James watched as the young man struggled to think through his next step. If he tried anything now, he was against four men. Yes, three of them were exhausted but it's surprising how much strength one can find when coming up against adversity.

Tristram turned to James. 'You shouldn't 'ave done that. You shouldn't 'ave untied them. They have to stay here.'

'To what purpose, Tristram? What're you going to do?'

'Teach 'em a lesson, that's what. Teach 'em you can't treat people like they do.' He jabbed a finger at James. 'Tie 'em back up.'

James straightened his shoulders and looked him in the eye. 'I'm not doing that. These men need medical attention.'

'They had food; I didn't starve 'em.'

Colm sprang to his feet. 'You might just as well 'ave. Half a pasty here, half a sandwich there. I need to eat, I need to see my Evelyn.'

'And do what?' Tristram scowled. 'Make her suffer like you always do? Little digs here, little digs there, sapping her confidence?'

Enoch eased himself up. 'ENOUGH.'

The bellow silenced everyone and appeared a good deal louder within the confines of the mine. As the echo subsided, James started at an unnerving *pop* above them. Their eyes turned up to where a new rupture ran the length of the cave.

Enoch turned. 'We need to get out. Now.'

'No,' said Tristram, his eyes darted back and forth, desperately seeking a way to keep control.

James yanked him to one side. 'It's not safe, Tristram, you'll get us all killed.'

Dust floated down; Bevis leapt up as a chunk of rock gave way and showered them with rubble. James turned and ordered everyone out. Colm, Bevis and Enoch scrambled over the debris. James went to head up the tunnel but Enoch's grip twisted him back. He swung round to see Tristram's leg trapped under a slab.

'Oh lord.'

The young man winced in agony as the colour drained from his face. 'I think my ankle's broken.'

To James' astonishment, Enoch, Bevis and Colm dashed forward to help and between them heaved the slab away to pull their captor free. Colm manoeuvred Tristram into a fireman's lift and headed up the tunnel, followed by his fellow captives.

As further rubble began to fall, James grabbed his rucksack and sprinted up the tunnel while considering the actions of the men. If they were happy to rescue their kidnapper, things must be looking up.

Emerging into dazzling sunlight, the men stumbled from the mine, shielded their eyes from the brightness and gratefully breathed in the fresh air. Colm eased Tristram off his back, fell to the ground and closed his eyes.

James squatted alongside Tristram. 'Those men just saved your life.'

Tristram acknowledged James exhaustedly. The man rolled his eyes. 'I don't know what I was going to do, Lord Harrington. I wanted to teach these men a lesson; I didn't know what else would do it. Hilda kept telling me about these women who came to the WI; how frightened they were. They had bruises on their arms, and I saw Evelyn once with a black eye. I hated it.' He turned to Colm. 'How can you do that to someone? She's half your size. She's a woman for God's sake.'

Colm kept his eyes shut, then covered them with his arm.

James asked Tristram about his father.

'That's where this stems from, isn't it?'

'Dad hit Mum all the time. When I was ten, I hit him with a poker. He'd ordered me to stoke the fire, pushed me toward the flames. He'd slapped Mum across the face for serving dinner late. I couldn't stand it anymore. I stoked the fire with the poker, let it get good and hot, then, when he was close enough, I swung out and hit him. Twice. He slapped me so hard I went flying across the room.'

James winced. He couldn't begin to imagine the effect that would have on such a young lad.

'Dad stormed out and Mum went straight upstairs and packed our bags. We went to live with Gran. She was strong and assertive but loving — a big bundle of love and support.'

'Like Hilda?'

He gave an enthusiastic nod. 'Yeah, like Hilda.'

'You can't kidnap everyone, Tristram. You can't right every wrong.'

Tristram ran his hands across his head and blinked back his frustration. 'I know. I know. This got me so mad though. It seemed a good idea at the time. I knew I'd have to let them go, face the consequences. I just wanted them to know what it's like — to live in fear. To be so terrified of what might happen that you're physically sick. To shake like a jelly as soon as that person comes in the room.' He wiped tears as they trickled down. 'I always wanted to be a son that went for a pint with his dad. I don't even know where he is but if I saw him now, I'd spit in his face.'

James glanced at Enoch. The old fisherman examined the ocean but it was clear he was listening. James peered over Tristram's shoulder and closed his eyes in relief as PC Innes came into view. An ambulance was parking up to one side. Behind Innes was Beth, who rushed to his side.

'Oh, James, are you all right?'

'I'm perfectly well, darling, and I believe that with a little sustenance and help from the medical team, these men will survive their ordeal.' He turned to Innes. 'Be careful with your man. I believe he has a broken ankle.'

Tristram held his hands out for Innes to pull him up and snap the handcuffs on. He hopped on one leg and faced the men. 'I'm sorry. I'm really sorry.'

James pulled him close and whispered. 'If it's any consolation, I do think you made a difference. But I wouldn't make a habit of this sort of thing.'

Tristram forced a smile and allowed himself to be taken away. Two ambulance men scurried toward the three men.

Beth linked an arm with him and flicked grime away from his clothes and hair. 'Are they going to be all right?'

'No physical injuries, but I believe those men are walking away from here with something to think about.' He turned to her. 'You took your time. I was beginning to wonder where on earth you were.'

Beth described her visit to the police station, saying that Wormstone was not due back until later. 'PC Innes was at lunch and sits as far away on the harbour wall as you can possibly get. I didn't realise it would take me so long.'

He laughed. 'All's well that ends well.

Let's get in the Austin and go to that farm. I know I look a mess but I could murder a decent cup of tea and soak up some of this sunshine.'

28

The following evening, James, Beth and the Merryweathers were seated in The Sardine. Jonah had decorated the table with candles, colourful place mats and thick cotton napkins.

It was early evening and Luke and Mark had stayed with the caravan site owners to help make fairy cakes for an upcoming birthday party later in the week. Anne playfully punched James on the arm.

'Beth and I were ensconced in that house helping the WI and all the time you were having all the fun.'

'I'd hardly call it fun,' said James.

'M–me and the boys had fun on our f–fishing trip. They caught a d–dab and they had it for tea.'

James congratulated him and suggested they all go fishing when they got back to Cavendish. 'We'll get the lads on the riverbank and see if we can nab a trout.'

Jonah approached and distributed menus to them. 'I can't believe Tristram was responsible for those kidnappings. He'd have been last on my list.'

'A–Agatha Christie says that she always goes for the most unlikely suspect when writing her novels. I–it clearly happens in real life too.'

They ordered their drinks and James insisted they push the boat out. 'Have a cocktail. Jonah, you have some spirits behind the bar, don't you?'

'I've a few, yes. I can't do the unusual things but I can do the popular ones.'

After some discussion, they settled on Vodka Martinis. Jonah jotted the order down and added that he was secretly quite pleased about what Tristram had done. He slipped his pencil behind his ear.

'I've not been a saint myself but hitting women is cowardly. I'll get your drinks.'

James and Beth updated them on what had happened since they'd seen the Merryweathers the previous evening. That morning, they'd provided a statement to Inspector Wormstone and, under his glaring eye, received a dressing down about going off half-cock and entering the mine.

'You should have waited' he'd said. 'A few hours wouldn't have made any difference. You could have got yourself killed. I spoke to DCI Lane about you earlier and he said you don't pay any heed to the authorities.'

James had accepted the telling off with a bemused look.

Anne was of the same mind. 'You had two attempts on your life just a couple of days ago. If Tristram had gone down that mine armed, well, I don't want to think about it.'

'You're forgetting something important,' said James. 'Tristram hates violence. He doesn't like to hurt anything or anyone although he was taking a chance cutting my brake-line. He knew I understood cars but I don't think he realised how dangerous it was. Snipping a brake cable is just as dangerous as cutting it. The attempts were supposed to be scare tactics. He asked that boat owner to speed by as closely as possible. He might have tied me up in that mine but he wouldn't have killed me. It's not in his nature. He said he was physically sick when he slapped those men in the mine.'

'But how did he manage to lure these men away?' asked Anne. 'That was what piqued your interest in the first place; I mean, he's not a big man.'

'He'd planned it out. He'd already established a place to keep them. The tin mine was nearby and he'd found it easy to navigate. He kept Colm in a different part of the mine until the police had done their cliff-top search. They did check it but not thoroughly. And the festival helped with his plans. Tristram took part in all of the parades but had his van parked up a side-street. He was in costume the whole time and had medication on him from the vet's office up at the Sanctuary. Where Colm and Bevis were concerned, he crept up behind them, injected them with something to make them drowsy and led them to the van where he blindfolded them. There were so many people milling around that no one took any notice. He had the needles up his sleeve. No one saw anything and the dose was high enough that they were willing to be led anywhere.

'With Flora, it was a little difficult. She wasn't in the parade but he left the procession just after he passed her, hid in a recess and then came up behind her.'

'A–and Mr Atherton recognised the v–van you say?'

James confirmed that the senses of a blind man were far superior. 'He felt Flora beside him. Even felt it when she reached for her neck. That was probably when Tristram injected her. There are relatively few vehicles down here and he knows them all. A hum in the engine, the pop in an exhaust. He even mimicked the sanctuary's Morris Minor. Quite extraordinary.'

Jonah came to the table with a tray of Vodka Martinis. He took their order of Dover sole, fresh garden peas and new potatoes. 'Be with you shortly.'

Anne questioned why Flora was released.

'Don't forget that Hilda was Tristram's fount of information. She'd told him about Flora and her nagging ways and he'd taken it the wrong way. Hilda was with Vic when he'd reported her missing. She told Tristram that Vic was devastated. I think he realised that he'd made a mistake.' He raised a glass. 'Listen, that's enough about mysteries. We're sitting here for a reason. Stephen and Anne, you are two wonderful people who've become valued and close friends. Happy anniversary and may you have many more to come.'

'And,' Beth added giving Jonah a quick wave, 'we have something for you that we purchased when we were in St Ives. Hopefully, it'll remind you of our holiday.'

Jonah reached down behind the counter and brought out a brightly wrapped frame. Anne clapped her hands and accepted it from him.

'How lovely. Stephen, help me open it.'

They tore the paper off to reveal a beautiful painting of Polpennarth and the coastline beyond.

'I–it's lovely, thank you s–so much. That'll take pride of place in the f–front room.'

Jonah placed a bottle of sparkling wine on the table. 'On the house, your Lordship. An anniversary gift and a well done for solving the mystery.' He returned to the kitchen.

'Have you seen Hilda?' asked Anne.

'Yes,' said Beth. 'She's as proud as punch of Tristram.'

The Merryweathers exchanged astounded looks.

'She didn't realise what he was up to, of course, but she's going to stand by him.'

James added that the villagers he'd spoken to were, on the whole, supportive of what he did. 'He's a popular chap and according to the Inspector, a lot of them have been giving him grief about charging him. The WI ladies have even signed a petition.'

'H–how extraordinary! What about th–the men who were kidnapped? I'm sure they don't f–feel the same.'

'That's the odd thing. They haven't pressed charges,' said James. 'They appear to have come out of this experience changed. The fact they dashed to

Tristram's help when he was trapped in the mine was quite a turning point I think.'

He went on to explain how Bevis and Debra had already departed for a couple of days away to fix their problems. 'I don't believe Enoch will change much but he has contacted his daughter, hasn't he Beth?'

'I spoke with Edith this morning. She was one person who was devastated by what Tristram had done and she's horrified that the details of their marriage are common knowledge, but, she had to admit she's delighted that Enoch's made the first move in repairing his relationship with their daughter.'

'A—and Colm?'

James explained that Colm had his work cut out. 'Learning to be a more tolerant, patient individual will take time and we must pray that Colm has the discipline to see that through.'

As if on cue, Colm and Evelyn entered the restaurant. Evelyn was dressed in a beautiful sky blue summer dress with a blue cardigan. Colm was in jeans and a loose short-sleeved shirt. He'd shaved and his demeanour was that of someone out on a first date, a man trying his best to impress.

Evelyn still had an air of suspicion around her; as if this new attitude was bound to end once the novelty had worn off. Colm struck a rather nervous pose and held out a chair for her. He avoided eye contact with them and sat opposite his wife where he reached across and held her hand with an apprehensive smile.

'L–Let's hope they're able to m–make a go of it.'

'And presumably,' said Anne, 'Tristram is going to jail.'

Their dinners came out as James explained that although the men hadn't pressed charges, obviously some charges would be made. 'I'm not sure how the courts will view it. The Inspector believes he'll get off lightly. His boss at the Sanctuary has promised him his job back if he has to go to jail, such is the popularity of Tristram Roscarrock. The fishermen are not so forgiving but they're in the minority.

'But something happened down that mine that none of us will understand and those men will not speak about it to a stranger. I can only assume it was of some good, otherwise they would surely have pressed charges.'

As they ate, they reminisced about their holiday; the people they'd met, the delicious food and drink, the vibrant festival, the characters and, above all, the beautiful views and coastline. James felt in his pocket.

'We have one more evening left. I've got us all tickets for The Minack tomorrow night. Luke and Mark too, I hope that's all right?'

The Minack was a unique theatre built into the cliff-tops just along from Penzance. It had been built back in the 1930s and offered panoramic views of the Atlantic as a backdrop to the stone stage.

'That is the perfect end to our anniversary,' said Anne, 'thank you.'

'Y–yes, I'm so p–pleased you came. And you didn't g–get withdrawal symptoms from playing the sleuth.'

'And you go back to a new kitchen,' added Anne.

'Goodness,' said James, 'I'd forgotten all about that.'

Beth said that she hadn't and was looking forward to trying out her new cooker. 'I may have a go at a Cornish pasty. Doesn't your grandmother have a recipe like that?'

'The closest thing we have is the Hiker's Lunch. Pasties are synonymous with Cornwall. I think every region has its own dish. Granny used to do something called Sussex Pond pudding.'

Anne pulled a face. 'That doesn't sound very appetising.'

'It's an odd recipe but tastes better than its name. It's called a Pond Pudding because it has the unfortunate trait of looking like a pond when you dish it up. I'll give you the recipe when we get home and you can give it a try.'

'And,' said Beth, 'your granny's scone recipe is just as delicious as those we had at the farmhouse.'

'Yes, I think you're right, although I may add a dash more vanilla. That made all the difference.'

At the end of the evening, Stephen knocked on the table. 'James, w—were those lights you saw definitely o—out to sea?'

'That's a strange one. Wormstone said he'd got onto the coastguard and there were no boats in that area at the time. The regulars repeated this story about ghostly fishermen giving a warning. I obviously saw Tristram's lantern on the cliff-top but I'm certain there were also lights out to sea.'

Stephen suggested it was probably a small fishing boat that had gone off course. Anne agreed and pooh-poohed the idea of ghostly goings-on. Beth was sure he'd been seeing things.

But James remained quiet. He knew what he'd seen. He didn't believe in ghosts but he knew he'd seen something. He'd seen the lights the same time every evening but strangely enough, now that the mystery had been solved, the lights had not appeared the previous night. Was his imagination playing tricks on him? Were the ghostly lights real and were the ancient legends true? He'd never know, of course, and had to put it down to Cornish folklore.

Stephen raised a glass. 'H–here's to our last day in Polpennarth.'

James raised his. 'And here's to returning to Cavendish and seeing our friends and neighbours.'

(See over for Grandma Alice Harrington's recipes)

Grandma Harrington's Sussex Pond Pudding and Plain Scones

SUSSEX POND PUDDING (serves 6)
This is an incredibly old Sussex dish and called a pond pudding because that is what it resembles once it's cooked!! It's full of flavour (and calories!!!) but, like James advised, give it a go, you may like it.

Pastry:
8oz self-raising flour
4oz suet
2oz fresh white breadcrumbs
Pinch of salt
Milk to mix

Filling:
2 lemons
7oz brown sugar
7oz butter

Mix the dry ingredients for the pastry using the milk to form them into a soft dough.

Reserve one third of the dough for the lid. Roll out the remainder into a circle and line a greased 2 pint pudding basin.

Leave some pastry overlapping the edge.

Place half of the butter and half of the sugar into the bottom of the lined bow.

Prick the lemons with a large needle or skewer so the juices can flow out. Then place them on the butter and sugar.

Place remaining butter and sugar over the lemons.

Roll out the remaining pastry into a circle.

Use this to make a lid, sealing it with a little milk.

Cover with greased paper and a cloth.

Steam for 3-4 hours.

PLAIN SCONES
(makes 8-10 scones)

Ingredients:
12oz self-raising flour
Pinch of salt
1 tspn baking powder
3oz unsalted butter
3 tbsp caster sugar
6 fluid ounces warm milk
2 tspn vanilla extract
1 egg, lightly beaten

Preheat oven to gas mark 7 and allow baking tray to heat up.
Mix flour, salt and baking powder in large bowl.
Rub in the butter until the mixture looks like breadcrumbs.
Stir in the sugar.
With the milk on one side, stir the vanilla extract into the milk.
Make a well in the mixture and gradually

pour the milk in and mix together until it forms a dough.

Turn the dough onto a floured surface. If you need to fold it a bit, do it gently.

Roll it, gently, to a thickness of 5cm.

Using a scone cutter, cut out several rounds.

Bring the dough back together and repeat the process. Should make 8 scones.

Brush the top with egg then place on baking tray.

Bake for ten minutes.

Switch on the wireless and enjoy with lashings of clotted cream and strawberry jam.

We do hope that you have enjoyed reading this large print book.

Did you know that all of our titles are available for purchase?

We publish a wide range of high quality large print books including:
Romances, Mysteries, Classics
General Fiction
Non Fiction and Westerns

Special interest titles available in large print are:
The Little Oxford Dictionary
Music Book, Song Book
Hymn Book, Service Book

Also available from us courtesy of Oxford University Press:
Young Readers' Dictionary
(large print edition)
Young Readers' Thesaurus
(large print edition)

For further information or a free brochure, please contact us at:
Ulverscroft Large Print Books Ltd.,
The Green, Bradgate Road, Anstey,
Leicester, LE7 7FU, England.
Tel: (00 44) **0116 236 4325**
Fax: (00 44) **0116 234 0205**

THE LATE MRS. FIVE

Richard Wormser

Soon after Paul Porter arrives in the small rural town of Lowndesburg, he is shocked to see his beautiful ex-wife Edith getting into an expensive limousine. He discovers she is now married to rich landowner John Hilliard the Fifth, to whose mansion he makes a visit hoping to sell agricultural machinery, only to find nobody home. But the local police know of his visit — and when they discover Edith's dead body there, he becomes the prime suspect as the slayer of the late Mrs. Five!

LORD JAMES HARRINGTON AND THE SPRING MYSTERY

Lynn Florkiewicz

James and his wife Beth are hosting the annual spring fair when wealthy recluse Delphine Brooks-Hunter is murdered. While James is summoned to the reading of her will and is tasked with solving an intriguing riddle, Beth tackles her own mystery after discovering a homeless man suffering from amnesia. As they delve deeper, a number of questions emerge. What links Delphine to the fairground folk? Who would harm such a refined lady? Are rumours of wartime espionage true? As they unravel the truth, they uncover more than they bargained for . . .

LORD JAMES HARRINGTON AND THE SUMMER MYSTERY

Lynn Florkiewicz

It's summer, and the annual tennis tournament between Cavendish and Charnley is underway; but a sudden spate of jewel thefts prompts James to put his sleuthing hat on. His investigation suggests that the criminals are using an ancient smuggling network. Can he convince his good friend, DCI George Lane, of his suspicions? Is the murder of the tennis umpire connected? Could a long-term resident really be a criminal mastermind? James desperately struggles for answers as he explores hidden tunnels, studies old maps and examines the motives of his fellow villagers.

THE RED TAPE MURDERS

Gerald Verner

Superintendent Budd's latest murder investigation begins with the murder of a solicitor, found strangled with red tape. Soon, two more local solicitors are murdered in similar fashion. Eventually Budd learns that two years earlier, a man shot himself when about to lose the bungalow he built, under a compulsory purchase order of the council. Two of the solicitors had acted in the sale of the land, and the third had acted for the council. Is someone seeking vengeance for the man who committed suicide — himself a victim of red tape?

GHOST LAKE

V. J. Banis

Its real name is Caspar Lake, but people call it Ghost Lake. Years ago, a ferryboat went down in a storm, drowning everyone on board — and some say their souls have never rested . . . Beth Nolan travels to the nearby town at the invitation of an old school friend, but no sooner does she arrive than she is plunged into the murky depths of the brutal murder of a young woman. Beth must find answers — or risk joining the dead in the haunted depths of Ghost Lake . . .

THE EYE STONES

Harriet Esmond

A shock awaits Deborah Ritchie when she arrives to stay with her recently married sister. She is told that the couple have both perished tragically in a fire which destroyed their home. Alone in the bleak Norfolk brecklands, Deborah is forced to accept hospitality from the forbidding Sir Randall Gaunt. She gladly leaves Sir Randall and his grim anatomical practices for the warm companionship of young Lord Stannard and his family. But before long, she is inextricably involved in a nightmare of mystery and unimagined evil . . .